REFUGE

AT PINE LAKE

A PINE HAVEN NOVEL

Rose Chandler Johnson

This novel is a work of fiction. Names, characters, places, and incidents are a product of the author's imagination or used fictiously. Locales and public names are sometimes used for atmospheric purposes. Any resemblance to actual people, living or dead, or to businesses, companies, events, institutions, or locales is purely coincidental.

Scripture references, whether quoted or paraphrased by the characters, are from the King James Version of the Bible.

Chanson Books, Augusta, Georgia
Book Layout ©2017 BookDesignTemplates.com
Author Photograph by Sharon Brisken

Library of Congress Control Number: 2019901551

Refuge at Pine Lake/ Rose Chandler Johnson. -- 1st ed.
ISBN-13: 978-0-9984933-1-2

Printed in the United States of America

As always for my children

A person's heart plans his way: but the LORD determines his steps.

—Proverbs 16:9

Contents

Chapter One

"When God burns down your house, you know it's time to move."

Deborah Lancaster shook her head as her lapis blue eyes flashed over the rim of red-framed reading glasses. Attractive and younger looking than her fifty-eight years, she sat curled in the corner of the sofa in the Marriott hotel suite with a Southern Living magazine on her lap.

Robin snuggled closer to her side. "Now, Mom. God didn't burn down our house."

"Well, he might as well have. We still have to move, don't we?" She sighed and looked around their temporary lodging. The suite with a kitchenette and sitting area was barely big enough for the two of them. Styrofoam takeout boxes sat on the coffee table, not yet cleared away from supper. A small tower of suitcases and banker's boxes, several family portraits, and plastic crates of art supplies lined the wall near the plate-glass window that overlooked a wooded field. Dusk had fallen.

"It's time I do this though. I should have gone to Virginia months ago, as soon as Catherine called saying she needed help with Mother. I held off making that decision way past the point that familial love and decency should have compelled me to go." She turned her face toward the window.

"It was only natural, Mom. You didn't want to leave our home. Don't be hard on yourself."

"Catherine and Mother are really happy I've decided to come."

"Of course they are. It's just what you need. And I'm happy to be staying here in Georgia. Living at the lake again will be awesome. And so will being on my own."

Her mom laid the magazine aside. Biting her bottom lip, she gazed blankly at her daughter.

"What is it?"

"Well ... I rented out the lake house." She pressed her hands over her mouth and then pulled them away. "We did talk about doing that a while back, remember? How was I to know *this* would happen and you'd need a place to live? But there's no need to worry. I've already talked to your sister. You can stay with them. It's only for six months."

"Six months!" Robin stood, and the dog jumped down at her heels and followed as she paced the floor. "As much as I love Emily and Ryan and the girls, I have no desire to live in Atlanta. Especially under someone else's supervision."

"But the kids will adore your being there." Her mom gave a weak smile.

"What about my plans? Even before the fire, you knew I wanted to spend the summer at the lake again this year."

"Wasting your time trying to catch that fisherman." Her mom's brows knitted.

Robin stopped her pacing and stared at her. "Oh, you just had to say that. That's not fair. You rented it on purpose to prevent me from spending time with Caleb, didn't you?"

"Didn't you learn anything last summer, dear? That man is not the marrying kind. And he's rightly observed that you are. You'll just get your heart broken again."

"Oh, Mom. I can't believe you did that without talking to me first." Robin picked up the empty food boxes, almost tripping over the dog on the way to the garbage can. "I am quite capable of choosing my own relationships. You and your bridge club are off the hook as matchmakers in my life. It's high time I made my own decisions. I certainly hope you aren't going to try to orchestrate my social life long distance."

Her mom's eyes widened and a rosy flush spread across her cheeks.

"I'm sorry." Robin softened her tone, but a note of defiance still rang in her voice.

"I'm sorry too. Really, I am. I just want what's best for you, baby girl."

"That's just it, Mom. I'm not a baby girl."

Lifting her arms, her mother motioned for Robin to come sit beside her. When the dog jumped onto the sofa, she nudged her aside to make room.

Robin plopped down and allowed herself to be pulled into a hug.

"Nothing was sweeter than our life together at the lake … with Dad," Mom said, no longer holding back tears. Tears for the beloved husband and father gone, and for their disrupted lives forever changed. So many tender emotions churned beneath the thin veneer of acceptance.

"Ah, Mom, I understand. It's okay."

What else could she say? No one knew better than she did how difficult the last seven years had been for her mother. During her dad's grueling battle with cancer, Mom was his constant caregiver. Robin had wanted to be with him more, but her parents insisted she continue her education. When he died the summer after she graduated college, she moved directly from the dorm into the condo with her mother and took a job at the local elementary school. All of her mother's decisions during those years had been based on what was best for her dad, and all of hers had been based on what she thought was best for her parents. She and her mother had helped each other through the grief, but now she needed to live her own life. The counselor had advised that as well.

"But the rental agreement, dear," Mom said. "Arrangements were made weeks ago. This man has planned six months of his life around it. It's too late to back out now. You'll just have to wait a while longer before you move to the lake. I'm sorry."

But what about her plans? She'd looked forward to the summer at the lake for months. Still, Robin gave in without further argument and allowed herself to succumb to the emotions, which brought forth her own tears of pure pent-up frustration.

The simultaneous impact and sound of crushing metal slammed Matt McLaughlin out of his tortured sleep. He squinted into the darkness, panting, heart pounding, body rigid. *Oh God.* The sirens. The terror.

The nightmare retreated as the bedroom came into focus. Muscles released. Pulse slowed. But he trembled. Cold in spite of the sweat that drenched his body, he pulled the sheet up to his shoulders. Anguish clung to his chest causing pain with each labored breath.

Months had passed since the last savage episode. Such debilitating torment to be thrust back into the horror of the accident. He had prayed to be done with them. Prayed that the combination of rest and medication would be the magic bullet. In reality, maybe he'd never be free of the nightmares or the grief that gnawed his soul.

Swearing under his breath, he grabbed a handful of the sheet and swiped it across his clammy face. He wanted to return to some measure of normalcy in his placid academic life. He wanted to resume writing. But after four years of misery and stymied efforts, he wasn't sure he could. Wasn't sure he had the will to try anymore.

When the nightmares continued to haunt his nights, and then more recently panic attacks stalked his days, he did not seek help. Only after he'd had an epic panic attack in front of a room full of students, bashed his fist into his best friend's face during the frenzied exit, and tumbled headlong down the university's granite stairs—then he was forced to get help. Three weeks in the medical center's third-floor psychiatric ward. During that time, he watched Tom Morgan's bruised face turn a multitude of plum-purple hues, and contemplated whether life was worth living and whether he cared or not.

Just the same, Tom cared. He had been there for him every day. And Lauren most definitely would care. With her characteristic passion, she would be flipping mad at him for how he'd let her death kill his spirit.

Something inside him stirred at the memory of her.

"You've suffered a tragic loss, and what's more, you blame yourself for Lauren's death." The doctor's words echoed in his head. "Grieving is different for every person, but I think you have gotten bogged down in the guilt and anger stage of grief. That un-healed wound is the seedbed of these dysfunctions."

You think? Matt closed his eyes and covered his aching forehead with his hands. *Must I wake every morning to this?*

"It's been four years since the car accident," the doctor had said. As if that was reason enough to have put it behind him. But in his days and nights, the freak accident that killed his wife might as well have happened yesterday.

While in the hospital, well-meaning folks who hemmed in his life formulated a plan that they said, with his cooperation, would alleviate the disabling symptoms and possibly result in his recovery in a

matter of time. What else could one do, if not coop-
erate, when one landed himself in a psych ward?

Matt glanced at the window. It had to be close to
dawn. He considered ways to get out of the trip to
Pine Lake, but none of them made much sense.
None would help him heal or stop his career from
hurtling headlong toward disaster. The stay in the
hospital along with the anti-anxiety meds had
brought a measure of calm. The sabbatical was supposed to complete his recovery, or at least stop the
free fall. Tom had spoken on his behalf to the dean,
as well as arranged for a house all the way across the
country.

"California is great, but you need to get away
from here," Tom had said with complete certainty
when he'd brought him home from the hospital a
week before. "Focus on something new. There's
clean air. It's the perfect place to write. You can start
a new chapter in your life."

Matt had to love the guy for his relentless opti-
mism in the face of his own persistent pessimism.
Start a new chapter, he'd said. "Hmph."

He got out of bed and took a shower. Then he
dressed, put his toiletries into his toiletry kit, and
forced himself to make the bed, the way Lauren had
always done. He picked up their wedding picture
from the nightstand. They were spectacular, she in
white satin and lace, he holding a glass of cham-
pagne. For a long moment, he looked at the image
before slipping it between the folded clothing in his
packed carry-on.

*Come to terms with the past. Eventually you must
turn the page.* The doctor's words insinuated them-

selves into his thoughts. How could he just turn the page and forget? The accident was his fault, after all.

With a sigh, he retrieved the picture and pressed his lips to the cool glass. After a moment's pause, he opened the drawer of the nightstand and laid it inside. "I can try, Lauren," he whispered. "I *will* try."

He closed the drawer, carried his luggage downstairs, turned out the lights, and locked the door behind him.

Chapter Two

A taxi took Matt to the airport, but he hadn't bothered to look at the ticket and misunderstood the departure time.

"That's what you get when others have to arrange your life for you," he muttered. The ten a.m. flight was, in reality, two p.m. Overbooking bumped him to the four o'clock flight. By then, he'd sat too long and drank too much in the airport lounge. Numb from watching countless passersby seemingly mind-controlled by electronic devices, he boarded the plane.

When he landed in Georgia, he had a devil of a time arranging a ride to the rental property. The shuttle pulled up to the house around two a.m. From inside the vehicle, all he could make out were dark shifting shadows of tall trees and the moonlight slivering across the silver-gray lake. Security lights popped on as they approached.

He stepped out of the van's silence into a cacophony of crickets, tree frogs, and bullfrogs. Dazed, his senses merged with nature's night sounds. He drew a deep breath and pulled himself upright. The night closed around him like a murky cloak.

"Want some help with that, bud?" The driver impatiently hopped out of the van. He came around to the side and removed one bag, then another. Matt grabbed one, and together they carried the luggage up the porch steps and dropped them in front of the door. Shoving his hand into his pant pocket, Matt retrieved his wallet, pulled out a twenty, and handed it to the driver.

"Thanks," the driver muttered before hopping back into the van and driving away.

An owl's call rose above the rest. *Who-who-who-who-who-are-yoouuu*?

Matt chuckled bitterly. *No one worth knowing.*

He fumbled in his pocket for the key and unlocked the heavy door. When he stepped into the wide, open foyer, he lifted his gaze to the skylight where the night sky formed a purple canopy. Moonlight shone through, falling on the room below. The expansive, window-filled rear wall gave the impression of infinity. Open space appeared suspended above ground and water. The house drew him in.

Shaking off sleep, he carried all the bags upstairs and dropped them inside the door of the room at the top of the stairs, destined to be his for the next six months. He sank onto the bed and pulled off his shoes, pants, and shirt.

So here he was. *Why did I let myself be talked into this?* With a heavy sigh, he pushed himself off the bed and trudged downstairs in the semi-darkness.

The wide planks of the wooden floor were cool and smooth beneath his feet.

His throat was parched. He expected the refrigerator to be stocked with bottled water, juice, and beer, at least, but he found only coffee creamer and a few eggs and condiments inside. He flipped on the kitchen light. Cans of vegetable juice and a case of ginger ale sat on the bottom shelf of the depleted pantry.

"What'll it be, Professor McLaughlin?" he asked in a phony genteel voice. "Lukewarm ginger ale," he said in his own low baritone. Before popping the top, he stood there a moment, considering the implications. It appeared he was not expected. He groaned, rubbing his hand over his tousled hair, and switched off the light.

A soft glow filled the place. He crossed to the windows and glass sliding doors, which covered two entire walls of the great room. The spectacular view of the lake, its dark, glassy surface shimmering in the moonlight, mesmerized him.

Jesus, I'd like to see you walk on that.

The thought startled him, and the voice of his preacher grandpa echoed in his mind.

Years and time suddenly fell away, and he found himself back where he had started beside a river in Tennessee. In the woods by the lake, time and place shifted in his troubled mind. A gentle breeze stirred the leaves of the trees that shaded the path to the dock where an aluminum jon boat rocked and bumped against the pilings. When he was seven years old, his grandpa taught him how to fish in a small paddleboat much like the one tied there. For the first time in years, he let himself think of his grandpa. Shivers ran down his spine, and he turned away from the window.

Light glinted off a metal frame on the sofa table. Drawn to its tangible reality, he picked up the picture frame and looked into a woman's beautiful blue eyes. Another pair of a similar hue, warm and smiling, stared back at him. He adjusted the picture perfectly reflecting a lovely woman and her daughter. It seemed they were looking directly at him. His hand shook as he set the picture back in place. After a deep calming breath, he exhaled slowly, and then tipping back his head, guzzled what was left of the tepid soda.

Somehow, Matt found himself upstairs beside the bed, not remembering having walked there. Dead tired, he breathed a prayer. "Let me sleep, Lord. I don't care if I ever wake up."

He dropped onto the bed and drifted helplessly into faraway regions of his mind. A profound quietness closed around him, and he slept dreamlessly under the spell of the place.

Robin breathed a happy sigh along with a silent prayer. The fire had begun to look like a blessing in disguise. All the irreplaceable treasures had mercifully been spared from the flames, even though many had been damaged by water from the sprinklers. With the first alarms, they hauled out her daddy's Bible, the family portraits and picture albums, laptops, her sketch pads, valuable documents, and favorite books. Some belongings they chose not to replace. Instead, they counted their blessings and settled with the insurance company, whose substantial settlement would ease the burden of relocation. Not only that, but Robin and her mother were forced to make some long-overdue decisions.

A month after the fire, Mom had moved to her mother's house in Virginia, where she assisted Aunt Catherine with the care of their aging parent, and she was pleasantly surprised to find life enjoyable there in her old family home. Robin was finally on her way to the beloved lake house in her Range Rover loaded with all her belongings. Callie, her dad's tricolored spaniel, secure in her harness, commanded the passenger seat.

Only yesterday Robin had completed what she hoped would be her third and final year teaching kindergarten. Because of the insurance settlement, she could quit teaching, at least for a year, to pursue her dream of writing and illustrating children's books. If that wasn't reason enough for excitement, at the lake she would be near Caleb Jackson, Pine Lake's most celebrated fishing and hunting guide.

Caleb had been her high school heartthrob. A lowly freshman herself at the time, he starred as the senior quarterback. He hadn't given her more than a cursory glance until their memorable meeting last summer.

That evening when she entered Joe's, one of the few restaurants in the lakeside town, she intended to pick up a veggie pizza to-go and head back to the lake house four miles away. She had checked out several DVDs from the town's rustic library, a small white wooden building across from city hall. That weekend marked the beginning of her summer vacation, and she planned to lounge on the deck and dock, swim in the cove, walk in the early mornings, draw and write, and watch old movies. That was before Caleb picked her up. Literally.

She laughed, thinking about it now.

Exiting the eatery, she'd paused in the entrance to allow the right of way to three kids chasing a hulk of a dog. They came to an abrupt halt in front of a harried woman, no doubt their mom. Robin lifted her free hand in greeting, but "Hey" barely escaped her lips when the mastiff sprang into action in chase of a wayward squirrel. Before she knew what was happening, the dog clipped her behind her right knee and sent her spinning, arms and pizza flying overhead. She surely would have landed badly had it not been for the strong arms that wrapped around her and brought her down easy on top of his own body. She felt the solid strength of a man's broad chest, and glimpsed fur and screaming kids fly by, all in a stupefying second.

"Whoa, girl! I gotcha!" A smooth masculine voice came from over her shoulder.

During a moment of stunned tunnel vision, she found herself gazing into the darkest green eyes she had ever seen. Those eyes as green as Georgia pines with flecks of rusty gold fastened on hers while muscular arms held her. She was sitting on the man's lap.

"Are you all right, honey?" Mr. All-American crooned. "Take a breath. Breathe … breathe."

"I am so sorry …"

"Can't say I minded," he said, amused.

Amid a tangle of helping hands and apologies, Caleb picked her up, set her on her feet, and stroked a hand down her back. For one so strong and agile, his touch was surprisingly gentle.

The pizza box lay open, its contents plastered to the sidewalk. The flabbergasted mom herded the kids to pick up the gooey mess with no lack of assistance from the unrepentant dog who wolfed down gobs of crust.

Still holding onto her upper arm, Caleb led Robin back inside the restaurant. He ordered pizza, one for her and one for himself, and while the pizzas baked, they chatted and sipped cherry soda. Introductions were in order since Caleb was sure he had never seen her before in his life. "How could I have forgotten such a beautiful girl?" he asked.

They soon figured out they were neighbors. That spring, Caleb had built a cabin just around the bend and past the cove, hardly more than a mile from the lake house.

Consequently, their carefree summer fling began. At least, that's what it was to no-strings-attached Caleb Jackson. But that hadn't prevented her heart from getting tangled in the line. When the time came to begin another school year, she returned to the condo in the city, and trips to the lake came less and less often. Summer waned, as did Caleb's interest. In spite of a few calls and another date or two, by Halloween their romance had all but ended.

"Robin, I love spending time with you. Fact is, you're my favorite. But if we take this any further, I'll have to marry you. I'm not ready for that. I'm not sure I'll ever be."

She had to give him credit for candor. But she hadn't expected summer's end to be the end of their romance. Evidently, Caleb thought otherwise.

She cried for the better part of a week. Her mother consoled her by saying that God in his own good time would bring the right man for her, but Caleb *was* the right man, to her way of thinking. He was handsome, successful, and had a good family. And she was attracted to him like to no other man she had ever known.

So now, why not try again to catch alpha-male Caleb Jackson? He was still eligible, and that meant fair game. Physically, she was in better shape than ever, which bolstered her confidence. And she'd gotten over her concerns for her mother and grief from the loss of her dad.

She embraced the idea of life on her own and envisioned Caleb as a part of it. So many thoughts raced through her mind as she drove. After an insane month, finally she was on the way—windows down, radio on, ready for the next chapter in her life.

The first order of business was getting the house ready for the new tenant. Robin would persuade him that her presence there was exactly what he needed. That was the only way for her to take up residence at the lake and get a second chance at romance with Caleb. Of course, she wasn't *supposed* to stay. After making the house ready and greeting the guest, she was expected to head to her sister's—except she had no intention of doing that.

Her plan made her feel disconcertingly like a six-teen-year-old plotting to sneak out of the house after the parents were asleep, not that she had ever done that. If her luck held out, her mom would be too busy tending Grandmother to check on her just yet. If necessary, she'd make up a story about being off the grid visiting a friend in North Georgia.

Her phone pinged and Robin looked at the screen on the dash. Of course, Emily. It was as if they had a telepathic connection. Her sister was expecting a call back from her anyway, after last night's lengthy conversation.

She tapped the screen. "Hi, Emmy."

"Hi yourself. Well? What have you decided to do?"

"I've decided to present my proposal to the tenant. I'll act like an innkeeper, and he can be the well-tended guest."

"So more than likely, you'll be staying at the lake. I can't say I'm surprised." She paused for a moment. "It might work. But like I've said, you have to heed your intuition. If he gives you any creepy vibes what-soever—"

"I know. I'll leave and come to your house," Robin said. "I'm en route now."

"You're driving? Well, be careful. I won't keep you. But you're going to have to tell Mom. Tell her the truth. You know how she is. When she realizes our minds are made up, she relents."

"I hope so."

"She understands," Emily said. "But again. Don't be naive. Well, that's not the right word since you are naive." Robin could imagine her sister rolling her eyes. "Don't be too trusting. And listen to that quiet voice in your head."

"Emmy, you are an awesome sister."

"I don't know about that. I have to remind myself sometimes you're no longer my little shadow with pigtails."

"Love you too," Robin said.

"Yeah, I love you, sis. Focus on your art. That's your gift. Don't worry about love. It truly will come into your life when you least expect it. Just like it did for me. You shouldn't have to work so hard to make it happen."

"Yeah. That's what you and Mom keep telling me."

"Don't forget I'm eight years older and wiser than you. Let me know immediately—tonight, if you are staying at the lake."

"I will. Thanks, Emmy."

"A text is adequate. You know I'll be getting the girls ready for bed before eight."

"I know. Now I have to get to the house and get everything ready—set the scene before the tenant gets here. First impressions are crucial."

"Good luck! And talk to Mom."

"Okay. Bye now."

Emmy had her back. She always did. She was right about their mother too, but how couldn't she be when they were so much alike. Case in point, Emmy really wanted her to stay with them in Atlanta, but after she'd understood how much it meant to her to be at the lake, she was her biggest supporter. Robin had been living her life by default. Now she wanted to pursue her dream. Having a sister to count on was great, but making this work was up to her personally. She sighed.

When Robin saw the vast lake giving off its aura and glistening in the morning sun, she knew she'd made the right decision. She drove over the bridge, suspended between the big blue sky and water, and happiness filled her heart.

She planned to drop off the groceries, along with Callie, before running into town to the farmer's market for fresh fruit preserves and local wines. She'd also stop by the church. After that, she would return and tidy up the place before the tenant arrived.

The incidental information her mother had given her about him came secondhand from the colleague who secured the rental. Her mother surmised that the middle-aged, burned-out university professor needed a six-month stay in a secluded environment to improve his health and revive his stalled writing career. Said professor did not own a car.

"Who doesn't own a car?" Robin had asked.

"Maybe he has an illness that restricts driving," her mother replied. "He's requested weekly grocery delivery and courier service by a trustworthy adult. Can you please set that up, Robin? Maybe check with someone at the church?"

That vital detail provided the perfect insight for securing the arrangement. Who better than her to provide the needed services? Plus, she would prepare meals and take care of housekeeping. Otherwise, she would be invisible. She could store her belongings in the downstairs bedroom behind the kitchen, and sleep in her dad's studio. The two-story apartment connected to the house by a breezeway was the perfect way for her to be there yet stay out of his way.

This had better work, Robin thought as she swung her jaunty vehicle onto the gravel driveway that led to the house. It was a just-right place to call home.

Callie lifted her nose and barked excitedly.

"Oh, you love this place, don't you, girl?" She glanced at Callie.

The dog sat at attention, head held high, nose pointing toward the house. Melancholy washed over Robin, and her throat squeezed tight. Her dad had gotten Callie as a puppy the summer before his health failed. The Cavalier King Charles spent puppy-hood romping in the woods, taking walks with her master, and snuggling in his lap. When the illness took all his strength, his small companion stayed by his side.

"I'm sorry, girl. He's not here," she whispered. "But we'll walk the same paths you walked together, and you can sleep with me every night." Robin petted her as the car rolled to a stop. Stroking the dog's back gave her own emotions time to settle. She unlatched the door and pushed it open with her foot. "You're going to stay here while I go into town. I won't be long."

As soon as she unfastened the harness, Callie sprinted across her lap and leapt out the vehicle, barking and running through the trees and back around the lake house, darting back and forth toward the water.

Robin stood, hands on her hips, watching her. Laughing, she carried the bags of groceries into the house. When she returned to the car for more, Callie was on the lake's shore. "Come on, girl!" Smiling to herself and humming, she went back inside.

She unpacked the bags on the kitchen counter, thrusting cold items into the refrigerator. When she returned, she'd put away everything else, tidy up and bake brownies so the place would smell inviting when the new tenant arrived. How could the professor resist friendly fudge brownies?

Callie met her on the way out. Robin held the door open, and the dog darted inside and dashed up the stairs and back down again. Her tongue lolled out happily.

"I'll be back in a little while," Robin said, easing the door closed behind her. The gravel crunched beneath her platform sandals as she headed for the car. Pausing to gaze out at the lake, she wrapped her arms around herself and inhaled deeply. It was good to be home, back in the place where she'd known only happiness.

She hopped into her SUV and drove away, absorbed in her plans.

Chapter Three

Awake, motionless, eyes closed, Matt lay in the large cozy bed, breathing slowly, amazed by the level of comfort he experienced. The events of the previous night came back to him little by little, strangely clouded in his mind due to a combination of alcohol and fatigue, he supposed. Too much time in an airport could give anybody brain fog.

Birds chirped loudly outside the window. A boat's motor hummed in the distance. He listened to the sound fading, drowned out, only to be replaced by another.

Reluctantly, he opened his eyes to semi-darkness and reached for his watch on the bedside table. Ten forty-five. How could it be that late? He'd slept solid for seven or eight hours then. He was still pondering that anomaly when he heard a vehicle approaching. Gravel crunched beneath tires on the driveway leading to the house. An engine shut off, and strains of an electric guitar drifted up to the room. Led Zeppelin, unmistakably.

He hoisted himself out of bed and peeked through the drapes just in time to see a foot clad in a white platform sandal step out of a cherry-red SUV. He heard a woman chatting softly. When lovely legs emerged, he couldn't take his eyes away. Long wavy red hair tumbled down her narrow back and blew like strands of sunlit copper across her face. A wispy white skirt brushed her thighs, and a tangerine-colored blouse floated around the curves of her body as she leaned in and out of the car. A rusty-brown and black dog darted back and forth from the vehicle to the lake.

Matt stepped back from the window. This wasn't the gray-haired widowed homeowner he'd expected. While he stood there trying to think, the door downstairs opened and lively steps moved in the direction of the kitchen. The woman was humming, then singing the lyrics to "Stairway to Heaven."

Well, like the song said, he wondered too. For a moment, he thought he might be in the wrong place. But then again, the key had opened the door. What was the woman doing there?

He'd have to get dressed, go downstairs, and introduce himself. But he didn't want to. Her presence was darn inconvenient. He needed privacy. He wanted solitude. While he stood rooted to the spot, the front door opened, closed, opened, and closed again. The vehicle pulled away from the house and disappeared.

He dropped onto the bed, intent on crawling back under the covers, when a bump at the door stopped him. Audible sniffing, a benign throaty growl, then the swish-swish-swish of rapid pawing on the door. Sharp barks followed in quick succession, building to an impossible-to-ignore crescendo.

"Ooh, good grief," he groaned, scrubbing his hands over his face. "She left the dog."

He squeezed his eyes shut tight, pulled a pillow over his head, and would have ignored the incessant noises had it been possible. Instead, he was drawn into an analysis of the range of emotions he heard in the animal's barks and moans. They had taken on a decidedly forlorn appeal.

On a scale of one to ten, where is your pain?

He stood and practically growled himself before flinging open the door. At first, the little animal trembled, looking up at him with dark chocolate eyes, tilting its head from one side to the other. Then she sprang into action, pawing excitedly at his knees, leaping on the bed and jumping off the other side to circle back around and come at him again.

"One would think you knew me." Annoyed, he glowered at the wet-nosed dog sniffing his ankles. Again, he slapped a hand over his face. Dispassionate indifference gave way to compassion, and he bent to pet the dog's head.

She calmed down at his touch and remained still as he scratched gently behind her ears. When he sat down on the bed, she jumped up and snuggled beside him. He sat motionless, tense at first, but as he relaxed, he didn't want to disturb their calm rapport. A cozy warmth spread over him.

"Since you're here," he said at last, "your mistress must be returning." After a few minutes of thought, he added, "I need to get up and make myself decent. First, come on. Let's go see what was in those bags."

Clad only in boxer shorts and with his hair disheveled, he went downstairs. He peered inside the bags on the kitchen counter, then opened the refrigerator. A gallon of milk, a carton of orange juice, and a six-pack of craft beer sat on the top shelf. He grabbed the milk. Spying the plastic bags of deli ham and cheese, he took them out and shut the door. After making himself a sandwich with the butter-top bread, he poured a tall glass of milk.

While he munched, he walked around the open living area. Natural shades of brown with muted shades of blue and red created a comfortable place. An oatmeal-colored leather sofa faced a large stone fireplace flanked by built-in bookshelves. Upholstered rockers and wingback chairs provided ample seating around a braided jute rug covering the dark wood floor.

He shoved the last bite of sandwich into his mouth, gulped the rest of the milk, and set the glass in the sink. Finally, he walked over to the sofa and sat down on the cool leather, running his hand across the back. It was a good place to relax. Like it had the night before, the picture on the sofa table caught his eye. Luminous blue eyes looked back at him, and he recognized the red hair of the woman he'd seen earlier. The daughter, he assumed.

The little dog barked once and stood unflinching, looking toward the entry door.

Matt tensed at the sound of the approaching vehicle. The red-haired woman would be walking through the door in a matter of minutes, and about the last thing he wanted to do just now was meet her. Hopefully, she would pick up the dog and leave.

While the dog pranced in the foyer, Matt ascended the stairs with long strides. He'd just closed the bedroom door when she entered the house.

Robin swept in, greeted enthusiastically by Callie, who quivered from her head to the tip of her shaggy tail. Robin knelt and briskly rubbed the dog's shiny coat. Callie yapped and sprinted to the base of the stairs, where she waited all the while looking at Robin. Suddenly, she ran to the top of the stairs, pivoted, and barked.

"No, Callie," Robin said affectionately. The adorable animal must be looking for her dad. "We won't be staying upstairs. And I don't have time to play." She continued to the kitchen, where she grabbed one of the shopping bags off the counter and walked over to the dining table. She lifted out a bowl of fresh fruit, a bottle of Georgia wine, and two bars of Godiva chocolate.

She sat down to compose a note. *Welcome to our lake house. It is a magical place. I hope you'll be as happy here as we always have been.* As a final gesture, she drew a pert robin perched on a flowering branch and signed her name beneath it. In the interest of time, she resisted the urge to sketch a cameo of the lake house setting. After standing the card on end, she took a moment to admire the arrangement before returning to the kitchen.

Callie continued to bark, which she chalked up to the excitement of being there. After Robin set out the ingredients for brownies, she turned on the oven. She'd just set a bowl and measuring cup on the counter when she heard footfalls on the floor above her.

Spine stiffening, she sucked in a sharp breath and froze.

A door opened upstairs, and footsteps descended the stairs. Callie's barking took on a frantic tone.

From where Robin stood, she couldn't see the person on the stairs. She stared unblinking, listening, waiting. She needed to swallow, but her throat squeezed closed. *Oh God. A squatter's in the house!*

A shaggy-haired, bearded man walked into view. She let out a sharp squeal while brandishing the spatula fisted in her hand.

The man jerked like someone had struck him, raising both hands in the air. "Hey! I won't hurt you! I'm Matt McLaughlin. I rented the house."

For one long heart-pounding moment, they stared wide-eyed at each another. Then Robin sent the spatula flying like a missile across the room and into the sink with a clatter. She exhaled and clasped both hands to her chest. Her stunned silence turned into laughter, and she did a snappy quickstep jig in place. "Oh, good heavens!" she gasped. "You scared me to death!"

He gaped, clearly dumbfounded, and her amused relief subsided as she noticed his silent stillness and scowling expression. With his shirt and slacks crumpled, he looked like a grumpy man who had just rolled out of bed.

"Have you just arrived?" she asked, straightening. "I wasn't expecting you until suppertime."

He shook his head. "Last night, two a.m. When you came earlier, I was in bed." His deep voice made him sound like the bear he resembled.

"Sorry I woke you. I apologize for not having everything ready. I must have gotten my days mixed up."

He continued to stare at her. Obscured by grisly facial hair, his expression was unreadable. Maybe a look somewhere between concern and pain?

"It's okay." He stepped aside to pet the dog. "It's my fault."

At least he seemed to like the dog. "I see you've met Callie. She was my dad's. He indulged her and now she's a bit spoiled."

He made no comment.

"I hope you don't mind her."

"She's fine." His response came after a too-long pause. Straightening his broad frame, he squared his shoulders.

Summoning all the people skills she'd perfected through three years of nurturing kindergarteners, Robin licked her dry lips and took a deep breath. "I'm Rebecca Rae Lancaster. Everyone calls me Robin. My mother and I own this home. I hope you'll enjoy your stay here." She lifted her palms in the air. "Welcome." Looking into his dark eyes, she felt momentarily drawn into their mysterious depths. Then she saw herself as he must have seen her, a kindergarten teacher talking to the new kid.

"It's nice to meet you." His deadpan expression said otherwise, and Robin wished she had more of her mother's Southern charm and her dad's unflappable fortitude.

"I'd planned to bake brownies and make a simple pasta recipe for your supper," she said, fighting down nervousness. "Would you like that?"

The man's penetrating stare morphed into a look of concern. "Don't put yourself to any trouble for me. I manage fine on my own."

"Oh, it won't be any trouble at all. I assure you. It's my pleasure." Her lips quivered, and she swallowed hard. The crack in her confidence had to be obvious.

He pushed his hand through his thick, tousled hair and then dragged it across his hairy jaw. "Well. Thank you," he mumbled, turning aside. "Excuse me. I'm going upstairs."

As he retreated, Robin stared after him. Her mouth twisted into a tight bow, and her nose wrinkled as she considered the baffling encounter. Their meeting hadn't gone anything like she'd imagined it would. Nor was he like anything she had imagined. He seemed depressed or maybe exhausted, or both. She couldn't tell. He'd definitely need to warm up a bit before she could broach the subject of her staying on.

The beep of the oven reaching temperature called her attention back to the brownie ingredients on the counter. She returned to her task with added zeal, knowing the desired outcome was not yet assured.

"Brownies, I need you to work some magic," she whispered.

Chapter Four

Matt sat on the edge of the bed and stared at the pale blue walls. His thoughts couldn't get passed the woman in the kitchen. Why was she here? Where was the solitude he sought? Wasn't that what he'd paid for? Tom hadn't mentioned this being a bed-and-breakfast.

Soon he heard the clatter of utensils on metal. Had Tom arranged for her to prepare his meal? That wouldn't surprise him, although he'd only asked for groceries to be delivered. On the other hand, maybe she was just being hospitable to welcome his arrival. Southerners were known for that, after all. No, that would be too presumptuous. Too familiar.

Nervous energy buzzed in his bones. He pulled out his laptop and plugged it in. But how could he relax with a woman flitting around downstairs?

Matt threw open the drapes to an astounding rush of sky, trees, and water. The blue-green water bordered by tall pines sparkled in the afternoon sun, the environment pristine and bright. The sky was the same blue as the woman's eyes. And what was that look on her face when he'd told her not to bother with supper? He probably should have thought to curtail the annoyance in his voice.

"Argh," he grumbled. "I'm not up for this."

After getting out a change of clothes, he went into the attached bathroom. A hard look at himself in the mirror showed a man he hardly recognized. When had he gotten so ancient? Gray hairs sprouted in his beard. Lauren used to trim his hair and beard with sweet words and a gentle touch. Now—in stubborn defiance, self-loathing, or both—he rarely bothered with such things as proper grooming. He'd grown a full beard since his wife died.

A long, warm shower soothed his nerves. He dressed in respectable khaki slacks and a polo shirt that clung too tightly to his thick belly. When was the last time he'd worn a polo? Stripping it off, he threw it aside and slid on the wrinkled long-sleeved collared shirt he'd worn on the plane. There was no need to tuck it in. He looked a mess and couldn't care less. He'd put on twenty-five pounds since he'd worn those knit shirts.

Drawn to the window again, he caught sight of a speeding boat full of laughing people awaiting turns to ski. A woman with one hand raised above her head glided behind it. Her fluidity and abandon … the gaiety … captivated him. He recognized the sounds, the experience, but not to the extent that his lips curved upward. He sank again onto the bed and tried to recall the purpose of this trip to Georgia.

Solitude.

Tom said he'd had enough of that. No, he needed to write—every day, even if only a few lines of drivel. Exercise every day, even if only a walk to the dock. He'd packed running shoes.

"Eat healthy. Lay off the beer," Tom said.

Now that was a different story. He didn't care if he watched his calories or alcohol intake or not. And eating a large bag of potato chips at midnight seemed to satisfy some primordial craving.

He glanced at the neat stack of polo shirts still in his bag, then snorted. It was doubtful he would be wearing those.

Hints of delicious aromas seeped into the room.

He crossed the room to the door, opened it slightly, and inhaled. Rich chocolate. Butter. Fish. How long had it been since he'd eaten a home-cooked meal? Months? Longer?

He checked his computer, hoping the Wi-Fi would connect automatically so he wouldn't have to approach the woman downstairs. This meal situation needed clarification. Knowing his sloppy dietary habits and how Tom had chided him to get healthy, did he even have to ask? Moreover, he didn't want to have that conversation. More than likely, Tom arranged for meals as well.

The internet connection failed. Matt sighed heavily, but not without a hint of appreciation. His stomach rumbled. The woman's presence was an intrusion, but a welcome-to-the-lake-house dinner would be a nice way to settle in.

It had to beat a giant bag of salty chips at midnight.

The sound of the shower running upstairs prompted Robin to dry her hands and scoot outside to retrieve her suitcase and cosmetic case from the car. She needed to freshen up before her guest came down for dinner. Carrying her bags through the house under Professor McLaughlin's nose would not send the right message. Until they agreed on an "arrangement," she would be discrete.

Scrumptious aromas greeted her when she walked back inside. Tonight's dinner was one of her favorite recipes. First, she sautéed garlic in olive oil with a touch of butter, adding heavy cream and chopped cherry tomatoes. She added a pound of fresh shrimp, which she stirred quickly into the steaming sauce. Next, she stirred in pesto, mozzarella pearls, and black pepper. She had given the pepper mill an extra turn. The combination of distinctive flavors in a creamy sauce was perfect over angel-hair pasta, along with fresh-baked bread and a crisp romaine salad. The sensory satisfaction of making great food pleased her, but she hadn't anticipated being nervous. After all, it would be no different from running a bed-and-breakfast. She could handle that. She liked people. She loved to cook. But the untimely appearance of the guest, coupled with his standoffish demeanor, made her uneasy.

She carried her bags into the room behind the kitchen, closed the door, and sat down in front of the vanity. Her thick hair was hot on her neck, so she pulled it up into a messy bun, then smoothed a tad of lotion over her face. She changed into a breezy cotton sundress. Its effortless simplicity suited her slender figure and classic style. Tendrils of shiny red hair curled on the nape of her neck, complimenting her peaches and cream complexion. She took another moment to study her appearance and tucked wisps of hair behind her ears.

Well, there's no way around it, she thought, returning to the kitchen. Try as she might, she looked more like a school girl than the proprietor of a B&B.

A door upstairs opened as Robin set the table, and moments later Professor McLaughlin entered the great room. He hesitated, watching her with not quite a smile on his face.

"The food smells good." He walked to an overstuffed chair and sat on the edge of it.

Callie, following close at his heels, rolled onto his feet and settled there.

He muttered something, leaned down, and rubbed the dog's belly. This time the smile was real enough. Watching his interactions with the dog, Robin relaxed a bit. He glanced up, and a fleeting glimpse of satisfaction softened his eyes, which appeared less tired than before.

Having set the last fork in place, Robin lifted a chilled bottle of wine. "Something to drink before dinner? A glass of wine perhaps?" When he didn't respond right away, she added, "The bread has about fifteen more minutes to bake."

"Yes, thank you. A glass of wine."

With a twist and a tug, she smoothly uncorked the bottle, then poured a glass of wine for her guest and a taste for herself. Picking up both glasses, she walked across the room and handed one to Professor McLaughlin, who searched her face as he reached for the glass.

She waited for him to taste it, and her brows rose.

"Sweet." He sipped again.

"It's Muscadine wine, made from native wild grapes. Not like California grapes at all. It has a unique flavor, doesn't it? Tastes like the fruit right off the vine." She smiled, but he didn't return it. "I have a serious red as well if you'd prefer it." Unsure of herself, her cheery voice faded.

"This is fine, thank you." But he sounded unconvinced.

The view of the lake caught her eye. She pursed her lips, walked over to the windows, and looked out. "It's lovely here, isn't it?"

"And quiet," he said.

"Yes, very quiet, I suppose." She continued to look out at the lake and the blue sky dotted with cotton-candy clouds. The tranquility of her surroundings never failed to sooth her.

The oven dinged, bringing her back to the moment. She turned to see Professor McLaughlin observing her, a frown across his brows.

"The bread is ready." On her way past the table, Robin set her glass by a plate. Heat emanated from the oven, and she put on thick mitts to remove the golden bread. While it rested, she arranged the pasta in an oval dish and poured the steaming sauce over it. The salad and dressings, soft butter, and a pitcher of water were already on the table. "Dinner is served. *À la table*."

He rose from the chair, cautiously displacing the sleeping dog at his feet, and came to stand at the table opposite Robin. They pulled out their chairs in unison. After sitting, she bowed her head and said a silent prayer of thanks. The dishes were passed around, and after a few moments, she felt much like she would have during an awkward blind date. Her confidence had fizzled.

Apparently, the professor was comfortable with silence. He gave no indication that he intended to open his mouth other than to eat. She was listening to the sound of her own chewing when at last he spoke.

"This pasta is delicious. And the salad quite good."

"I'm glad you like it." She breathed a little sigh of relief.

"Thank you for making dinner."

"It was a pleasure. I'd be glad to cook for you every night. You could just let me know which foods you prefer or if you follow a particular diet."

Professor McLaughlin lifted his head suddenly and raised a dismissive hand. "I didn't know Tom Morgan arranged all this." He paused with the fork in his hand, the utensil hovering above his plate. "He means well. I'm not much of a cook." Watching her, he set the fork down, then picked it back up and resumed eating. "*Heart healthy*, *low carbs*," he said, between bites, "were the terms the doctor mentioned."

"Oh. Sure." Robin blinked. "I enjoy cooking. I loved cooking for my parents. I have lots of great recipes."

"Certainly. Make whatever you like."

"Really? That would be great." After pulling the breadboard closer, she cut a slice of bread. "Would you like a piece?"

He took the slice and buttered it.

"There's a great farmer's market in town where I get the best fresh produce."

He nodded dismissively as he returned his attention to the food on his plate.

Robin ventured a glance at his downcast eyes. His dark hair fell over his forehead and curled around his ears and collar.

"And what would you think of my using the bedroom suite behind the kitchen?" she asked cautiously, holding out her hand in the direction of the pocket doors that led to a short hallway to a bedroom and the entrance to the garage. "For my occasional use. I'll spend most of my time in the studio apartment through the breezeway, so I won't be in your way."

A furrow crinkled Professor McLaughlin's forehead and he shook his head a bit before he found his voice. "You stay here?" he asked with a distressed look on his face.

"I'll take care of meals and errands, and your stay will be carefree." Robin swallowed the lump in her throat and held her breath.

Color had risen to the part of his cheeks visible above the beard. "Fine," he blurted out. "Whatever the arrangements."

"So ... that will work for you?"

"Whatever." But the crease in his brow only deepened.

It was Robin's turn to lose her voice. No doubt he assumed her preparing his meals had been prearranged. Her staying here was a logical leap. Should she cut right to the chase and clarify that point, or would that be biting off more than she could chew?

Professor McLaughlin drank the last of his wine.

Robin seized the opportunity to serve him. "Here," she said graciously. "Let me pour you another glass."

He glanced at her with gray eyes the color of the sky before a storm. His expression was solemn but otherwise unreadable.

She raised her glass to his. For this rare moment, she decided that the less said on her part, the better.

The dishwasher's hum buffered the space between Robin and her guest while she ruminated on the pros and cons of making an explanation. The dinner had been a success in spite of stilted conversation. However, as soon as it ended, Professor McLaughlin excused himself from the table, crossed the room, and stood silently gazing out at the lake, making further conversation difficult. In fact, his detached demeanor discouraged conversation.

Robin cleared the table and stacked the dishes unobtrusively while he made his quiet watch with his back to her. Callie, eager for her evening walk, paced around his feet.

When she finished the dishes, she mustered her enthusiasm. "How about a walk around the cove? Callie is begging to go for a walk. We'll show you our favorite trail."

Professor McLaughlin slowly rubbed the side and back of his neck while continuing to stare out the window. Callie now pirouetted at his feet, understanding quite well the word *walk*. He looked down at the twirling dog.

Robin pulled in her bottom lip and held it between her teeth, resisting the urge to say more. Finally, when she could stand it no longer, she took a deep breath. "Uh … then you want to go?"

The man bolted across the room, a stricken look on his face. "No. I mean, go without me!" Halfway up the stairs, he halted. "Good night."

Taken aback, she stared in stunned silence. Then she grabbed Callie's leash from the hook beside the door and slipped into her walking shoes. After closing the door noiselessly behind her, they headed down to the lakeshore.

Robin allowed her face to scrunch in perplexed bafflement. "Good grief. What have I gotten myself into?" She retied her shoes while the dog relieved herself. "He's tied in knots, poor guy. He *needs* rest and relaxation."

A gentle breeze had picked up across the lake. The well-beaten path, about ten feet from the water's edge, meandered around the point of the cove for a mile or so and ended at a manmade beach. Due to its secluded location and the *Private Property* signs, rarely did anyone stop there except its residents. She walked faster as she neared the beach, her mood lifting with each step. When her feet sank into the soft sand, she slowed again. Callie tugged impatiently, so she unsnapped the leash.

Three picnic tables stood under the trees at the back edge of the clearing. Robin sat on a bench and watched Callie play. As her mood adjusted to the rhythm of the place, thoughts of Caleb filled her imagination. In only a few more days, she would see him again. His handsome face came to mind. He'd promised to call her as soon as he returned from the fishing tournament.

Butterflies filled her stomach, and sweet anticipation rose within her. Summer vacation had begun.

Oh, wow, she thought with a smile. *My future starts now.*

Chapter Five

Silence settled around Matt as he sat on the edge of the bed. He was still breathing hard. Finally, he crossed the room to the computer. Another attempt to connect to the internet failed. He couldn't send Tom a message and calling him wasn't an option. No way was he going to subject himself to a barrage of questions.

Dinner had been delicious, and his hostess gracious. If only things had stayed that simple. Something about the view, the lake, the colors of the sky had jolted a memory. He'd stopped himself before saying aloud, "Look, Lauren. Remember ..." An image of his wife's sunlit face had struck him so hard he lost his breath. It had been months since he had remembered her smile precisely. Without reason, his heart pounded and he struggled to draw a breath. He'd seen the confused expression on Miss Lancaster's face, but he was halfway up the stairs before he could stop himself.

Now, standing at his computer, his heart continued its frantic pace. His mind raced. He needed to escape. He bolted through the bedroom door and stumbled down the stairs. Once outside, he bent at the waist, grasped his knees, and gulped mouthfuls of fresh air. Driven by panic, he trudged up the gravel path and through the wide gate that opened onto the property.

He was jogging by the time he got to the dirt road that led to the highway. Blinded by misery, he ran until sweat rolled down his back. Pain stabbed in his side, his chest clenched, and he faltered, vying for balance. He lost his footing, falling with a thud onto the side of the road.

Some dark place inside him seemed to crack open, and grief erupted. Sobs wracked his body. He lay in the dirt for a few moments before rolling over, drawing himself up, and putting his head between his knees. When the tide finally stemmed, he moaned. What a ridiculous scene he had to be making in the otherwise quiet woods. The whole situation seemed unbearably ludicrous.

He chuckled, and then laughter erupted, exploding into spasms of hysteria, as joyless as it sounded.

A sharp explosive noise, almost like a gunshot, split the air.

"My God, man. You all right?" A thin old man struck a walking stick hard against a metal mailbox, causing Matt to jerk to attention. A brown Labrador retriever with a graying muzzle stood against the old man's legs and made throaty half-hearted growls.

He and the animal locked in a stare, eventually judging each other harmless. The dog pushed into Matt with his snout, rubbed its body along his side, and wagged its tail.

"Hey!" he cautioned the dog. He propped himself on his arm to keep from falling over, then looked at the old man. "I'm fine."

The stern face quizzed him. "No, you ain't fine. What's wrong with you? You lost your mind?" The words sounded concerned, without insult or rancor.

"My wife died." Matt spat out the words matter-of-factly, as if he had known all along the reason for this latest bout of madness.

Recognition lit the old man's face. "Oh, so that's it. I get that. Same thing happened to me." After a moment, the old man stuck out his hand.

Matt took it, and they both swayed as he got to his feet.

"Sorry about banging the mailbox. Couldn't get your attention otherwise. Bradford is the name. Charlie Bradford."

"Matt McLaughlin."

"Why don't we walk up to the house? Sit a spell."

Matt looked down at himself, brushed dirt and debris from his shirt and pants, and then fell in with Mr. Bradford on the walk to the rustic cabin nestled in a grove of trees. They climbed the wooden steps and sat in rocking chairs without saying a word. The dog collapsed like a flat tire on the porch.

The old man looked in the direction of the lake along a path through the pines. The setting sun painted striated shades of pink and tangerine across the sky.

"Nice weather we're having, ain't it?" Mr. Bradford began to rock slowly.

"Yes." The moment seemed surreal. He was sitting on a stranger's porch after the most maudlin outburst of physical and emotional dysfunction, and he felt none of the humiliation that usually followed such an episode.

"Ain't no shame," the old man said, like he intuitively knew Matt's thoughts. "It's the mind and body's way of getting rid of the rot after devastation. I know. I lost my son and my wife."

More than five minutes passed. The dog dreamed and its tail thumped on the floor. Traffic on a distant highway somewhere off behind them became audible through the woods. Matt felt slightly disoriented. Yesterday seemed ages ago. He couldn't remember the drive from the airport to the lake house the night before, and he wasn't sure how far he'd come down the road tonight.

"You're not from around here, are you?"

"No. I'm renting a house."

"Oh, yeah. That must be the Lancaster place. Nice house Martin built. He was a talented fellow. Great fishing partner too. When he got cancer, they moved over to the city to be close to the hospital for treatments. Said he'd be back. From the looks of him, I knew better. I'd seen that look before. But pretty Birdie and his wife Deborah, I expect they'll be back."

"Birdie?"

He chuckled. "Her name's Robin, but her dad and I sometimes called her that."

"She's there now. At the lake house, I mean."

"How about that. Good. And how long are you here for?"

Matt followed his gaze toward the lake. A tiny point of light flashed among the trees, followed by another, and another.

"Lightnin' bugs," he murmured to himself, surprised by fireflies long lost in his memory.

"How long you staying?"

"Six months. To get myself together." That also made perfect sense just then.

"Huh. Well, you're in a good place for it."

Matt gave a slight nod and pushed himself up.

"Come on back anytime. We'll fish. You like to catch largemouth bass? Crappy?"

"Sure." He hobbled down the steps.

The dog lobbed down the steps behind him.

The old man stood and stretched his bony frame, then pointed toward the north. "House is about half a mile up the road there."

"Sure. Thanks." Matt willed himself to stand up straight in spite of the fatigue that stiffened his body. "I'll take you up on fishing sometime."

"Well, don't be a stranger." Charlie watched him walk up the road.

Before he got out of sight, Matt glanced back over his shoulder. The man stood there, still holding onto the porch post and watching him.

Charlie understood. Thank goodness somebody did.

Matt let himself into the lake house as quietly as possible. To his relief, all was dim and quiet except for soft music emanating from beyond the kitchen.

He had just stepped onto the flight of stairs when the little dog darted through the kitchen, followed by Miss Lancaster. In his current state, the bright look on her face was about enough to knock him on his rear.

"Oh, you've been out," she said. "We thought you had already turned in for the night."

"I went for a walk after all," he mumbled, not taking his eyes away from hers.

"I'll be going over to the apartment in a few minutes. Can I fix you something before I go? How about some of those brownies and a glass of milk?"

In spite of the fact that he felt sluggish and awkward, he stepped back off the stair. He patted the dog's head and nodded.

"Oh, good. I didn't want to have any until you did." Her smile spread all the way to her twinkling eyes. She turned on a small lamp on the kitchen counter and took two dessert plates and glasses from the cabinet. Then she took out a knife and cut the brownies in the metal pan.

"Could you grab the milk out the fridge?" Robin tipped her head toward him, sending her long hair swaying over her shoulder.

He complied and set the plastic jug on the table. Didn't she find the situation odd? They were strangers and yet she acted like they were friends. Her smile never let up.

"I didn't ask you if you prefer nuts or not," she said.

Matt studied her face, trying to figure out if she was making a joke. She wasn't. "Nuts," he said, feeling foolish.

"Me too. Definitely nuts. Chopped pecans." Her grin returned. "Sometimes I add crushed toffee bars, but I decided to keep them simple this time around."

He returned to the place where he'd sat at dinner, and she joined him with the brownies and napkins. He put a brownie on his plate and started pouring himself some milk.

"Mmm."

Slowly setting the jug on the table, he looked at her.

"Oh. Excuse me," she said. "I try not to do that in public." She pressed the tips of her fingers over her mouth and her eyes widened. Pink bloomed on her fair cheeks.

"It's fine." Matt noticed a smattering of freckles across the bridge of her nose.

They continued to look at each other. For some reason, he felt a bit light-headed. He forced his attention back to the brownie on his plate, and they ate in companionable silence until drowsiness overtook him.

"Thanks, again. Those are delicious. Now …" He gripped the edge of the table and stood. "It's been a long day."

Robin got up too. "Good night, Professor McLaughlin. Sleep well."

Walking to the stairs felt like wading through deep water. *Now if only I can make it up the stairs.*

Robin eased back into the chair and willed herself not to watch him walk away. His tired eyes seemed to guard something painfully personal and private. *This place will be good for him.*

Noticing a brownie crumb on the table, she pressed it with the tip of her finger and licked it off. The bedroom door clicked closed upstairs, and she gathered the dishes and carried them to the kitchen sink.

With tail wagging, Callie brushed against her legs.

"We'll go outside in a minute girl. Then it's bed-time."

The dog barked in response.

"Shhh. Let's not disturb our guest."

It seemed that Professor McLaughlin needed all the rest he could get.

Chapter Six

The rich aroma of fresh coffee roused Matt from a sound sleep. Sunlight gilded the edges of the soft linen drapes. There had been no waking in the night, no midnight foraging. He lay in the comfort of satin sheets for several moments, as close to pleasure as he'd come in some time.

Weighed down with fatigue the night before, sleep had closed around him as soon as his head hit the pillow. Mercifully, he slept in oblivion. The soft surroundings made him forget where he was, and his heavy eyelids closed for one more minute of normalcy.

A dog barked outside and a woman's laughter like bells of a wind chime followed. Then he remembered. The friendly dog. The blue-eyed girl. Their situation intrigued him. She spoke in a soft voice, her words rolling out in a way part refined intelligence, part childlike transparency. Nervy yet delicate, with a genuine smile. The dog's bark resounded from farther away. He couldn't resist getting up.

Pulling back the drape, he glimpsed a furry tail whipping into the woods followed by Miss Lancaster in blue shorts. She disappeared from view, and he lifted his eyes to the open sky, rainbow colored in the morning light.

After a brisk shower, he pulled on some jogging pants and a college T-shirt and padded down the stairs. The coffee was hot. A large white mug sat on the counter beside the pot, the word *perk-a-tory* defined on its side. Unexpected humor at such an early hour brought no smile to his face. Just the opposite. Instead, he defined *purgatory*. *My life now*.

A note stuck out from beneath the cup.

Fresh pot of coffee made before our walk. Bacon, sausage links, and scrambled eggs are in the covered dish on the stove. Twenty seconds in the microwave is all it needs. You'll find a fresh fruit tray in the fridge. Hope you like honeydew and cantaloupe. You have several options to choose from for lunch. Check in the fridge. Supper at 6:00. See you then.

Matt relaxed his shoulders as he lifted the lid on the covered plate and leaned close to smell the delicious aroma of maple, hickory, and pork. A half-dozen slices of thick bacon and as many plump sausages surrounded a mound of golden scrambled eggs. While the plate warmed in the microwave, he poured himself a mug of steaming coffee. He carried his breakfast over to the table, pulled out the chair slowly, and sat down. Fresh bread and butter, peach preserves, and a small clear pitcher of thick brown syrup sat on a round lazy Susan in the center of the table.

Glad to be alone, he devoured the bacon and juicy sausage, then spread a thick slice of homemade bread with preserves. The chunks of fruit burst fresh peach flavor into his mouth, reminding him of the peaches he'd eaten—the juice running down his chin—during Tennessee summers long ago.

"Mmm." Remembering Miss Lancaster's similar reaction to the brownies the night before, his stomach clenched, giving him a startled rush. He poured himself another cup of coffee.

When he finished breakfast, he walked over to the wall of windows. The sun warmed him, and drawing a deep breath, he lifted his shoulders high around his neck and rolled them back, down, up, back, down. His muscles relaxed. He drew a deep breath and exhaled slowly. Here it might be possible to do the breathing technique the therapist suggested. He stood there for a long time, listening to the birds and wanting nothing more than to merge into the midst of the sunshine and the air and sky. Reluctant to let go of the moment, he hated to move away from the window.

It feels far away … from grief.

He returned to the kitchen for one more cup of coffee and carried it upstairs to the bedroom, where he opened the drapes wide for the view.

Soon he saw them—Miss Lancaster walking with a bounce in her step, her head erect, the sun shining on her bare shoulders, and the happy dog skipping by her side. Her red hair, fiery in the sunlight, shone against porcelain skin. He couldn't take his eyes off her.

Suddenly she looked up, waved, and smiled.

He twisted his lips into a reluctant smile before backing away from the window.

A few minutes later water could be heard running through the pipes, and several minutes after that, a door clicked closed. She was keeping out of the way, just as she said she would.

A glimpse of the neglected computer reminded him of Tom. But the urge to communicate with his friend, or any other living soul, had flown out the window. He picked up his dead cell phone and didn't bother to plug it in before tossing it on the unmade bed. After fishing the running shoes from his bag, he put them on, went downstairs, and slipped out the front door before inertia could set in.

The cool breeze carried a hint of pine and the sweet wistful scent of honeysuckle. As he neared the water, ripples lapped against the shore. The boat tied there swayed and bumped ever so slightly against the dock. He stopped and watched the almost imperceptible movement. Then he followed the path Robin had taken.

As if he had checked his past at some invisible door and walked into a mystical place, he looked at the lake and the sky and became an element in the environment. His thoughts, if he had any, were wordless impressions. When he came to a clearing around the peninsula, he sat on a weathered picnic table facing the water and propped his feet on the wooden bench. All around him was the vast expanse of sky and water.

In the distance, the lake appeared to encircle a floating stand of stunted trees. A solitary angler stood at the bow of his boat, near the small island, waiting with his line cast into the water. Across the lake, two or three houses peeped through the woods, and where the elevation rose higher on the horizon, a white wooden cross seemed to sit on the treetops.

Morning gave way to the clarity of midday. Peace had lulled him into a deep stillness. Matt sat idle for some time, forgetting about everything, until a large brown bird caught his eye. He watched in awe of its wingspan and the effortless beauty of its flight, its freedom and grace as it dipped and soared. The white-headed bird landed some forty feet away on the tallest spire of a leaf-stripped tree. Whether lightning struck or diseased, the tree looked like so many old bones. The eagle was even more striking against the juxtaposition of the bleached skeleton tree. The bird's stance suggested majesty, its flight artistry. It spread its wings and soared, flying off to some faraway place.

Matt shivered. An unexpected though not un-pleasant emotion touched his heart. Gratitude? Yes, that was it. Then there it was again. His grandpa's voice murmured in his soul.

Under his wings you will find refuge.

Within a few days, a routine effortlessly took shape. Matt ate delicious breakfasts alone while Miss Lancaster took long walks, and then he jogged and explored the woods after she returned to disappear into the left wing of the sprawling house or into the separate studio apartment.

Besides occasionally spotting her from the window, he saw her only at dinner. He would grab something simple for lunch and return to the room upstairs to read or nap or stare out the window with the spectacular view. His days were effortless. At six o'clock, dinner was served.

He'd been there five days when finally he decided to get in touch with Tom. He plugged in his cell-phone and determined to ask about Wi-Fi at dinner.

Midafternoon, he heard Miss Lancaster enter the kitchen, and within minutes Callie was sniffing at his closed door. He opened it and left it ajar. The spaniel scampered in, wagging her whole body in excitement.

"Callie, come back down here," Robin called. "Callie."

No sooner had he plopped down in the plush lounge chair, Callie jumped into his lap. He petted the dog's head and lightly scratched behind her ears.

"Callie, no."

Matt looked up to see Miss Lancaster framed by the doorway.

She smiled and tilted her head to the side, putting her hand on the doorframe beside her head. Her long red hair swung over her shoulder as she tilted her head. Her hip curved slightly to the left. "Excuse us. I'm sorry to bother you."

"Not at all." Before he realized what he was doing, his eyes trailed down the length of her.

Her arm dropped to her side and she straightened as if some disconcerting thought had struck her. "Come on, Callie." She took a step forward to retrieve the dog.

He'd been gawking. "She can stay, Miss Lancaster," he said, looking down. "She's very comfortable."

The dog cut her eyes at Robin, then closed them lazily and nuzzled closer to his side.

"The little rascal." When he glanced up, she wrinkled her nose for a second. "Robin. You can call me Robin."

"Robin, it is." He raised his eyebrows with a little nod. "And call me Matt."

"See you at dinner, Matt." She retreated down the stairs.

He returned his attention to the tenderhearted dog snuggling in his lap. She was such a softie, lounging there and loving the attention. Comfortable, and comforting too. Something about her easy devotion got to him.

He had experienced that in his life. Twice. As a child growing up with his mother and grandpa in Tennessee, his poor, simple backwoods-self thought life couldn't have been better. But all that vanished, through no fault of his own, leaving him as maimed and wounded as an animal that had chewed off its own leg in a trap. The struggle had cost him. Then quite unexpectedly, Lauren came into his life. But he lost her too, and that had been of his own doing.

Bitterness rose in his throat. Loving cost him dearly.

Might it be even more costly to never love again?

The thought hit him like a gut punch. He sucked in a breath and shut his eyes. In the years since Lauren's death, the thought of loving again had never crossed his mind. He'd had his chance and lost it. He deserved no more. Now perhaps all the idleness was affording him too much time to think, and with an absence of familiar routines, he had lost perspective.

Petting the dog, he tried to recapture a sense of calm, but the tension grew. When it became intolerable, he slid Callie off his lap and headed for the shower. The warm water would relax him and he would look decent for dinner with the pleasant proprietor.

That was the least he could do to redeem himself.

Chapter Seven

Chicken seasoned with herbs de Provence along with onions and tiny new potatoes roasted in the oven while Robin prepared the garden vegetables for a salad. Caleb's handsome face, ruddy and tanned from hours spent in the sun, came to mind, as did his muscular build, lithe from his active lifestyle. Every now and then, her heart fluttered. Tonight he would return from the fishing trip in Louisiana, and he had promised to call.

Hopefully the much-anticipated bass challenge had been a success. Caleb thrived on the comradery of those competitive events, and dreamt of the day when his would be the winning catch. Always out in the woods or on the water, he'd channeled his love of outdoor sports into becoming the area's top hunting and fishing guide. He'd landed some prestigious sponsors and business partners during the time he'd been in business for himself. He had his life together.

According to Caleb, he hadn't always been so focused. As the oldest of six children, accustomed to responsibility and structure, he'd gone a little wild at university when he'd gotten out from under his father's thumb. Everything came easy for him, not only sports and academics, but also women and opportunities. He'd reined himself in as graduation approached, earning a degree in electrical engineering to satisfy his father. Instead of going to work in the field, he took a chance on his dream.

Some would say she and Caleb were polar opposites, but any woman would be attracted to him. His innovative spirit and wholesome good looks were not his only admirable traits. He also had a great sense of family loyalty, and regardless of what he'd said last summer about not wanting to get married, she knew someday he would. He'd make a wonderful husband and father, and she intended to catch him for her own before someone else snagged him.

About the time she heard the shower upstairs, Callie padded into the kitchen.

"Oh, now you want to be with me. I see how it is." She skirted the little dog while murmuring words of caution as she opened the oven door. Savory aromas wafted over her face. "I'll just let this rest a while."

She placed the roaster on top of the stove, then set the table, adding a whimsical bouquet of primroses she'd picked on her morning walk. She'd ladle vegetables into bowls once the shower turned off, but she could start to carve the chicken. But maybe she should reserve that privilege for Professor McLaughlin.

Matt. Remember to call him Matt. Although in her opinion, the title suited him. He appeared grumpy beneath the shaggy beard. His voice was deep, and sometimes he mumbled rather than speak outright. More often than not, he wore rumpled clothing. Thank goodness he had brightened somewhat since their first evening together. Something in his dramatic dark eyes spoke to her that night. She'd seen that look in her mother's eyes when her dad was undergoing chemotherapy. So what had caused such sadness in his?

Just as she put the final touches on the table setting, Matt came down the stairs. Callie dashed to meet him, and Robin turned.

Suddenly, the landline rang.

"Oh. I forget that archaic device is here. It seldom rings." Robin swept her hand toward the dining table while crossing the room to the phone situated on the top of a small bookshelf. "Please, go ahead and sit down. The Lancasters'. Robin speaking."

"Hello, this is Tom Morgan. Is this Mrs. Lancaster, the homeowner?"

"Miss Lancaster, actually. You must be calling for my mother. I'm sorry. She isn't here. May I take a message?"

"I'm trying to reach Matthew McLaughlin. I believe he's staying there?"

"Oh, sure. Of course. Just a moment, please. I'll get him." Robin turned to Matt and held out the receiver. "For you."

Matt lifted an eyebrow and walked over to take the phone, wondering who could be calling him. "Hello?"

"Matt! I'm glad to hear your voice. It's Tom. How are you?"

"Fine. I apologize for not getting in touch with you." He knew he had no excuse, but he added, "The internet connection is down."

"It's no problem. Since I hadn't heard from you, I thought I'd better call. Make sure you made it. Well? How are you? How are the accommodations?"

"Oh, I'm fine. This is a great place."

"And you're not alone?" Tom sounded intrigued. "Miss Lancaster sounds like a nice *young* woman. What's up with that?"

"Uh …" Matt glanced toward the kitchen. Robin had disappeared. "She is. She's working out nicely. Thank you."

Tom laughed. "Hey, no need to thank me. I think that's great."

Matt felt slightly discombobulated. Had he missed something? But Robin reappeared, and he had no interest in continuing the conversation with her nearby. "I'm glad you called. I appreciate all you've done. I don't deserve you, really. Right now, dinner is waiting. Can I call you back later?"

"No problem. I just wanted to make sure you'd made it to your destination. Take care, man. Enjoy your dinner and the company."

"I will. Thanks again." He set the phone back into its cradle, then turned to Robin.

She regarded him intently, her eyebrows raised and chin tucked. "And all is well?"

"Yes." Matt returned to his place at the table.

As well as it had been in a long time.

For a moment, Robin thought the conversation had shifted to her and that Mr. Morgan would give her away. After all, he wouldn't have expected her to be there. She was relieved when the call ended with seemingly nothing said about her.

"Would you mind carving the chicken?" She carried the platter with the golden-brown chicken to the table, then set it down.

Matt paused but then picked up the knife and fork. "I don't mind." He proceeded to cut up the chicken, effortlessly removing the legs, thighs, and wings, and carving the breast into thin, even slices.

Robin stood close by, observing, but when he stopped and looked up at her, she smiled and took her seat at the table. "It looks good? Not dry?"

"No, not dry. It looks good."

She hoped so. "I have yet to roast a chicken as beautifully as my mother does. Sometimes I over-bake it." Realizing she was rambling, she changed the subject. "Please, serve yourself first."

Matt chose several pieces of chicken, then passed the platter to Robin, who chose one small slice of white meat. The vegetables and gravy made the rounds, and she continued to serve herself minuscule portions. The prospect of Mr. Morgan calling her out, coupled with her anticipation of Caleb's phone call, had left her without an appetite.

Matt probably could have eaten the whole juicy chicken if he were alone. But with Robin as his dining companion, he exercised restraint. No need to call attention to his boorish habits. Odd, how her presence provided him more self-control than he'd had in years.

Already accustomed to her, he detected a subtle change in her mood and appetite that evening. Usually she was more talkative, quite chatty really, and tonight her blue eyes seemed guarded. While she watched Callie sit patiently by his chair, Matt eyed Robin.

Suddenly, Callie bounced up and rushed to the front door. A bump sounded on the porch floorboards outside, and the doorbell's non-stop chime brought a barrage of sharp barks.

"Excuse me. Again." Robin pushed back from the table. "I wonder who that could be. I'm not expecting anyone." She crossed the room and opened the door.

A tall, lean, blond-haired man stepped inside and swooped Robin up into his arms as she squealed with delight. "You're a sight for sore eyes, girl!" He lifted her off her feet and twirled her around like a rag doll.

"I've been waiting for your call," she said breathlessly. "But you're here!"

"I couldn't wait for no dang phone call. I hurried over here." Setting her back on her feet, he held her at arms' length and grinned broadly. "Let me get a good look at you." He looked her up and down in an exaggerated manner, obviously enjoying himself.

"Caleb!" She giggled. "Stop it. You're embarrassing me."

The chair scraped against the floor as Matt stood, and the two turned toward him. Heat flooded his neck and cheeks. Mercifully, his beard hid the evidence of his discomfort.

"Well, hey." Caleb took a step back from Robin as his eyes widened in his suddenly blank face. He glanced at Robin, then back at Matt. "It looks like I've interrupted your supper."

"Not a problem." Matt couldn't have sounded any more dispassionate.

"Oh, it's quite all right. Join us. I've made roasted chicken." Robin chattered in her usual upbeat manner, clearly oblivious to the men's discomfort. She awaited a response, admiring Caleb's tanned face while he stared at Matt.

"I was headed over to Zach and Jenny's," Caleb said, his voice flatter. "Thought you might want to come. That's why I stopped by."

"Sure. I'd love to." Robin sounded delighted.

Caleb looked back and forth between them. "Aren't you going to introduce us?"

"Oh. Of course." Turning, she extended her arm toward Matt. "Caleb Jackson, I'd like for you to meet Professor Matthew McLaughlin."

"One of your old professors?" Caleb asked, incredulous.

Robin sucked in a breath and shook her head. "Oh no." Her usual ready flow of words bottlenecked in her throat. She was both amused and mortified at Caleb's ridiculous question. "He's not one of my former professors."

Matt stepped forward and stuck out his hand. "Associate Professor of History, University of California San Diego."

Although Caleb shook his hand with a casual air, he was visibly flummoxed.

"We've just met this week," Robin said. "Mom arranged for Professor McLaughlin to rent the house. I'll explain everything on the way to Zach and Jenny's. Give me five minutes to change." She spoke so quickly and animated that no one else could get a word in.

Making her exit, she clandestinely directed her raised eyebrows and down-stretched mouth at Matt. Apparently, this wasn't the way she'd meant for Caleb to make his acquaintance.

Matt didn't move.

After a long moment, Caleb broke their stare and sauntered over to the windows. With his hands thrust into his pant pockets, he looked out at the lake. "Great view. When did you say you got here?"

"Monday." *If it's any of your business.*

"Huh. What's this about renting the house?"

The man's tone annoyed Matt. He was loath to respond to intrusive questions, but for Robin's sake, he gave a noncommittal reply. "I'm on sabbatical."

Caleb whipped around as quickly as a fisherman might throw out a line. "Well. Don't you think you've hit the jackpot." He spoke the words evenly, with no effort to disguise the mistrust in his voice.

Matt tensed but held his silence.

A few minutes later, Robin returned wearing a light blue sundress. Her wavy hair, previously up in some kind of bun, fell loose down her back. She stopped beside Matt, her eyes searching his. "Please excuse us for interrupting supper. I hope you'll enjoy your meal and the rest of the evening."

Matt dipped his head in a nod.

Caleb, who now waited by the door, rested a hand on Robin's back when she reached him, drawing her to his side. "Yeah, man. Enjoy your dinner. Nice to have met you." He smiled with no hint of hostility, then ushered her out and pulled the door closed behind them.

Matt sat back down at the table. He picked up his fork but didn't eat. Instead, he dissected the previous scene until the food was cold. "An *old* professor? And don't I think I've won the jackpot?" he grumbled. "I didn't like his tone one bit."

Callie gave a short sharp bark. She looked up at him from beside his chair, her ears perked up.

"What do you think, Callie? You don't think much of Mr. Smart-Aleck either, do you?"

Callie's tongue lolled out and her tail thumped in sympathetic support.

"What on earth could she see in him?" He took a bite of chicken, which now tasted like cardboard. He reached down and allowed Callie to nibble it off his fingers. His appetite was gone anyway. He got up and scraped his plate and Robin's into the garbage disposal, then cleared the rest of their dishes and wiped the table with a dishcloth. He covered the serving dishes with plastic wrap and set them in the refrigerator.

The evening stretched out before him, silent and empty. He plopped onto the sofa with the intention of sorting out his thoughts, but instead he found himself brooding. Callie sprang up beside him, but within minutes uncomfortable feelings needled him. He stood so abruptly that he bumped the coffee table.

Callie tipped her head, looking at him quizzically.

"And why should I feel"—he raised his arms like an orator— "aggravated? Makes no sense the guy got under my skin." His arms fell to his sides and he began pacing in front of the windows. Sunset's soft light refused to let him sulk. After a few minutes, he folded his arms across his chest and scratched his beard just like the proverbial absentminded professor. Then he stopped. He closed his eyes and listened. There was no sound of her nearby. Yet still he listened.

The sound of silence gave way to the beating of his heart. He no longer listened outside of himself, but to his soul. Thoughts gathered like clouds on the horizon, and words registered in his mind like the rat-tat-tat of Morse code. He squeezed his eyes tighter shut, trying hard to comprehend. Then he opened his eyes, grabbed the back of his head, and looked upward.

Callie growled at the sudden gestures.

Matt turned away from the windows and headed for the stairs. "Come on, Callie."

For the first time in four years, all he wanted to do was shut himself in a room and write down the words running through his head. A mystery unfolded.

And the old desire rekindled.

Chapter Eight

Sitting beside Caleb in the cab of his truck, Robin pressed her hand to her chest. Her heart still raced due to his unexpected arrival. He had his eyes on the road, and his silent distraction contrasted greatly to his demeanor when he'd walked through her door.

She leaned toward him. "Hey, you. You're a sight for sore eyes too."

He turned to her with an odd, almost angry look, which was quickly replaced by a smile. Then he pulled her closer, draped his arm around her shoulders, and gently caressed her upper arm. "I didn't know I missed you this much." Tipping his head down, he looked at her.

"That's sweet of you to say. I missed you too."

He returned his attention to the road. "Well, aren't you going to tell me about this professor?"

"There isn't much to tell. Mom rented the house to him some months ago without telling me a thing about it. After our condominium burned, I told her I

71

would live at the lake. That's when she broke the news."

"Are you living there now? Or were you just there for dinner? I'm confused."

"I am living there, yes … in the studio apartment. He rented the house, so he has complete run of it. We have an arrangement. I'm preparing meals and taking care of things, much like an innkeeper for a bed-and-breakfast."

His expression hardened. "I can't believe your mother would allow it."

Robin sighed softly, remembering the somewhat nerve-wracking conversation she'd had with her mom on the topic earlier in the week. The dreaded call actually hadn't gone as badly as she'd anticipated. She held her ground with her mother then, and she could do it with Caleb if needed. "Well. She wasn't thrilled when I told her I was staying on at the lake, and in what capacity, but she knows I can do this and how much I want to be there. I don't want to live in Atlanta with Emily or move to Virginia with her."

"I wouldn't want that either, but do you think you can trust this character? He looks like a throw-back to Woodstock."

"Oh, Caleb." He did have a point, but still. "He's fine. He's taking a sabbatical from the university. I really don't know anything about him though, except that Callie is crazy about him."

"And you think because the dog likes him, you can trust him?" He sounded even more peeved.

"The real estate company vetted him. They did a background check, I think. Now let's talk about something else."

"When were you going to tell me about this?"

"When I saw you this weekend, of course. There's no need to be concerned. I see the man at suppertime. The rest of the day, I keep to myself and so does he."

"It sounds like you're putting a lot of trust in someone you don't know anything about. Have you googled him?"

"Certainly not. There's no need for that. Besides, it's an invasion of privacy."

"I think you should."

"I honestly couldn't feel safer." Maybe a bit intimidated, she thought, but perfectly safe.

Caleb made a disgruntled sound. "You call me if you need anything. I'm always close by. And let him know that."

"Oh, for goodness' sake, don't worry. It's a temporary arrangement. He'll be gone by the first of the year. Look on the bright side. I'm here!"

An uneasy silence fell between them. Fortunately, Zach and Jenny lived right up the road and the conversation could soon end. She settled against him. Dusk had turned to darkness by the time they left the wooded lake area and neared the lights of the village where Caleb's brother and sister-in-law lived.

"You could always stay at my house, you know." Caleb gave her arm a squeeze. "If you need to."

"Oh no, I couldn't. You can't be serious. This arrangement will work out fine with a quiet, serious person like Professor McLaughlin. I assure you of that."

He met her gaze, his eyes serious. "It better, or I will send him packing."

Caleb pulled into the driveway of the craftsman bungalow where Zach and Jenny lived. Several dogwood trees stood on either side of the front yard, and a large oak in the backyard towered over the house. Multicolored impatiens grew in abundance around the front porch, shining in the glow of solar lights in mason jars. Another one of Jenny's Pinterest projects, probably.

When Robin had met Jenny last summer, they'd quickly learned they had a lot in common. Besides being the same age, Jenny was also an elementary school teacher with an interest in art. And they were both smitten with Jackson men.

Zach, handsome and tall like his brother, opened the door to welcome them, and Jenny came to his side. Zach was a CPA, a livelihood much too tedious and confined for Caleb. He and Caleb were brothers the closest in age.

"Hey." The men exchanged hard and fast bear hugs, slapping each other on the back. "You outdid yourself, man! Great job!"

Caleb laughed heartily and gave him an affectionate jab on the shoulder.

Jenny hugged him. "Good to see you, Caleb. Congratulations." Smiling, she turned to Robin. "And it's great to see you too."

"Come on in and sit down. We just started watching a season of *The Office.*"

"Yeah, we felt like binging on comedy, Zach style." She giggled. "It's Netflix. Pause it, Zach. I'll go get some drinks and snacks."

"A Coke for me," Caleb said.

"I'll help." Robin followed Jenny into the kitchen.

The guys had already kicked back in the recliners on each end of the over-stuffed sofa, in rapt conversation about the tournament. With shining eyes fixed on his brother, Zach was the perfect audience for the minute-by-minute descriptions of the competitive events and trophy catches.

"Gosh, it's good to see the two of *you* together," Jenny said as they walked into the cozy kitchen. "You're dating again?"

"Well, I think we are. This is the first time I've seen Caleb since we went out to dinner in April. He'd come into the city on business and we went out. We've kept in touch ever since. Not so much over the winter, you know."

"He told us about the fire. How awful! We were sorry to hear about that. You've already been through enough with your dad's illness and passing."

Robin nodded slowly. "We were fortunate not to have lost everything like some of the residents did. Our unit was on the end of the complex. But for the grace of God, right?"

"Absolutely. So now you're at the lake. That's great. I really enjoyed your being here last summer."

"Thanks. Me too. I'm glad to be back. I love that house. And you know how I hope things will work out for Caleb and me." The women exchanged knowing looks. "Besides that, I want to focus on illustrating my children's stories. Maybe look into publishing. Daddy and I shared that dream."

"Aww, that's a wonderful dream. With your talent, you really should. I wish I could draw as well as you do."

"Are you kidding? You're multi-talented. Your signature is all over this place, inside and out."

A smile spread across Jenny's round pretty face. She took ham and cheese slices and pimento cheese out of the refrigerator and started making sandwiches. After pouring Tostito chips into a bowl, she grabbed a large plate spread with layers of chili, bean dip, sour cream, salsa, chopped onions, and cheese.

"That taco pizza looks yummy."

"I make lots of snacks for the weekend. Zach loves to eat. You'd never know it by looking at him. He has a high metabolism. I, on the other hand … well, let's just say everything goes to my fanny."

They both laughed, and Jenny handed Robin the plate of sandwiches. Together they carried the food into the den.

The men ate and chatted for at least an hour about fishing while the women caught up with snippets of information about their lives and families, teaching, and summer plans. The friendly atmosphere made it seem like no time at all had passed since they'd hung out together last summer.

Then Caleb caught Robin's eye and patted the cushion next to him. "Come sit over here."

She did, and Jenny moved to the seat beside Zach. They turned on an episode of *The Office* and joked around for the rest of the evening.

"I hope we'll be seeing a lot of you this summer," Zach said when he and Jenny walked Robin and Caleb to the door.

"I'm already looking forward to working with you in your studio," Jenny added.

Robin couldn't wait. "We'll certainly do that."

Caleb gave a lopsided smile. "That is if Robin's professor doesn't mind."

Both Zach and Jenny looked at her, and she couldn't think of a thing to say. "*Caleb!*" His name came out like a plaintive moan.

Jenny arched an eyebrow. "Your professor?"

"Oh, Robin didn't tell you? She has a renter at her house for six months. A bearded guy with wild hair who I mistook for one of her old professors."

Robin cut her eyes at him. "My mom rented the lake house to a professor on sabbatical. One of her friends manages rental properties, so she arranged it. I didn't know anything about it until recently. For the most part, I'm staying in the studio apartment."

"But she's cooking for him," Caleb added, stepping behind Robin and draping his arms around her shoulders. "What do you think of that?"

Zach looked from Caleb to her but said nothing.

Jenny shook her head. "Oh, stop it, you two. Robin is a sensible adult. Women manage B&Bs all the time, and the guests don't molest them. This isn't any different." With a roll of her eyes, she backhanded her husband's arm. "You guys are so territorial and old-fashioned." After spontaneously grabbing Caleb in a hug, she turned to Robin and did the same. "I'll call you and we'll plan to get together soon."

Zach nodded at Caleb. "Call me when we can go fishing."

Caleb reached for Robin's hand on the way to his truck. He held the door for her, and they got in without a word. When they waved at the couple standing on the porch, he smiled. "Aren't they something?"

"They're such fun. I enjoy spending time with them." Robin looked down at her hands in her lap. How she'd love to have what they had.

"Hey. I'm sorry I brought up the guy renting your place."

"Oh." She sighed. "It just … it kinda felt like you were calling me out."

"It did, didn't it? I'm sorry. I'm over it, okay? Jenny's right. You're responsible and sensible. Besides, you have me to keep an eye out for you."

Robin glanced at him and smiled. "I feel better knowing you've accepted this inconvenient arrangement."

When they arrived at the lake house, Caleb walked her to the door. "But shouldn't I take you around to the apartment?"

She raised her eyes to his. "I have to clean up dishes and Callie's inside."

"I'll come in and help."

"I don't have free run of the house, remember. Bringing a friend in at almost midnight isn't quite appropriate." Against her wishes, an apologetic tone crept into her voice. Just the same, she wasn't going to back out of the arrangement. She intended to follow through with her plan.

Caleb nodded. "It's all right. I get it, honey." He placed his hand on the back of her head and drew her into his arms. Their lips brushed softly as they looked into each other eyes. "I've wanted to do this for days."

Their lips met again as they melted into each other's arms. When at last he pulled away, she was breathless. She touched his cheek and he leaned close to kiss her again.

"Good night, Caleb."

"Wanna go to dinner tomorrow night?" He kissed her once more.

"Uh-huh."

"Pick you up at seven?" His hands slowly slid down her arms to grasp her hands. Their fingers intertwined.

"Okay."

"Okay." Another tiny kiss brushed her lips.

"Good night," she said with a giggle.

"Good night." He backed away slowly.

She watched him walk to the truck, then took out her keys and lifted her hand in a timid wave. He waited as she unlocked the door and stepped inside.

She closed the door silently, leaned back against it, and listened to the sound of the truck as he drove away. There was something terribly appealing about him … his dynamic personality that could fill up a room, his aura that made her as weak as a kitten.

"Slow down," she whispered in the dark, closing her eyes and putting a steadying hand to her heart. "Don't get ahead of me again."

Matt heard the truck crunch down the gravel road about the same time Callie did. He stopped typing and listened. The dog jumped up from her place at his feet and sniffed around the closed bedroom door. Then she returned to touch her nose to his arm.

"Wait a second, Callie." He stared at the screen in awe. "I'm writing." He clicked *save.*

Keys jangled downstairs, and Callie's tail swished a quick tempo on the floor. Matt stood and stretched before crossing the room. As soon as he opened the door, she scooted out and disappeared into the dark.

Matt waited in the doorway. A light clicked on downstairs, and he heard Robin murmuring to the dog. Muted sounds drifted from the kitchen, and he took a step into the doorway. Unwillingly, he felt a tug to join them, but he stepped back and closed the door.

Well, maybe old Charlie was right. He had lost his mind.

Instead, he went to the window. The lake shone under a sky full of stars. He had no reason to join them. She wouldn't be there in the first place if Tom hadn't made the preposterous arrangement. Still, it had been easy to get used to her being around. He listened for a few minutes more, imagining what she would be doing, picturing her graceful movements. Then he returned to the desk and sat down. Somewhat reluctantly, he leaned closer to the screen and read what he'd written.

They were powerful words. As if by magic, he slipped under their spell—forgetting failure, forgetting loss. His mind soared, leaving the present as well as the past behind for some better place he was creating.

Chapter Nine

The summer began in earnest, and soon several weeks had passed. Robin rose early each morning, dressed in shorts and tank top, and put on her running shoes. Callie followed her out the door of the studio, and they crept into the house to make breakfast for her tenant before taking a long race-walk down the dirt road and into the cool woods. Some days, she stripped off her shoes to enjoy a dip in the lake afterward. She'd then shower and return to tidy up the kitchen without so much as a glimpse of Matt. By then she was eager to work in the studio on illustrations for her stories, and in midafternoon she returned to the kitchen to make supper. Sometimes she dined with Matt, but most evenings she went out with Caleb.

Since the night of Caleb's surprise visit, Robin felt a change in rapport with her guest. He remained an enigma, closed off to her. He seemed more relaxed and somehow more alight with an inexplicable intensity. Yet if they'd had a budding friendship, it had withered on the vine. In its place sprouted a more professional working relationship. Few words passed between them.

It was just as well, Robin surmised.

Even though Matt had stayed up writing until after two, he awoke before dawn, going over and over plot details in his mind. Writing derailed when the birds' chorus reached a crescendo outside his window. The sound reminded him of rain on a tin roof. He closed his eyes, remembering the tin-roofed home of his boyhood, then dozed on and off, pleasantly content to stay burrowed under the covers.

Already the day had a different vibe. He heard Robin and Callie come in downstairs, whereas normally he slept right through it, only occasionally hearing a vague sound through the veil of sleep and then discovering that she had indeed been there and made a full breakfast. Sometimes the delicious aromas stirred his sleep, but he got up only when he knew she had already gone out.

Today was different. It seemed awfully early, and something was different about the smells and sounds. He wanted to see for himself what she was doing.

Matt got up and pulled on a white T-shirt and black sweat pants. He had to tighten the drawstring since the pants had gotten loose. In the bathroom, he combed his fingers through his hair before splashing cold water on his face.

At the top of the stairs, he hesitated, listening. "Good morning down there!"

A little laugh came from the kitchen, and Callie's nails scraped across the hardwood floor. She was up the stairs and licking his ankles within seconds. He chuckled. Slowly he descended the stairs, careful not to step on the dog or trip over her.

Robin stood in front of the stove with a large two-pronged fork in her hand, tending a frying pan. Wearing shorts and an oversized T-shirt that fell off her shoulder and with her hair framing her face, she was prettier than a sunrise.

"Good morning." She spoke quietly, as if trying not to wake anyone, then offered a shy, quirky smile. "I *am* going to make your breakfast. I promise. As soon as I fry this chicken. I'm sorry I woke you."

Did she always look so vibrant first thing in the morning?

"You didn't wake me." Matt looked from her to the chicken sizzling in the hot oil and raised his eyebrows, smiling slightly. "You compete with Colonel Sanders?"

"Ha. No contest. Fried chicken was my daddy's forte. I'm making enough for you. I'm making potato salad too, for a picnic later." That explained the large pot that steamed on the back burner of the stove.

"That's nice." He moved closer to watch what she was doing.

She glanced at him a few times while turning the chicken. Her elbow bumped him.

"I'm in the way." Matt stepped over to the coffee pot and took out the carafe. "I'll make the coffee." He filled it with water, added scoops of coffee, and pushed the button. Then he set out the coffee mugs just the way she always had them arranged when he came down for breakfast.

She glanced at the cups, then up at him. Her lips curled into a smile. The rosy blush of her cheeks was the same color as her lips.

Suddenly self-conscious, Matt took a deep breath and walked out of the kitchen into the living room. Callie followed on his heels. He sat down and began rubbing the dog's head. "Aren't you the pretty girl? Yes, you are. Oh yes, you are." He talked to the dog like he might talk to a child.

Callie jumped into his lap.

"How do you like your coffee?" Robin asked. "I'll bring you a cup."

"You're busy enough. I can get it." He set the dog on the floor and got up, then eased past Robin to the other side of the kitchen. "How do you take yours?"

"With lots of cream and sugar."

He felt her eyes on him as he put a teaspoonful of sugar in the cup, then added cream and stirred in the coffee. Just as he was about to set the cup on the counter beside her, he looked into her eyes. The world faded, and almost like an out-of-body experience, he drew closer. Without thinking, he lifted the cup to her lips.

Her blue eyes searched his as she took a sip of the hot coffee. His lips parted too. Still looking at him with wide eyes, she moistened her lips with the tip of her tongue. A surge of pure desire rose up his belly, catching him totally off guard. He hastened to set the cup on the counter and turned away.

He took his time pouring himself a cup, then headed for the stairs. "I'll get out of your way and come down at the regular time."

If Robin responded, he didn't hear her for the rush still surging through his limbs.

Robin's knees felt weak. She leaned against the counter and considered sitting down for a few moments. Instead she blew out a slow, silent whistle. Once she'd regained her composure, she opened the refrigerator and pulled out mayonnaise and sweet pickle relish for the potato salad.

A nice pickle I'm in. She set the relish on the counter and stared at the pattern in the granite. What had just happened?

For one brief, blissful moment, something passed between them—like some sensual symbiosis. His beautiful deep gray eyes drew her in, and she couldn't pull herself away from them. Now her hands were shaking. He hadn't acted anything like himself, but neither had she, which made no sense at all. Mercifully he'd gone upstairs.

Robin drained the potatoes and dumped them into a large bowl, then stirred in seasoned salt, pepper, and diced boiled eggs, or at least she hoped she had. Her mind kept replaying the tremulous moments. Matt stirring her coffee, their eyes meeting, his holding the cup tenderly to her lips.

She hurried to get the food ready for the picnic so she could make breakfast. Strawberries, blueberries, and whipped cream were already in bowls. She wrote a note on a napkin—*Happy Fourth of July!*—and stuck a little American flag in the bowl of mixed fruit. She wrapped several pieces of crispy chicken in aluminum foil and dished some of the potato salad into a plastic bowl that she put in the refrigerator for dinner. The rest of the food went into a small cooler.

Since Matt had gone upstairs, Robin hadn't heard a sound. Now the shower was on.

"Let's go, Callie."

They needed to leave before he came back downstairs. She didn't dare look at him right now. For some reason, she felt vulnerable and out of place in her own house—for the first time all summer.

Matt had to be losing his mind. What had gotten into him? He had a few choice words for his Neanderthal self. Her eyes the color of summer skies had captured his, and in that moment, he lost his grip on reality. They were the only two people alive. But what must she think of him now? Heat rose to his face at the thought of it.

After a shower, he lingered in his bedroom until he was sure she had left. How was he going to look at her the next time they met?

Downstairs, his breakfast—decorated with a little flag and note—waited for him. Already the Fourth of July. The weeks had flown since he started writing again. Progress had continued steadily without a hitch since the story's conception, and he thought through the plot again while he ate his cleverly prepared red, white, and blue breakfast. This morning he'd been elated with the novel's progress. Maybe that explained why he had acted the way he had. Still, he couldn't get Robin out of his mind.

I hope I haven't jinxed myself. I must have come off like some kind of weirdo.

He'd waited too late for a run, although he hated disrupting the new habit. He had to get out before nine to avoid the heat. It was just as well. He needed to resume where he'd left off with the story in his head this morning. At the rate he'd been writing, he'd finish the novel by the time the sabbatical came to an end. Writing was working wonders getting him out of his funk. Lauren would be happy.

Lauren. He hadn't thought of her yet today. A wave of sadness washed over him. Writing loosened his grip on the past and on her as well.

While he struggled to refocus his thoughts, his cell phone chirped.

He picked it up. "Hello, Tom. Happy Fourth of July!"

"How are you, Matt? Lydia sends her love."

"Give your charming wife a hug for me. I hope she and the kids are well. You're up early. What are you doing to celebrate the holiday?"

"There's a cookout on campus. We went last year, remember? Lots of fun things for the kids. A magic show, fireworks. Will you be celebrating?"

He grinned. "Well ... I'll be working on my new novel."

"Is *that* right? Oh man, you've made my day. That's great news. You pushed through the wall. I knew you would."

"It wasn't anything I did, really. The story came to me in a burst of clarity. It's been like rolling out a scroll. Totally unlike anything I've experienced before. Now it's a matter of getting it out before I do something to screw it up."

"You're writing again. That's a breakthrough. There's no reason to believe you won't finish it."

"I take nothing for granted, Tom. Nothing." Momentarily, he thought of the happiness he and Lauren once shared.

"Understood. Still, it's good news."

"Thanks. You know, you really did me a service with this gig. Now I see the method in your madness with the added amenities. I'm eating right and feeling better. Hey, I'm even running again."

"Impressive. But what do you mean, *added amenities*?"

"Miss Lancaster preparing my meals, of course. You're a sly one. But I won't lie. I cursed you at first and resented the intrusion." He chuckled. "She's a great cook."

Tom was silent for a few moments. "Uh … I'd like to take credit … but only where credit is due. The homeowner is cooking for you? The lady from whom you're renting the house?"

"Okay, Tom, pretend you don't know about it. Seriously. You're the best."

In the background, kids called, "Daddy!"

"I guess you hear that chorus of happy voices." Tom chuckled. "They've been like this since the crack of dawn. They're ready to pile into the car, so I need to go. But I can't tell you how glad I am to hear you're doing well."

"Thanks, and give my best to the girls." He hung up and stared at the phone.

Although Tom hadn't said it, Matt knew that he and his wife had been praying for him. He was grateful for friends who hadn't given up on him even when he had given up on himself.

Chapter Ten

As soon as she heard laughter and the honking of the boat's horn, Robin grabbed her sunglasses and tote, along with her contribution to the picnic, and hurried out the door and down to the lake. The day was clear and sunny, perfect for a holiday.

The boat was full of smiling women waving at her exuberantly. Caleb loved entertaining his sisters. She couldn't wait to join them.

"Hi, y'all! Is there room for me?" Robin came to a stop at the edge of the wooden dock.

Caleb stood and stretched out his arm to her. "Sure there is, honey. You're next to me."

She looked into his eyes, as green as grass in the sunlight, and took his hand. A warm flush of pride put a wide smile on her face.

Claire, who looked much like her brother, slid out of the passenger seat and onto the edge of the boat beside the other girls on the backrow seat. All were dressed in swimsuits and flip-flops, while Robin wore a light sundress over her suit, red Keds, and a floppy brimmed straw hat. She had slathered on plenty of sunscreen earlier. After years of living on the water, she knew what she had to do to avoid the blistering effects of the sun on her fair skin.

Caleb leaned over and planted a kiss on her cheek before revving the engine and heading out to the center of the lake. The boat jerked as he shifted gears and picked up speed. Robin squealed and slapped her hand on top of her head to keep the hat from blowing off.

"It's nice to see you," Claire called.

"You too." Robin shifted so she could look at the girls in the back. Claire was attractive and tanned, with sandy-blond hair. She was closest to Caleb in age, while Mary Beth, who sat beside her, was next in birth order. "Hi, Mary Beth. Where are the kiddos?"

"On the beach with their daddy and Zach and Jenny, setting up the picnic site. You know everybody, right?"

"I think so, in spite of the fact you all look alike." Looking at each one, she said their names in her head. *Claire, Mary Beth, Rachel.* "Rachel, you're the youngest, right?" Next to Rachel sat a girl she didn't recognize.

"I'm Kaitlin." The young woman combed slender fingers through blond hair heavily streaked with strawberry pink. "Rachel and I were conjoined twins separated at birth." She tilted her Audrey Hepburn sunglasses down to peer at Robin, then tossed her head and laughed.

Robin laughed, trying not to make a face at the girl's odd response.

Rachel pursed her lips and rolled her eyes. "We've been best friends since first grade."

That made more sense. "Oh, that's great. Almost like having another sister."

"Something like that." Kaitlin gave Rachel a sly look.

Unlike the other women, Claire didn't laugh, nor did she smile at Kaitlin's introduction. In fact, she gave Kaitlin a look that would have set most polite women back on their heels. Robin tried to ignore the uneasiness that poked her. It was a look of disapproval, possibly even disdain. She glanced at Kaitlin to see her reaction, but she wasn't paying any attention. Nor was Caleb. He smiled into the wind, and she reached over and gave his arm a squeeze. When she glanced back at Claire, the baffling look had vanished.

"I've been looking forward to this." Robin raised her voice so he'd hear her over the engine.

Caleb winked at her. "Me too."

Robin turned her face to the wind, content to be speeding across the water by his side.

"Are you going to let me get you up on skis first?" he asked, a twinkle in his eyes.

"Why not? I definitely don't want to follow any of these class acts." She pointed her thumb at the girls behind her.

"As soon as I get a bit farther out."

They raced along for a few minutes before Caleb slowed the boat. Robin took off her shoes and hat, then slipped off the dress and shoved it into her bag. Claire handed her a life jacket and Robin strapped it on.

Caleb grinned. "Ready to get out there?"

"You bet." Robin jumped into the water and swam to the back of the boat. Claire leaned over to hand her the skis, one at a time. Robin bent her knees and carefully fitted them on, then grabbed the tow rope Rachel tossed to her. After aligning her body in the proper position, she took a deep breath and blew it out slowly, reminding herself to relax. This was her first time on skis for the season. She was liable to be a bit shaky. "Hey! When I'm ready, don't pull me up too fast."

Caleb nodded and held up an okay sign.

Robin took another deep breath. "Hit it!" Bracing herself for the tug of the rope, she leaned back slightly. Exhilaration rushed through her body as she rose. A collective cheer went up from their party, and she smiled feeling the wind and spray on her face.

After a few minutes going straight ahead, she raised her arm and signaled for the boat to turn around. She glided smoothly across the wakes. About fifteen minutes later, she signaled for the boat to stop and then let go of the rope.

The boat came back around for her, and Mary Beth jumped in. "I've got to take my turn now so I can get back to the kids." In a matter of minutes, she was up and gliding across the water.

"Good job, honey." Caleb leaned toward her for a quick kiss as she dried herself with a towel.

Robin looked behind them and smiled. "Wow. She skis like a pro."

"Let's not compare our ability to these other ladies'," Claire said. "It's a serious advantage to have been on the university waterski team."

"Yeah, sis." Rachel turned from watching Mary Beth and looked right at Claire. "And if I remember correctly, you disapproved."

Claire shrugged and lifted a brow. "At first, maybe I did."

"Nothing I'd dare attempt," Robin said.

"Nor I," Claire agreed.

"We'll have time for one more before lunch." Caleb interrupted the sibling banter. "Who's going next?"

Kaitlin and Rachel spoke at once, then laughed at themselves.

"You go," Kaitlin said. "Might as well save the best for last. I'll go this afternoon."

"Great." Rachel grinned confidently. "I've been doing this since I was six years old. Y'all watch and learn."

As soon as Mary Beth took off the skis, she passed them to Rachel, who was eager to prove her prowess. Her slender figure glided swiftly across the water and hopped effortlessly across the wakes. She bent her knees from time to time and lifted her leg to hop on one ski, then another, every move controlled. Robin watched in awe.

"She's such a show-off," Claire said with a smile.

The traffic on the lake had picked up. All the while Rachel was on the water, other boats passed by, their occupants smiling and waving. It was easy to keep a safe distance on the wide lake, and Caleb kept a close watch all around.

Suddenly, a sleek speedboat approached as another boat towing a kid on a watercraft passed by. Rather than go on the wayward side of the boats, the speedboat cut a path close to the side of Caleb's boat.

"Watch out!" Caleb shouted at the reckless driver. "Are you crazy?"

Robin looked back and gasped. The water behind them churned like a maelstrom. Rachel crouched down on the skis, close to the surface of the choppy water. Just when it seemed she'd weathered the worst of it, one of her knees bounced up much higher than the other and the ski veered off on its own. Rachel continued to hold the rope, and her body and the skis twisted and flipped. She hit the water hard.

Mary Beth and Kaitlin screamed and grabbed one another. Claire never took her eyes away from where Rachel went down. Caleb swore under his breath as he turned the boat around and headed back for Rachel, who still hadn't raised her arms out of the water to indicate she was okay. Before Robin knew what was happening, Claire jumped out of the boat, and Caleb yelled for Mary Beth to take the wheel. Then, he dove in.

Moments later, Caleb surfaced with Rachel in his arms. Claire was right beside them, as calm as could be. Rachel, at first flailing and gasping for air, dissolved limp and groaning onto the floor of the boat. Claire supported her upper body in her lap. A hush fell over the group at the sight of her leg, which lay in an unnatural position, visibly twisted and fuchsia colored at the knee. An ugly knot protruded beside where her knee should have been. Before they got to shore, she was writhing in pain.

Caleb passed Robin the orange signal flag to hold up so those on shore would realize they had an emergency, and then he headed in. Everything happened so quickly. As soon as they reached shore, people rushed toward them and Caleb shouted orders. He grabbed his youngest brother Paul by the shoulders, said something inaudible to him, and then ran back to Rachel. Paul jumped in a truck and took off down the dirt road.

"We have no time to wait for the EMTs," Claire said. "Her knee is dislocated. We have to move fast." Although she sounded calm, her face had taken on an ashen hue.

"I know. We can't wait for them. Our cells won't work anyway. I'm going to the station in town so they can transport her by ambulance to the hospital." Caleb and Zack started carrying Rachel to his truck.

Claire protested.

"If Paul gets us the police escort, we'll drive straight there," Caleb told her.

Claire climbed into the back seat and cradled Rachel in her arms. Kaitlin jumped into the passenger seat.

Caleb, his face grim, looked over his shoulder at Robin. "I'll call you."

Mary Beth clung to her husband, and Jenny grabbed Robin's hand.

"Poor Rachel," Robin whispered. "She's in so much pain."

"She's in good hands. Claire and Caleb know what they're doing," Zach said.

"Claire will make sure of that, the way she mothers you all," Jenny added.

"I think she became a PA just so she could take care of this family." Mary Beth smiled weakly.

Mary Beth's husband led her toward the picnic table. "Honey, why don't we get the kids fed, then we'll go home. I'll watch the kids at the pool while we wait for news."

"Right. We won't get phone reception here." Zach looked around at them all. "We need to call Mom and Dad too. But first, let's pray for Rachel."

They all drew together, pressed close and held hands, while Zach prayed for Rachel and Jenny added requests for all those who would take care of her.

Robin walked away somewhat encouraged but still greatly concerned for Rachel's welfare and feeling wretched about the accident. No one had seen it coming on what was supposed to be a fun-filled day.

"Thanks for bringing me home." Robin clutched her hat and tote in one hand as she got out of the truck, then grabbed her little cooler off the floor. She stood beside Jenny's open window, shifting uneasily from one foot to the other.

Zach and Jenny both looked at her with solemn faces. "Of course," he said. "We didn't mind."

"We'll let you know as soon as we know something." Jenny offered a faint, joyless smile.

"Please do." Robin watched as they drove away, then sighed as she turned toward the house. She walked around to the studio, where Callie greeted her as she opened the door. "Hi, girl."

Callie bounced around her to scoot out the door and run willy-nilly.

Robin dropped her things beside the door and followed Callie through the woods. Eventually they made their way to the dock, and Robin sat down and let her feet dangle over the side. She gazed across the lake and thought of all that had taken place in the last few hours. They were thinking only of the fun they were having. In an instant, everything changed.

Fortunately, both Caleb and Claire were amazing. Robin admired the family's collective response to the emergency.

She clasped her arms tightly around her body, still shaking a little. At the same time, she realized her skin was burning hot. She rose and headed back to the lake house so she could sit in a shady spot and wait for a call.

Chapter Eleven

It wasn't that Matt was spying on Robin, but when he heard the truck outside and then her voice, he couldn't help looking out the window. He hadn't expected her back until late. For a few moments, she stood by the truck talking to its occupants. Her shoulders seemed to droop.

He walked away from the window and returned to his computer. Writing resumed, but after several wasted minutes of type-delete, type-delete, he gave it up. It was barely two o'clock, and she hadn't come home in Caleb's truck. He felt an uneasy certainty something had gone wrong.

Callie's bark brought his attention back to the window. Sure enough, the frisky dog was on the dock and Robin sat on its edge, dangling her feet in the water with her back to him. He willed himself to sit down and write, but it just wasn't happening. His concentration was completely shot. He saved the document, closed the computer, and changed into swim trunks.

As soon as he walked outside, Callie ran up to him. Robin followed behind her.

"Hi! I didn't expect to see you back so soon."

"Hi, Matt. Where are you off to?"

"I thought I'd go for a swim."

She barely made eye contact. "Enjoy yourself." As she headed toward the studio, she called, "Come on, Callie."

Matt paused to look after her, then turned and walked down to the dock, pulled off his shirt, and dove in. The water was cool, and it might have cleared his mind if he hadn't been so preoccupied with Robin. She'd completely lost her usual light demeanor. Something had to be wrong.

He swam until his lungs burned. When he returned to the house, there was not a trace of Robin or the dog. He climbed the stairs to his bedroom and fell asleep on the bed.

Robin was talking downstairs when he awoke. He quickly showered and dressed, hoping to catch her before she went out again. But when he got out of the shower, the house was quiet.

His mood picked up when he found Robin at the kitchen table, sipping a glass of iced tea while gazing out toward the lake. "Hi there."

"Hi."

It was early yet for supper. Not knowing what else to do, he made himself a glass of iced tea. "Okay if I join you?" He pulled out a chair.

"Sure." She looked at him then.

"I can't help noticing that you don't seem like yourself. Is everything okay? Can I do anything?"

"My, that was practically a speech coming from you." Her taut expression gave way to a little smile.

He tightened his lips and felt the crease appear between his eyes as he studied her beautiful face. Maybe she was making fun of him. He didn't care. "Seriously. Are you okay?"

"I'm fine. But Caleb's sister Rachel was hurt today in a skiing accident."

He flinched. "That's awful. Is she … bad?"

"They had to transport her from the local hospital to Atlanta. Her leg was pretty messed up. She dislocated her knee. I just got off the phone with Caleb. He's on the way to Atlanta."

"I'm sorry. And you've been waiting all afternoon for news."

She closed her eyes and nodded.

"I'm sorry."

They sat in silence. Finally, Matt stood up and went into the kitchen. He opened the refrigerator and took out the fried chicken, potato salad, and a head of lettuce. It crossed his mind that even though food was his go-to sedative, it wasn't everyone's. Just the same, he wanted to do something. "How about we eat supper early and sit on the porch afterward?"

"That would be nice. I didn't eat lunch."

He took two plates out of the cabinet and put some lettuce on each one. Then he sliced a tomato and laid slices on top of the lettuce. He carried the plates to the table along with the container of potato salad and the foil-wrapped chicken. "An indoor picnic."

Robin smiled weakly.

"Hold on. I'm not done yet." Matt returned to the kitchen and came back with a bottle of vinaigrette, silverware, napkins, and a bowl of fresh strawberries and blueberries. "There." He placed the items on the table.

Robin's face brightened. She seemed genuinely touched and surprised by the attention. She studied him as he sat down. "Thank you, Matt."

"Of course." He waited for Robin to serve herself before helping himself. "Mmm. This chicken is good. Really good." He glanced up at her. "Absolutely no contest. Your fried chicken is better than the Colonel's."

Callie yapped, staring right at him.

Matt looked down at the dog and attempted to shush her with a frown. To play it off, he sat up straighter and shrugged.

"Is she begging?" Robin asked, a perplexed look on her face.

Callie inched closer to Matt's chair without taking her eyes away from him and barked again.

"She *is* begging."

Matt chuckled nervously under his breath.

"Callie! Stop that. Bad girl!" Robin shifted her gaze to Matt, her eyes wide. "I can't believe it. She's never begged at the table."

"Hasn't she?" The half-smile on his face had to betray him.

"Has she? Matthew McLaughlin, have you been feeding her from the table?"

"Maybe once … or twice," he responded sheepishly.

She shook her head. "She really is spoiled now. I can't believe you did that."

Matt didn't care that she'd caught him red-handed. Her disbelief amused him. To his relief, Robin laughed too. "I'm sorry. I couldn't help myself. She's just so darn cute. And when you're not around, she's a little tyrant."

"A *tyrant*?" Robin sputtered in mock disbelief.

Matt howled with laughter. For a delicious moment, joy melted over them like butter on hot biscuits. At last Robin sighed and shook her head again, her eyes twinkling. More relaxed now, they finished the meal with no more pleas from Callie. Afterward, they put the food away and went out onto the porch.

"I can be a good listener if you need to talk," he offered.

Robin stretched out on the chair beside his and let her sneakers drop to the floor. "What an unusual day this has been."

Callie curled up by her side.

Matt flipped on the ceiling fans and lit the citronella candles on the wicker tables. Then he sat on the chair beside them and determinedly looked at the lake. Anywhere other than at her fine pair of legs.

Cheerful sounds, shouts, and laughter mingled with the boat motors and drifted on the breeze as he watched the boats on the water. They seemed safe and secluded in a private place, and he liked the feeling. If the truth be told, he liked being with Robin.

When had he begun to care where he was or with whom? Maybe this *was* a magical place, like Robin had said on the first day he arrived. Peaceful vibes surrounded him. He looked at Robin, who had fallen asleep, and smiled. At least for the time being, she wasn't worrying about the accident. After about an hour, he crept inside to refill his glass.

Bottle rockets exploded in the sky from across the lake as he walked back out onto the darkening porch, and a cloud of stars floated down to the water. Callie barked and sprang onto the floor.

Robin sat up. "Whoa. Did you see that?"

Another bright display erupted, and showers of sparkling embers sprayed across the sky.

"Couldn't miss it. We have a front-row seat." But their smiles were short-lived. Callie began to run around like her tail was on fire.

"She really freaks out when she's near fireworks," Robin groaned.

They both stood and lunged for Callie, but she evaded their grasp. Matt opened the door to the house, and she darted inside. As she cowered on the sofa, he successfully nabbed her. He took her in his arms and sat with her on his lap.

Robin sat beside them, and together they soothed the trembling animal. "It's okay, Callie," she crooned. "You're safe with us."

Matt felt the dog's heart racing as he held her. Robin spoke softly and stroked the dog's back. He stilled as his attention shifted to the woman by his side. Robin seemed to pay no attention to how her hair draped over his arm as she leaned over Callie. While the minutes passed, he wrestled with the desire to sink his face into her silky hair. The sound of her breathing filled him with a longing that made his chest ache.

Suddenly, Robin turned her face to look at him. In her eyes he saw the same awareness of him that he was feeling for her. He might have drowned in the flood of senses washing over him had reality not intervened with the ringing of a phone.

Robin jumped, her eyes wide and her jaw slack. They stared at each other for a moment, then she fumbled for the phone in her pocket.

Matt resisted the urge to groan. Instead he tightened his grip on Callie.

Robin moved to the far corner of the room while she talked curled up in a chair perpendicular to him.

All the while, he stroked the animal's fur and rubbed behind its ears. Muffled pops and explosions continued to punctuate the sky as it erupted with color and light. "It's okay, Callie," he whispered, continuing to stroke and sooth. "All we need is a minute to recover from all the blasted fireworks."

"Caleb, how's Rachel?" Robin asked, her voice wafer thin. She hugged her legs.

"She's out of surgery." He sounded tired. "The doctors said she did well."

"Thank God for that."

"The injury was bad, but not as extensive as it might have been. We were able to get her to the hospital fast, and the doctors were great. Still, recovery will take weeks, maybe months."

"You must be exhausted."

"Not so much, considering the adrenaline rush, but it's going to be a challenging week. I have new clients coming in tomorrow for several days of fishing." Caleb paused. "Honey, Mom and Dad just walked in. I need to talk to them."

"Of course, go ahead. Thanks for calling."

"I miss you. Today was supposed to be our time, and tonight."

"It's okay. Take care of yourself while you're taking care of everyone else."

"We'll talk soon. Bye, sweetheart."

"Good night." Robin ended the call, but didn't move. She was relieved to hear his voice and to learn of Rachel's condition, yet she'd only half attended to his words. Rachel, Caleb, Callie, Matt … too many thoughts scurried through her mind like mice in an empty barn.

Flashes of light continued to light up the sky, and her emotions sparked like embers. The candles flickering outside made her realize the room was now completely dark. She clicked on the lamp beside her and turned to look across the room.

At first, she couldn't see him, but as her eyes adjusted, she saw Matt looking back at her. Simultaneously, they looked away—he at the dog in his lap and she at the skylight above. That feeling of vulnerability washed over her again, just like it had earlier in the day. What on earth was the matter with her?

Callie trembled still.

Robin stood. "I think … the room behind the kitchen is quieter and darker than the studio. Callie needs that. If that's fine with you …"

"Of course. Sleep there tonight."

"Thanks." She clapped her hands softly. "Come on, Callie."

Matt held out the dog as Robin approached. "Go ahead. Go on."

Cuddling the dog in her arms, Robin crossed the room to the dark kitchen. She didn't say good night. That would have required more mental wherewithal than she could muster. What she needed right now was to retreat to a quiet, cozy place.

Maybe then she could recover from the day and make sense of her exploding emotions.

Matt blew out the candles on the porch, locked the doors, and turned out the lights before heading upstairs for the night. That phone call had saved him from making an embarrassing mistake. Another moment and he would have kissed her. He couldn't have helped himself. And for a fleeting second, he thought he saw the same tender emotion in her eyes. Even now, he imagined his mouth on hers, his arms pressing her to his chest, her arms around his neck. Twice now, powerful sensations all but forgotten had caught him off guard. Four years. Nothing. Grief had buried that part of him. So why had it reawakened now?

At this rate, he'd be lucky to keep this house until Christmas. She was liable to toss him out at any time.

Matt took his laptop from the desk and sat with it in a chair. He turned on the lamp over his shoulder and picked up where he'd left off with the story hours before. Enmeshing himself with the lives and aspirations of fictional characters aided his escape from his own burgeoning desires.

The day's celebratory fireworks had all but stopped when he heard a vehicle outside, the sound of it amplified by the stillness. A glance at the digital clock showed one a.m. He scrubbed his hands over his face and went to the window.

A truck pulled up and stopped. The door opened, slammed closed, and then the distinctive crunch of footfalls crossed the gravel. Someone was walking around the side of the house.

"Who the devil is that?" he grumbled. Then he recognized Caleb's truck. He must've come by to see Robin and was going around to the studio. A few minutes passed before Matt thought to go downstairs to call to him, but he didn't have a chance.

Bam! Bam! Bam! Someone pounded on the door loud enough to wake the dead, or at least seriously disrupt the living. Matt hurried down and flung open the door. Caleb shoved in, cursing and accusatory.

"Wait a second, man! What the heck's wrong with you?"

"Where is she?" Caleb demanded, looking up the stairs through squinted eyes.

Matt shoved the heel of his hand hard into Caleb's chest. "Wait one second," he said through gritted teeth. "Keep your voice down. We can talk outside."

Callie ran barking into the mix, stopped abruptly, and growled at Caleb.

"Hey, what's going on?" Robin drifted through the kitchen, seeming not to have heard their exchange. Her voice was husky with sleep. "Caleb?"

Both men let their arms fall and stepped back from one another. Chests heaving, they watched Robin, slipping on a gossamer robe as she approached. Her tousled hair tumbled around her face onto her shoulders, and she had such a look of innocence on her face that it was all Matt could do not to punch Caleb for the heck of it. Instead, he shook his head and went back upstairs.

"Hey, sweetheart," Caleb said softly. The rest of their words became inaudible as Matt closed the bedroom door.

His heart pounded as he stood in the middle of his room. He knew exactly what that jerk had been thinking. It would have served the guy right if he had punched him. But what good would that have done. He had no right to interfere. He was only renting the place.

But from the first night, somehow, he'd known. Something about Robin captivated him. Increasingly he was drawn to her. And now? He was so in over his head.

Chapter Twelve

Robin attended church the following day, glad to have something uplifting to brighten her day. The peaceful atmosphere had a restorative effect on her soul. She needed it after yesterday.

Joyful anticipation, pride, and happiness from being with Caleb, then having that dashed by fear and worry—it had left her exhausted. Definitely not how she had imagined the day. Caleb stopping by to kiss her good night was endearing, but he hadn't been himself. His embrace lacked its usual passion. Naturally, he was preoccupied with graver matters.

If all that wasn't troubling enough, something had happened between her and Matt—twice in one day. A connection. Something deep inside. His eyes questioned her. Or had she just imagined it? It wasn't like anything she'd experienced before.

Robin determined she would concentrate on her drawings and—if she could manage it—see as little as possible of her tenant. She didn't need confusing vibes shaking her love boat. She was intent on being with Caleb, and she wasn't too naive to realize that when a man and a woman are together in a small space, some tension might occur, as indeed it had. She'd have to avoid all such situations between her and Matt in the future.

As Robin walked out of the sanctuary, someone called her name. She turned to see Margaret Hurston quick stepping in her direction. As always, her bouffant hair was perfectly sprayed in place, and her polished oval nails matched her raspberry-colored lipstick. Miss Margaret dressed up even when she went to the grocery store. She looked especially nice for church.

"Hi, Robin. Your mother told me I'd be seeing you." She hugged Robin tightly.

The woman's signature fragrances, Shalimar perfume and cherry almond lotion, surrounded her. Approaching eighty, Miss Margaret was a fixture in the church and town. She had been a member of the school board for decades, served as mayor during her sixties, and remained the chief event planner for the town counsel. Had there been a Junior League, she would have been its president. She had taken Robin's mother under her ample wings decades ago and they'd become friends.

"Good morning, Miss Margaret. You look so nice."

"You too, sweetie." She released her and took Robin's hand between her soft wrinkled ones. "Now your mother says you won't be teaching school this year, that you've moved back to that grand house on the lake and you're illustrating your children's stories."

"Yes, ma'am. That's right."

"Well, that's perfect. For you and for our little town. I'm not getting any younger, you know."

Robin smiled and waited for Miss Margaret to finish her line of thought.

"I don't quite manage like I used to. I need help planning events for our town."

Robin had trouble believing that. "You're forever young, Miss Margaret. A true marvel. Mom always said she didn't know how you did all the things you do. She loved working with you."

"And I loved working with her. She's a real lady. I'd like to work with you too. That is, if you will agree to help me. The next big event is the fall festival, and it's fast approaching," Miss Margaret continued. "Do you think you, and maybe your friend Jenny Jackson, could join me and the rest of the committee for planning the event?"

"Well, I—"

"Now, Robin, there are only five of us old ladies left. Our members under forty are too busy with babies and T-ball and jobs outside the home."

The town had dwindled over the years.

"You remember how wonderful the fall festival used to be. My children loved it back in the day." Miss Margaret choked up a little when she said that. Although Robin hadn't known them, both of her children had passed away young—her son decades before in Vietnam, and her daughter not many years after that from a congenital heart defect. Miss Margaret had poured herself into the community all the years since. "Can you help me make it great again? I want to see children and old folks all enjoying it … at least one more time."

How could she say no? "Of course I'll help. I'd love to."

"Thank you, sugar." She hugged Robin again. "It means so much to me."

They agreed to start meeting the first week in August to plan the festival, and Miss Margaret beamed as she walked down the street to her house, her leather handbag hanging from the crook of one arm.

When Robin returned home, she took Callie for a ten-minute romp. She was eager to get to work on her illustrations, and ideas were forming in her mind for art projects for the fall event. They'd have face painting. She'd draw caricatures and set up easels so the kids could paint as well. Jenny would be sure to have great ideas too. She'd ask her about it the next time they spoke. Right now, Robin was in her happy place.

The apartment loft was the perfect artist's studio. With a bank of floor-to-ceiling windows on the lake side, she had a beautiful view and natural light. A custom-built drafting table stretched just beneath the windows. Dozens of identical glass containers holding every color pencil imaginable and artist brushes of every size lined the back edge. She'd spent many happy hours there with her dad, she sketching nature drawings and he sketching free-hand or on designs for construction projects.

After the house was built, during her teenage years and before the illness struck, she and her family were more or less sequestered here. Her parents were involved with church and a few community projects, but they expected to spend a pleasant retirement here. She'd attended the local high school.

She smiled, savoring the sweet memories, content to be close to her dad in spirit. After choosing the pencils she'd use on her illustrations, she began drawing.

Predominately in soft blues, greens, and natural colors found in nature, whimsical pictures of big-eyed characters came to life—all modeled after herself and her sister, on adventures on a farm, in the barn, or at the pond, with lots of flowers and butterflies, green hoppy frogs, puppies and animals, in all kinds of situations that make children's eyes grow wide with wonder. Her illustrations, which won Robin her first art award at the county fair when she was twelve, brought smiles to young and old.

She had yet to share them with Caleb, but maybe she would when she finished this project. Right now, he and several of his family members were at the hospital in Atlanta with Rachel. For the upcoming week, Mrs. Jackson and Kaitlin would be with her much of the time. The family would ensure that she had all the support she needed as she healed and regained the use of her leg. As soon as Caleb had a day off, Robin hoped to go with him to visit his sister.

The afternoon passed quickly just the same. Robin left her work as it was and took Callie over to the house for supper. As she made herself a salad and a sandwich, the dog whimpered at the door to the bedroom at the top of the stairs, but Matt didn't open it to her. Robin thought he might. Typically, he did, but not this evening. She almost hoped he would and felt vaguely affronted by the fact that he didn't.

Today being Sunday and her day off, he wouldn't expect her to make his dinner. "Let's go, Callie," she called to the dog. After grabbing a few items from the back bedroom, they silently made their exit. It was probably best to keep her distance, she reminded herself. Apparently, he felt the need to avoid her as well.

As she walked around the yard with Callie, a presence seemed to follow her. She turned and looked up. Only a slight flutter of the drapes at his window, but enough to confirm that indeed Matt had been standing there. Somehow, she'd known it was his eyes she felt on her.

She huffed. This was silly. He could have at least acknowledged her with a wave.

He was so … confusing. Not as closed off as she'd thought at first. His eyes were appealing and melancholic. Yesterday he'd shown sensitivity and kindness when he'd kept her company. She should thank him, but … actually, she already had. She shook her head to refocus her thoughts.

Breaking into a slow jog, she called to Callie, eager to get back to her perch in the loft to watch the tangerine-colored sun go down.

Matt pushed back from the computer and rubbed his eyes. So this was what he could do when his writing was going right. He'd put in five solid hours of work. Real progress on novel number five.

His first novel had been a bestseller—for about a nanosecond anyway—and he and Lauren had reveled in it. He had written that book on a dare from her. She'd challenged him after he shared a plot that wound round and round in his head. She pushed him to make it more real, earthy, tantalizing. The second and third books sold decently, securing his publisher's good graces. He garnered a nice following of readers who enjoyed edgy romance laced with mystery and suspense.

The fourth novel surpassed all expectations, staying on the *New York Times* bestseller list for ten straight weeks, or so he'd been told. It hit the shelves the week Lauren died. He'd done nothing to promote it—no book signings, no media events, no pitch articles. Nothing at all. And he had not written a word since. Until now.

He was lucky his agent and publisher had stuck with him. And he wasn't going to try to explain the fact that they had, or why he could write now. What was it his grandpa said? *Don't look a gift horse in the mouth.* He didn't care why. He was writing, and today he had been especially focused. He'd ignored Callie when she whined at his door, and he hadn't allowed his mind to wander to the sweet red-haired girl. When he caught himself wondering what she might be doing, he turned back to the story.

Granted, it was nice having her around, but he could take no credit for the fact that she was there. Her presence was a sly perk from an insightful friend. He didn't intend to forget that, nor would he take advantage of the situation. He hadn't expected to meet a woman here, or anywhere else. He certainly hadn't expected to be attracted to one. Better to channel all passionate surges into writing. At least for today, that approach was working.

Matt walked over to the ribbon of windows, now his favorite spot from which to view the world. The sky had turned to liquid silver. The setting sun shimmered with a honey-colored glow like candle-light. His eyes trailed to the boat tied at the dock.

"It's about time I went fishing," he said. "I'll give Charlie Bradford a visit and see if I remember how to bait a hook and cast a line."

Right then, Robin walked into view. She looked incandescent. And as much as he would have liked to quietly observe her for a very long time, he stepped away from the window. He hesitated, just briefly, before crossing the room and returning to the plot that still held the power to beguile him.

Chapter Thirteen

As soon as Matt finished eating breakfast, he headed to Charlie Bradford's cabin. The day was going to be a scorcher, he could tell. Regardless of what the thermometer said, Georgia was hotter than California. Besides the humidity, hordes of insects and biting creatures made themselves a nuisance.

He slapped a yellow fly stinging his arm, then rubbed the spot. The next time he took to the woods, he would round up some bug repellent.

Thick brambles and vines draped on the spindly trees mixed among the tall pines that bordered the dirt road and obscured the view of the lake. A dog barked as he approached the road leading to Charlie's. The dog and his master came out on the porch and watched his approach.

"Hey there!" Charlie called. "You done missed breakfast, but I can fix you something if you ain't eat yet."

"Thanks, but I've already eaten." Matt stopped and put his hands on his hips, mirroring the stance of the man on the porch.

The dog descended the steps and clumsily slithered around his legs in friendly greeting.

Charlie grinned. "Sammy likes company. That's for sure. We don't get much."

"Well, I thought I'd take you up on that invitation to go fishing," Matt said, scratching the dog's head. "When's a good time?"

"The mood's struck you, has it? Why not right now? It's late, but there's still time to get out before the sun's too high."

"Good. Can't say I'll know what I'm doing. I haven't fished in decades." He gave the dog's side a brisk rub.

"It's like riding a bike." The old fellow chuckled. "A lot of things are. Come on in the house a minute." He led the way into the dimly lit interior and cleared a ceramic plate and cup from the table. After walking through the house onto the back porch, he pulled a worn leather tote off a large hook and snatched a ball cap from another. "You need a cap. Grab yourself one. A rod too."

Charlie took a few minutes putting together the jigs, crankbaits, and plastic worms he wanted in the tackle box, then slid it into the tote. A fishy smell emanated from the gear. He opened a small waist-high freezer and pulled out a bag of ice, which he dumped into a cooler. "About ready now. Carry the cooler, why don't you."

Matt pulled the cap onto his head and picked up the cooler and a rod.

"Today we'll go out on the boat so you can practice casting your line. Come back tomorrow morning at daylight. We'll get in some good fishing."

They trudged down the slight hill to the old wooden dock. Charlie untied his green aluminum jon boat, stepped into it, and started the motor. Matt stepped in and sat down. The old fisherman eased out into the lake, then sped up a bit. Soon he was pulling over close to the weeds protruding from the water along the bank. He shut off the motor, moved to the front of the boat, and turned on the troll motor.

"We'll troll the coves and work our way back toward the cabin." He glanced back at Matt and the fishing tackle. "Take your time choosing your lure." After pulling out a black jiggly bait tied to a silver disc, he held it up and shook it gently. "This here is the one I like best. Catch a lot of two- and three-pound largemouth on this."

"Really?" Matt looked up from his lure. "Do you release them?"

"All depends. Today I'll be keeping what we catch."

Over the next couple of hours Matt had a few hits, but he didn't manage to set the bait properly. He did, however, succeed in snagging his hook on a dead tree branch half submerged in water. He took off his cap more than once to swat the mosquitos that buzzed his head. Sweat trickled down his neck and the center of his back, and his beard itched. While he scratched and swore, Charlie chuckled. Matt was sure the seasoned angler laughed at him as much as anything else while reeling in one fish after another.

"Let's call it a day," Charlie said. "We can come back out early in the morning. I can tell the heat and that beard aren't agreeing with you."

"Hmph. Let me cast one or two more times. I want to find that spot where you caught the three-pounder."

Sure enough, after only a few minutes, Matt got a hit, pulled up on the line at exactly the right moment, successfully set the hook, and reeled in his first catch.

"Hold steady!" Charlie said. "It's a keeper!"

"Whoa! Look at that! Just look at that." Matt admired the bass and held it up for the old fisherman to judge. "What do you think? It's more than three pounds, right?"

"Looks like a three and a half pounder. Biggest fish of the day. See there. I told you it would come back to you."

Matt chuckled as Charlie headed back to the dock.

"We'll have to have a fish fry. How about tomorrow night?" Charlie asked.

"If you fry 'em for us, I'll eat with you." He smiled.

They tied up the boat and brought in the gear. Together they cleaned the fish, then dropped them into a pan of cold water. As Matt held the slimy fish in his hands and scraped the scales, he felt like some of his own hard shell was falling away. A bit of the delight and freedom he'd felt as a child came back to him.

He considered those emotions as he walked back to the lake house. Odd how such an ordinary event could have such a poignant effect. He thanked God for Charlie Bradshaw's willingness to entertain strangers and for his grandpa's love. The memories of their years together came back to him. He didn't expect the happy feeling to last, but he'd enjoy it while it did.

The emotional baggage he carried back to the lake house was lighter than it had been earlier.

Early that morning, soon after she'd returned to the studio from making breakfast, Robin caught sight of Matt through the trees, walking on the dirt road. He was dressed in a baggy shirt and shorts. Not wearing running clothes, nor jogging near the lake as he usually did. She wondered for a moment about the change in routine, but then the sound of a boat on the lake turned her thoughts to Caleb. He was taking some businessmen from Kansas out fishing for striped bass.

Robin walked over to the computer and turned on the iTunes playlist that best suited her work mood. The soft upbeat music enveloped her in a protective bubble conducive to concentration. Gathering her materials, she set to work. As she sketched nature scenes from the story and set her young characters in them, she relived similar events from her childhood. Trips to a farm, catching tadpoles around the edge of the pond in Mason jars while Granddaddy and Daddy fished off the bank, running through the tall grass with Emmy. The hours ticked by as her memories and story came to life.

Now she pressed her hand to her aching stomach, which had been growling for hours. She didn't want to stop drawing yet, but her phone alarm reminded her it was time for dinner preparations. "It can't be this late," she murmured, giving the phone a stern tap to stop the alarm. "Callie, have I neglected you all day?"

The dog jumped down from the daybed where she'd been sleeping. She stretched her short, furry body and looked up at Robin as she poured cool water into the dog's bowl. Robin took a long drink from the glass she had poured for herself earlier. The ice had melted and condensation formed a wet ring on the table. She wiped it away and took one last look at her work before she and Callie exited the studio.

She followed Callie around the shady woods before going into the house. According to the oversized outdoor thermometer, the temperature hovered at ninety-five degrees.

A good week to cloister inside and draw.

The following morning, much to his surprise, Matt woke thinking about fishing. Before going down for breakfast, he took a hard look at himself in the bathroom mirror. His beard had become a bona fide nuisance yesterday. Something needed to be done to prevent an aggravating recurrence. He opened one drawer, then another, but found them empty. Fortunately, the last drawer contained generic grooming tools—a set of plastic combs, a brush, a lint roller, extra toothbrushes, and a six-inch pair of scissors.

Lifting his chin and gathering his beard in his fist, he tightened his grasp and pulled down gently. Snip. Snip. A soft tuft of black hair dropped into the sink. Holding the beard along his jawline between his fingers, he trimmed more from ear to ear. He aimed for comfort. A proper trim could come at another time.

After grabbing a banana and an English muffin for breakfast, he wrote a note on the white board on the front of the refrigerator: *Gone fishing!* Then just because he could, and because it was something Robin would do, he drew a school of fish. Matt chuckled at his primitive sketch as he walked out the door.

Charlie was waiting for him. In the first light of day, a smoky fog hovered over the surface of the lake. The sky was getting progressively brighter in the east, transforming the gray into layers of pearl and pink and baby blue.

They got in the boat and eased along the same path as the day before, trolling along the weed beds, cove to cove. From time to time he heard the plop of a fish as it hit the surface of the water. Were insects, frogs, and birds always so noisy? Or was it that with civilization momentarily hushed, nature simply rose to fill the void? Whichever it was, his thoughts were pure in this environment. Two men in a boat, reverent in the act of fishing. Not much to see from the outside, but each within his own breast housed an unseen world of soul capacities and human experiences, quietly contained, presently content to concentrate one heartbeat at a time on the prospect of catching a fish.

And catch fish, they did. Matt lost count of how many Charlie caught and released. Around eleven a.m., when they called it a day, Matt had caught four bass and Charlie had seven keepers. As they had the previous day, they worked together to clean the fish, talking all the while about life in general and their lives in particular.

Matt talked about how he had lived the first thirteen years of his life in the mountains of Tennessee with his mom and grandpa—the good years, simple times with simple things. "My biological father was a man just passing through our whistle-stop town," he said. "I never knew him. My mother didn't know him either. She'd met him at the one and only general store in town, and at his invitation, met him at the coffee shop when she left her job at the library at the end of the day. He bought her a hamburger and a soda. I remember she said he didn't eat himself, just watched her while she ate. He offered to walk her home. Well, he did more than that."

Matt paused to push his hair out of his eyes, catching a whiff of the fish smell strong on his wet hand.

Charlie continued his task without comment.

"Grandpa was hoeing at the back of the field when they walked up, but he didn't see them. When the dog started barking, he assumed it was her coming home. The man soon had Mama in his grip, but he didn't let go until he'd gotten what he came for. By the time Mama realized his intentions, her screams came too late."

Charlie paused a moment, then shook his head. "Shameful man."

"Grandpa was running up to the yard as the scoundrel ran down the steps. The police never caught him. No one knew who he was. He got in the car he'd left parked in front of the diner and drove away before Grandpa could run the two miles into town."

"That's bad," Charlie said.

"Yeah. Devastating for my mom. But for me, growing up there with Grandpa and her were the best years of my life. I didn't lack for anything. I had no idea we were poor until my mama married and we moved to California."

"I can understand."

"Yeah ... I haven't thought of that in decades."

After a few minutes of silence between them, Charlie took up the conversation. "My wife and I had a son. David." He continued cleaning the fish while he talked. "Those years with him were the best years for us."

"What happened?" Matt asked.

"He'd gotten himself a summer job. Intended to go off to college in the fall. That morning, he left us sleeping and walked down the dirt road to meet his ride at the crossroads, not far up the road from our house. The friend he was supposed to meet woke us up a little while later blowing the horn in front of the house. David hadn't showed up. We found him lying in a ditch beside the road. He looked like he had laid down and put his head on a boulder. Not a mark on him, except for on the side of his head. We think he jumped out of the way of a car in the half-light of dawn or slipped on the bank of the road."

"I'm sorry." How heartbreaking that must have been, he thought.

"It was the worst thing that could have happened to us. My wife … the light went out of her eyes that day and didn't come back until the week she died."

Matt groaned.

"Now that was something. When she knew she was dying, the light came back into her eyes. I thought it meant she'd get better. It didn't. She knew she was fixing to go to heaven and be with her child again." He nodded. "We had twenty-five years together after we lost David. Peaceful years. We moved down here and ran a little store on the out-skirts of town. I'm grateful for that. She was a good wife. Just couldn't get over the loss of our boy."

"How did you … endure it?"

"God. That's all I had. By his grace, I have this un-shakeable faith. We're all in His hands."

"Hmm. Sounds like Grandpa."

"Wasn't for that, when I was knocked down by the terrible things in my life, I couldn't have never got up."

They finished cleaning the fish, rinsed the table surface clean with a hose, and washed their hands.

When Charlie spoke again, the hush of reverence had passed. "We have a big mess of fish here. I'll freeze some. We'll have plenty for supper. How about you come back down here at five o'clock?"

"Sure."

"I'll have the fish in the frying pan when you get here."

"Sounds good."

"Bring Birdie with you."

Matt paused and raised his eyebrows. "You want me to ask Robin to come for supper?"

"Well, sure. Why not? There's more than enough fish. It's been a while, but she's eaten here before."

"All right."

On the way back to the lake house, of all the things he could have thought about, Matt couldn't get Robin out of his head—inviting her to supper, and how to go about inviting her.

You're a big boy, he scoffed at himself. *Handle it.*

He went directly upstairs to shower, definitely needing to clean up before he approached Robin. For two days, he'd managed to avoid her. But maybe what was to him an intimate moment on the sofa—that sudden jolt of awareness—was nothing at all to her and he was being foolish. The look in her wide eyes, however, said otherwise. But who was he to judge? His emotional malaise had required intervention and treatment.

When Matt entered the kitchen to make lunch, the drawing on the refrigerator caught his eye. The sketch he'd drawn earlier was still there, but Robin had embellished it, transforming the fish into winsome creatures swimming through weeds. He chuckled.

Her talent was clearly on display in her cooking as well. Matt was pleased to find homemade chicken salad with grapes and pecans among his food choices. He took his time enjoying a salad with lettuce, cherry tomatoes, sliced cucumbers, and a generous portion of chicken salad along with a bottle of sparkling water. With his dishes put away and the kitchen back in order, he went in search of Charlie's invitee.

At the door of the studio, he knocked lightly. No response. He rapped on the door more boldly, and this time Callie started barking. The dog and her owner neared the door, and he took a deep breath.

"Hello." Robin raised her eyebrows in surprise.

Callie jumped on Matt's legs.

"Callie, don't bowl him over!" She laughed, stepping back to allow him entry. "Come in."

"Am I interrupting?" he asked as he stepped inside.

Light flooded the space. Sliding glass doors across the back of the room opened onto a small patio with the lake beyond. Canvases were propped on the floor against one wall. Large framed murals covered the walls. A metal staircase spiraled up to a loft.

"No, not at all." They both stood there awkwardly for a minute, and then a dazzling smile lit her face. "Would you like to see my work?"

"Sure." He wondered what that might be.

She chattered as he followed her up the stairs. "The apartment is rather sparse, but perfect for my needs. My dad wanted a quiet place where he could leave out all his drawings and building plans."

The room was open and full of light.

"This is my workspace." She held out her hand to present the room, then walked over and stood in front of a long drafting table.

Matt stopped beside her, his eyes scanning the drawings on the table. They were incredible. "You're an artist." He turned to her, his eyes narrowed with curiosity. After a moment of staring at her, he turned back to the illustrations. "They're beautiful. Such vivid detail."

"Thank you."

"You're telling a story here." He leaned down for a closer look.

"I'm illustrating one of the children's stories I've written."

She'd written children's stories? "The scenes are captivating." He looked at a picture of two little girls playing along the bank of a pond, a shaggy dog beside them. The smaller of the two girls had long red pigtails. He studied the drawing of the younger girl, and then looked at Robin.

"Yeah. That's me. The story was life before I conceived of it as a book."

"I knew you were talented, but—"

"Even though I'm a kindergarten teacher, my real passion is art and bringing delight to children with my stories. My dream is to write and illustrate children's books."

She looked so happy telling him this that he frankly didn't know what to say. He was reminded of the times he and Lauren used to talk about her social work and the small daily victories that fueled her passion. Robin was more complex than he imagined.

"Gosh, forgive me for going on and on. I didn't even ask you the reason for your visit. I'm sure it wasn't to look at my drawings."

"Not at all. I like seeing them. But I came over on Charlie's behalf … to invite you to his house for supper."

"Mr. Charlie? Aww. He's so nice."

"He's frying the fish we caught for supper."

"Oh? Cool. Sure, I'd like that. Daddy and I enjoyed lots of fish fries with him when I was a girl."

"Is five o'clock good for you?" They had walked downstairs and were now standing by the front door.

"That's perfect. He goes to bed at dark, you know." She opened the door.

Matt stepped outside but turned around to face her. "Well … I'll see you later." For mercy's sake, he didn't want to leave.

"Do you want to walk down there together, or do you want me to drive us?"

Matt shrugged. "We can walk." As he turned to go, Callie started to follow, but Robin kept her back.

He hurried to the lake house alone. Before he escorted Robin to Charlie's for supper, he wanted to take another stab at trimming his beard.

Chapter Fourteen

Standing before the mirror again, Matt gathered his grooming tools and leaned forward for a closer look. He twisted his mouth to each side and his head turned along with it. This wouldn't be easy. He raked the comb through the thick hair.

Never had he intended to grow a bushy beard. It just happened. Shaving—even showering—after Lauren was killed had required a herculean effort. A car picked him up and took him to campus where he taught, mostly sleepwalking through the days, usually not even remembering coming and going. He'd walked away from the accident without a scratch on his body. But his soul was shattered. Two weeks afterward, with the memorial service behind him, Lauren was laid to rest beside his mama and grandpa in Tennessee. The months passed, and his outer appearance came to reflect more of what he was inside—a ruined man. Now here in this place, a little more each day he felt less like a freak and more like the man he'd once been.

Little by little he combed and clipped, then shaved his neck and the top of his cheeks. Twenty minutes later, the beard looked neater. A little patchy, but a marked improvement. He decided to rinse off quickly in the shower.

Matt switched back to story-writing mode as the cool water pelted his skin. Once out, he quickly dried himself, combed his hair and beard carefully, dressed, and settled in to write all afternoon. Not one day with a blank page since he'd started writing again, though he dared not let his mind dwell on that. The sabbatical felt like the best thing that had happened to him in years.

Robin and Callie stirred down in the kitchen, and not long after that, something sweet and chocolaty teased his senses. He stopped typing, closed his eyes, and breathed. Here it wasn't hard to breathe. Robin was baking her chocolate chip cookies. He glanced at the clock and saved his work. It was time to go to Charlie's.

Matt and Robin made the short walk to Charlie's with Callie skipping along beside them. Despite the temperature, walking down the shady dirt road was pleasant. They strolled in silence for a while, glancing back and forth at one another and chuckling at the dog's antics.

"Mr. Charlie is proud of his fried fish," she said. "My dad and I used to come for supper sometimes after they caught a bunch."

Matt nodded.

"I haven't visited much since my dad got sick." She felt a little guilty.

"When was that?"

"About seven years ago. We were living here when he was diagnosed, but then my parents bought a condo in the city to be close to the hospital. He had colon cancer that spread to his lungs, liver, and brain."

"I'm sorry." By the sincerity of his tone, he was.

"He died three years ago. We miss him. My mother especially. But we have happy memories."

A pensive look sobered Matt's expression. The little smile Robin flashed in his direction seemed to have no impact.

She pointed to a vine full of exotic purple and white blossoms. "Oh, look at those. Aren't they lovely?" She swooped off the road and picked one of the large star-shaped flowers.

"I've never seen flowers like those."

"Passionfruit. As in the passion of Christ." She admired the flower up close, then held it steady before Matt to give him a closer look. She let her arm drop and went back to the vine.

Suddenly, she stomped on a ball of green fruit on the vine, making a loud distinct *pop*. Callie jumped and Robin laughed. "Or another name is Maypop." She stomped on another one.

After a moment of silence during which Matt seemed to be holding his breath, he burst out laughing. Callie danced at his heels.

After that little episode, their pace quickened and soon they were in Mr. Charlie's front yard. Old Sammy barked a welcome.

"Come on in," Mr. Charlie called. "Y'all better get on in here. I about got supper ready. Bring that little Cavalier in too. She's all grown up now."

Matt held the door for Robin and Callie, and they scooted in.

Mr. Charlie and Robin stared at each other a moment before the thin old man opened wide his arms and hugged her. "It's nice to see you, Birdie."

"You too, Mr. Charlie," she said warmly. "Nice of you to have me. The food sure smells good."

"Well, it does because it is. And I wanted a chance to see you. Now y'all go ahead and sit down. I'm just putting everything on the table."

They pulled out the ladder-back chairs and sat around the table. The vegetables served were fresh from Mr. Charlie's garden—a bowl of coleslaw and a sliced beefsteak tomato. A large platter of fried fish fillets and hushpuppies sat in the center of the table.

Robin poured glasses of sweet tea from a plastic jug.

"Let's bow our heads and say grace." Mr. Charlie folded his hands on the edge of the table. "Lord, thank you for this food to the nourishment of our bodies, and thank you for friends around the table to bless the soul. Amen."

"Amen," said Matt and Robin in unison. They glanced at each other, smiled, and then began to serve themselves. Mr. Charlie and Matt talked about their first fishing trip and the successful venture that had provided supper and stocked the freezer.

"Yeah, I was surprised you came back down here, boy, after yesterday."

"Of course I came back," Matt said. "I had to prove I knew how to fish, didn't I?"

"You proved it. Wish I had a picture. The grin on your face this morning was about as wide as that string of fish we caught."

Matt nodded.

"Now, Birdie. I remember your days fishing in my boat."

"Yes, sir." Warm memories filled her heart. "Once when Daddy and I went out fishing with you, I caught a bream. I remember how it wiggled on the hook. It was hardly as big as Daddy's hand, but I was proud of it."

"Well, sure you were. And we were proud of you," Mr. Charlie said. "Your daddy loved to bring you with him. Those were good times. We'd sit on the porch talking for hours."

"I remember."

"You were his sidekick. He liked calling you his little Birdie."

"Yes, he did," she whispered. Suddenly, her stomach felt a bit shaky.

"Are you doing all right now?" he asked quietly.

Matt's fingers touched hers and gently covered them.

"Yes, sir. I'm doing fine."

"And how about your mother?"

"She's doing well. She's in Virginia helping care for Grandmother."

"That's good. Your daddy was a happy man. He lived a good life."

She nodded. "That's one of the things that helped us with the grief. He did live a full, rich life."

"And that's what we all should do—be happy and enjoy life the way God intended."

Matt looked down at his plate. Robin hoped her cheeks weren't flushed. She glanced at him again.

"Well, don't stop eating," Mr. Charlie said. "There's lots more where that came from."

Matt sighed and pulled back his hand. Ignoring Callie when she stuck her nose to his leg, he took another piece of fish from the platter. When Robin offered Callie a pinch of her hushpuppy, he smiled.

They sat around the table talking long after supper ended. Robin insisted on clearing the table and washing the dishes while the men continued to talk. Mr. Charlie said she could wash only if she left them for him to dry, but Matt said he would dry and Mr. Charlie could put away. After cleaning up the kitchen, they went out on the porch and ate cookies.

When the sun started going down, Robin caught Matt's eye. "Mr. Charlie, I think we need to be going. It's about bedtime."

"Thanks for having us, Charlie. The food was delicious. Best fried fish I've ever eaten."

"We'll have to do it again. Thank y'all for coming. Me and Sammy don't get much company, but we like it." He kept rocking slowly and didn't get up when Matt and Robin rose to leave. "I need to ride to town tomorrow. Matt, why don't you come ride with me? Nine o'clock?"

"Well, I have other plans. But maybe next time."

"Okay, then. Good night, y'all. I'm just gonna sit here a little while longer."

Sammy followed them down the steps and up the path a ways before he stopped and watched them go. When they got to the mailbox, they turned and waved to Charlie, who seemed content to wave goodbye and watch the sun go down.

"That was nice," Robin said when they had walked about halfway home. She smiled at him. "The two of you interacted like granddaddy and grandson."

"He does remind me of my grandpa."

"Really?"

"Yeah. I grew up with my grandpa in Tennessee. He taught me how to fish."

"Is he still there?"

"No, he died one winter after my mother and I moved to California. He's buried on the side of a mountain in the place he loved."

"I'm sorry for your loss. And your grandmother?"

"She's there too. I didn't know her. She died young."

"Tell me about Tennessee. Did you like growing up there?"

"I loved it. It was an easygoing place, kinda like it is here. My mom and I moved away when I was thirteen. Haven't thought of Tennessee and Grandpa in years. For some reason, right now, here, it doesn't seem so very long ago."

Robin looked at him attentively, then gave an understanding nod. "Do you think he's lonely? Mr. Charlie, I mean."

He hadn't thought about that. "Oh, I don't know. I hope not."

Suddenly, her cell phone rang, disturbing the spell created by conversation and crickets on the dirt road in the twilight.

Robin's pulse picked up at seeing Caleb's name on her phone. "Hey, how are you?" she said cheerfully.

"Great. I'm over here at the pizza joint in the city with my fishing partners. We're celebrating catching a monster striper today. Can you come join us?"

"Right now?" She glanced at Matt. She was reluctant to end their conversation.

"Sure, right now. We just got here. I'll order for you. I want to introduce you to the guys."

"Well … okay. But don't order anything for me. I've already eaten. And it'll take me about forty-five minutes to get there."

"I'd wait for you all night, babe. See you soon."

Robin ended the call and looked at Matt. "I guess I'm going to have to run, literally." She picked up her pace, then turned and started walking backward up the road ahead of him. "Caleb wants me to join him for pizza in the city. Can you take Callie?"

"Sure. Go on."

Matt picking Callie up was the last thing she saw before jogging toward home.

Chapter Fifteen

The popular vintage pizzeria dominated a corner of a block in the city's historic downtown. Robin found a parking space on her second time around, just at full dark. She dropped coins in the meter and hurried to the restaurant. The old brick structure with high ceilings and hardwood floors was packed with dinner guests. As she stepped inside, she caught sight of Caleb and his party sitting in a three-sided booth across the dining room. The pizzeria's logo was painted in white on the wall behind them.

"Hey." Robin mouthed the word with a wide smile and waved.

Caleb quickly rose and crossed the room to meet her. They hugged and kissed each other on the cheeks. "You made it, and you look great." He slipped his arm around her back. "Thanks for coming on short notice."

As they approached the rectangular table, she smiled at the two men sitting there.

They both stood halfway before greeting her and sitting back down. "Ted Wilkerson," the stout middle-aged man introduced himself. "It's so nice of you to join us."

The other man, red-faced, grinned and nodded. "John Reynolds."

"I'd like for you to meet Robin Lancaster," Caleb said. "She's my neighbor at the lake, and I also have the pleasure of calling her my girlfriend." He winked at Robin, who leaned slightly into his arm.

"I bet you do." Mr. Reynolds chuckled and elbowed Mr. Wilkerson.

Robin looked from them to Caleb, who didn't seem to pay the comment any attention. "Well ... I hope you're enjoying your meal."

The two men had plates of lasagna, and Caleb was eating slices of his favorite pizza. A pitcher of beer sat in the center of the table.

"It's very good," Mr. Wilkerson said. "Excellent choice for dinner."

She sat down. "Caleb and I like the food here. It's authentic, freshly made Italian."

At that moment, a waitress arrived at the table. "Your order of bruschetta, sir?"

"Thanks. Right here." Caleb gestured to Robin. "I ordered you some bruschetta, honey. I know how much you like it."

"Thanks." Robin wrinkled her nose. Hadn't she told him not to order for her? She met the waitress's gaze. "Ice water, please." She picked up an appetizer and raised it to her mouth.

Mr. Reynolds picked up his glass and asked for a refill, then leaned across the table and leered at her.

"Would the little lady like some wine? They have a very good Ruffino Chianti on the menu."

She stopped chewing and looked at him. "No, thanks. I'm good."

"Then let me buy you a drink. How about a Bee's Knees?"

"You're very kind, but really, I wouldn't like anything."

He looked back at the waitress. "Just bring me a refill. Gin and tonic. This little lady is hard to please." Again he elbowed Mr. Wilkerson. "Unlike the pink-haired girl," he added in a lower voice, then belted out a laugh.

Mr. Wilkerson sternly shook his head. "We had an amazing day fishing"—he nodded at Caleb—"and a first-rate fishing guide."

Caleb was looking at Robin. He reached over and rubbed her back. "We had a great day. You caught a true trophy striped bass, Ted."

"It was exciting. I've never seen anything like it! I thought it might pull me out the boat before I reeled it in!"

"A toast!" Mr. Reynolds raised his glass. The others raised theirs. "To the best darn fishing guide in the South."

"Here, here," Mr. Wilkerson said. "Sign me up for the same time next year."

Caleb smiled. "You bet."

"I'd like a do-over." Mr. Reynolds shook his head. "I was all thumbs today. Heck, the highlight of my day was flirting with that girl with pink hair who took our pictures."

Robin glanced at Caleb, who had stopped eating.

"Ah, you've been fishing well, John," Mr. Wilkerson scoffed. "What's one bad day?"

"That's right," Caleb said. He gave Mr. Reynolds a hard look, but the man seemed oblivious to the discomfort that the others felt. Caleb put his hand on Robin's thigh under the table, gave it a little pat, and squeezed it gently. "Honey, didn't you say you had to make this an early evening?"

Robin stared at him at first, but then caught on. "I did," she lied, doubling down. "It's been nice meeting you both. I'm glad you're having a great fishing experience." She rose and Caleb and the other men stood too. "Enjoy the rest of your evening. Good night."

"I'll just walk her out, guys. Be right back." As soon as they got outside, Caleb stopped and pulled her toward him. "I'm sorry for what happened. I didn't see that coming. He got drunk fast. I'm going to have to go back in and tell the waitress not to bring any more drinks. Fortunately, I'm the one driving them back to the hotel."

"That was awkward. I was getting so uncomfortable." Confused and somewhat insulted, Robin started walking toward her car.

Caleb stepped into pace beside her. "I'm really sorry. The man's drunk."

"Who was he talking about? The girl with pink hair. Kaitlin?"

"Yes. She came over and took pictures of us with the fish. She has a great Nikon, and the guys had to have pictures of that giant fish."

"Ooh." Robin pursed her lips and raised her brows.

"I'm really sorry about him. Really. He was out of line. I'll make it up to you this weekend, honey."

When they got to her vehicle, Caleb took Robin in his arms and kissed her, and for a moment she almost forgot how aggravated she was. Caleb seemed annoyed as well. "So I'll see you Saturday?" He smoothed his hand down the side of her face and tucked a wisp of hair behind her ear, looking at her sweetly.

Robin's irritation eased. "See you Saturday."

In the car, driving home on the dark highway, her thoughts ticked back and forth like a clock's pendulum. The entire scene replayed in her head. Every word, every glance and nuance.

The man had been rude. And why had Caleb asked her to come to the restaurant in the first place? When had he ever called her his girlfriend? That was nice, but she didn't like to be displayed. And so what if Kaitlin had a nice Nikon. When had she started photographing Caleb's catches? She had questions, and Saturday was days away.

Tomorrow she'd get some answers, or at least talk out her frustrations. She'd invite Jenny over for coffee.

As soon as she parked the car at the lake house, she pulled out her cell phone and texted, *Hi Jen. Coffee and muffins at my house at 10? I need some girl time—boyfriend drama!* That should do it.

Moments later, her phone dinged. *OH. Sure. See u then.*

Robin couldn't remember a time when she had been in such a foul mood. Coffee with Jenny would help. After all, two heads were better than one.

As Robin returned from her morning walk, Matt approached dressed in a black T-shirt and running shorts. It looked like he was just beginning his morning run. "Good morning."

"Morning," he said with hardly a glance as he passed.

She picked up Callie to prevent her from following him. "Calm down, girl. You aren't going anywhere. We need to get ready for Jenny's visit." She set Callie down inside the door and headed for the shower. Afterward, she returned to the house to make muffins. She wanted to serve them piping hot from the oven.

She cut butter into flour and brown sugar for the streusel topping, added a few chopped pecans and some cinnamon, and set it aside. Next, she peeled an apple and grated it, then finely chopped another. These were Jenny's favorite muffins. The perfect coffee cake muffins. While they baked, she made fresh coffee.

She could hardly wait for her friend to arrive. Her night had been restless. Maybe she was making too much of it, but her foray to the pizzeria had left her with a bad taste in her mouth. Along with the bruschetta, she'd gotten an unwanted side of sexual harassment and tidbits of disconcerting revelations.

As soon as the coffee was ready, she carried the carafe over to the studio. She set the table with dessert plates and silverware, cream and butter, and headed back over to the kitchen to check on the muffins in the oven. The aroma of baked apples and cinnamon soothed her senses. The magic of comfort food.

At five after ten, Robin heard the sound of a car in the driveway. But five minutes later, Jenny still hadn't knocked on the studio door. She went in search of her and heard voices out in front of the house. Jenny—and Matt.

"Well, it was nice meeting you," Jenny said.

"You as well," he replied.

Turning in her tracks, Robin hurried back inside and closed the door, waiting until Jenny knocked on the apartment's door before opening it. "Oh, I'm glad you're here." She gave Jenny a hug.

"My goodness." Jenny laughed. "What's going on? You're so excited."

"I need your company, girlfriend."

Jenny glanced around. "I smell something yummy. Did you bake my favorite?" They started toward the table. "Oh, you did. Apple crumb top." She smiled brightly. "Thank you."

"I know how much you like them. Go ahead. Sit down. I'll pour the coffee."

"These are going to kill my diet, you know." But Jenny was already biting into a warm muffin. "Mmm."

Robin poured their coffee and took a sip of hers. "Well, I asked you over—"

"Wait, wait." Jenny licked her lips and her fingers, tilted her head, and held up her hand like a school crossing guard. "Before you get started, I want you to know ... I just met your house guest. The one you said looked like a bear. Uh, no. I don't think so. Nor is he *middle-aged*. Forty? Forty-two at most. What were you thinking?" A silly smile played across her face.

"Well. He did look like a bear when he first arrived." Robin returned the smirk. "He's lost weight, and last week he cut off half his beard."

"Are you sure you weren't trying to downplay his attractiveness for Caleb's sake?" Jenny leaned forward slightly and pinned her with a stare.

Robin rolled her eyes and her shoulders. "Certainly not. I didn't think he was attractive."

Jenny chuckled. "Yeah? You've changed your mind now, haven't you?"

Robin let out a little shriek before laughing.

"He came running down the road wearing that tight black Nike shirt, and my eyes almost popped out when I saw him heading for your house."

"Oh stop. Enough already." She sighed in defeat. "No more about the tenant. I have some real issues to talk about with you."

Jenny buttered her muffin. "I don't like how your face just got all serious."

Robin sighed. "I don't know where to start." She lifted her hand helplessly and let it fall back on the table.

"What happened?" A scowl furrowed Jenny's brow.

"Caleb called me last night on the spur of the moment—close to seven o'clock, I think it was—and asked me to come to the city to meet him and those fishermen."

"Uh-huh."

"I changed my clothes and drove over there as quickly as I could."

"Oh. Where did you meet him?"

"The Village Pizzeria. You know the place. The four of us, we've been there together."

"Nice place." She nodded. "And then what."

"Well … everything seemed fine for about … five minutes. Seriously, five minutes! Caleb introduced me to his clients. They were nicely dressed, around fifty."

"You're killing me here."

Robin huffed. "Well, immediately one of the men starting ogling me and practically insisted on buying me a drink."

"Haha." She gave a dismissive grin. "So what's new?"

"No. It wasn't typical. He made me uncomfortable. He was rude and drunk and told the waitress that I was hard to please."

"What?" Jenny grimaced. "That wasn't nice."

"Yeah. And I'm not done yet. Caleb just ignored him until the man added that the pink-haired girl wasn't."

Jenny's mouth fell open and she covered it with her hand. "The pink-haired girl," she whispered, behind her hand.

"Yeah. Kaitlin."

They just stared at one another. "Huh?" Jenny shook her head. "I have no idea what that could've meant."

"Long story short, Kaitlin took pictures of the men with the fish they had caught."

Jenny blew out a breath through rounded lips.

"Why would Kaitlin be there taking pictures of them? That's what I want to know. I mean, Caleb has a camera and a cell phone that takes perfectly good pictures."

Jenny had stopped eating.

"Jenny?"

"I didn't think you knew," she said, almost sounding whiny. "I'm sorry I didn't say something sooner. Kaitlin was probably taking pictures to put on Caleb's blog."

"Caleb's blog?"

Jenny nodded. "Last fall, when you and Caleb weren't talking, Kaitlin helped him design a blog for his business. It's actually very good."

Robin raised her hands, palms up, and stared up into space. "No one has ever once mentioned a blog to me."

"Sorry." Jenny gave her a pained look.

"But why not? Why didn't he tell me about it?"

"Probably because he didn't want you to think that he and Kaitlin were an item. Because they aren't. She might have thought so, but Caleb always denied it. I think he and Claire might have even argued about it over the holidays."

"Oh. My. Gosh. And you didn't tell me! So the whole family knows about this partnership and has voiced opinions about it?"

"Yeah. Kinda. The family is really close, you know. Anyway, everyone thinks Caleb ought to be with you. The two of you are great for each other. Kaitlin, on the other hand, well ... you've met her. I don't mean to be cruel, but quite frankly, she's a bit flakey. I didn't see the point in gossiping about ... gossip."

"But you could have told me." She couldn't help feeling a bit betrayed. "You've seen them together?"

"Well, yeah, but it was nothing. Once before Christmas. She was at his cabin working on the blog when Zach and I stopped by one afternoon. It seemed innocent. I'm really sorry I didn't tell you."

Robin shook her head. "But the real question is, why has Caleb never told me about the blog and Kaitlin's assistance? We talk."

"Because to him it's probably not important. He's with you. Not her." Jenny shrugged. "Men think differently than women." She nibbled bits of muffin and sipped the coffee.

Neither of them spoke for several minutes, then Robin took a deep breath and sighed. "I'll just have to talk to Caleb about this on Saturday." She smiled impassively. "There's no sense in being upset about it in the meantime. It's probably like you say. Not important."

"Exactly. A non-issue. You'll see. After y'all talk, you'll be fine." Jenny smiled slightly. "Forgive me for not mentioning it?"

Robin twisted her mouth to the side. "Of course, but please don't keep things like that from me."

She nodded. "Now tell me about the festival. I want to help."

"I knew you would. Miss Margaret will be happy to hear it."

"It will be fun, us creating art activities and events for the kids."

"It will be. Let's save that until another day though. I'm not feeling very creative right now." She struggled to pull her focus away from the Kaitlin situation.

Jenny held her gaze. "Don't worry about Kaitlin. After you talk to Caleb about it, you'll see there's nothing to worry about."

"My other question might seem strange, or not, in the light of what you just told me. I wanted to ask you if there was any reason, that you know of, why Claire doesn't like Kaitlin. I noticed she gave Kaitlin a scalding look when we were out on the boat on the Fourth."

"Well." Jenny paused. "Claire does have a protective instinct when it comes to her brothers and sisters. She's the oldest girl. She's been serving as their big sister, little mother her whole life."

"A protective instinct?"

A flush rose in Jenny's cheeks. "I hope I don't regret telling you this stuff. I hate gossip, and so does Zach."

"Jenny please. I need to know."

She sighed. "It's like Claire is running defense. Like she's afraid Kaitlin might latch onto Caleb. The girl has had a crush on him since she was a teenager."

"I don't like the sound of that."

"Really, Robin. There's no sense in speculating and worrying about moot points. I'm sure he can explain."

"I'm sorry." Robin tried to put on a happier face. "I can't believe I'm quizzing you like this. I'm putting you in an awkward spot. I just don't like feeling this way."

After a pause, Jenny said, "That's understandable. You're in love with Caleb. But I think you'll see there's nothing to worry about after you talk to him."

Robin nodded.

Jenny glanced around. "Can I see your illustrations? I hope you're going to let me have a peek before I leave."

"Of course." Robin brightened. "I want your perspective. But first, I need you to show me the blog." She pushed back from the table. "Let me grab my laptop. It'll just take a minute. No more questions and backbiting. Afterwards, we'll talk art."

Chapter Sixteen

For the third morning in a row, Matt walked the dirt road to Charlie's house. Robin's question about the old guy being lonely preyed on his mind. At least Charlie asked for company and wasn't ashamed to speak his mind. Matt respected that. And in spite of the time away from his computer, the fishing trips had taken nothing away from his writing. He could spare some time for his neighbor.

Sammy barked when he walked up on the porch. The front door swung open. "Hey! We were just about to walk out the house."

"Thought I'd go with you after all."

"Good. You won't mind Sammy riding along, will you?"

"Of course not." But Matt didn't know how they'd all fit in the small cab of the truck.

Charlie let down the tailgate, and the dog jumped into the back. "He likes riding with his face in the wind." He chuckled.

The two men climbed into the old truck, which smelled like the dog, fish, and the evergreen air fresher dangling from the rearview mirror. "I go to town every month after I get my check. Go to the bank, get a haircut, buy groceries. Sometimes, if I'm lucky, the farmer's market will be open and fresh pit-cooked barbeque or boiled peanuts will be for sale."

"It's been a long time since I've eaten barbeque or boiled peanuts."

"Stay around here long enough, and you'll have some good eating."

Matt enjoyed the scenery as they drove. The dense woods along the country roads bordered fenced fields dotted with cows, goats, and horses. They reached the small town of Pine Haven, population 6100, in no time at all.

"That number ain't right," Charlie said, nodding to the sign as they entered the city limits. "Hasn't been that many people here in years."

Just the same, the charming Southern town centered around an imposing historic courthouse on Main Street, with a Civil War canon in the middle of the roundabout. Charlie parked in front of South Regional Bank, and Matt got out and fished some change from his pocket.

"Hold off on doing that. You'll just waste your money. Our little town hasn't used the meters for years."

Matt dropped the change back into his pocket.

"After I'm done here, I'm going to walk over to the barber shop." Charlie pointed across the street. "Why don't you look around? Meet me over there."

"What about Sammy?"

"He'll stay right here with nary a problem until I come back for him." Charlie patted the dog on the head. "Good boy, Sammy. Stay."

Matt strolled down the tree-lined sidewalk, noting the shops open for business as well as those that used to be. Fischer's Fine Jewelry, established 1952, no longer dazzled passersby, but Susie's Sweet Confections served patrons fresh coffee and other beverages, sandwiches and fresh baked goods. The Sunshine Shop delighted its customers with vintage signs, glassware, handmade goods, and baskets of colorful silk flowers. The Bookworm looked quaint, and from the number of kids coming in and out, summer reading was popular. Fred's, a modern-day general store, had antique mannequins in various stages of dress standing in the deep display windows and a little bit of everything else for sale. An attorney's office, an insurance office, a family dentistry, and a house museum filled out the square.

Matt was about to cross the street when a familiar bright blue truck decorated with logos and wildlife decals stopped across the street in front of K & K's Beauty Salon. Matt stopped and watched as a slender blond woman slid out of the front seat and hurried into the shop. The truck's driver revved its motor and drove on, disappearing down the street.

About that time, Charlie exited the bank, went to his truck, and let down the tailgate. Sammy jumped out and waited by his master's feet until he was directed to walk with him across the street. Matt lingered in front of the beauty shop, which was next door to the barber's.

"That didn't take long, huh? Let's go on in and get our hair cut." Charlie held the door for him and Sammy to enter.

"You're getting the haircut. I came along for the ride," Matt said. "This place looks just like Floyd's Barber Shop. I used to watch Andy Griffith with my grandpa." The old barber even wore a white jacket.

"The only folks who say that are folks not from around here," the barber said with a scowl.

"No offense," Matt added. "I like your place."

"Well, have a seat in my chair. You can go first. I see you're in bad need of a haircut and shave."

"Oh. Well, I wasn't—"

"Go on and sit down," Charlie said. "Hal here has been cutting hair for fifty years. Cutting mine for most of 'em. You'll be pleased."

"You could shape up the beard. No shave though. Just trim it, and my hair as well."

Charlie sat down in a metal straight-back chair with a black vinyl seat and back.

Just then, an attractive woman with Dolly Parton's sense of style walked in. "Hey, Mr. Charlie. How have you been?"

"Fine, Kathy. How are you? How's business at your new beauty shop?"

"Slow but steady." She smiled broadly. "I'm not complaining. Suits me and my niece fine."

"You still cutting hair over here too?" Charlie asked.

"I sure am. I can't leave my regular customers," she said, putting her hand on her ample hip.

"I didn't want her to leave," Hal said, frowning. "But who am I? Might as well be chopped liver. She wanted a fancy woman's shop."

Kathy laughed and kissed him on the cheek.

"Stop that. You're going to make me mess up this man's hair." In the mirror, Hal winked at Charlie.

"That won't happen. You're the master, Mr. Hal." She walked around the chair as if appraising Matt. "You should let me trim the beard. You know beards are my favorite."

Charlie chuckled and petted Sammy's head.

Hal grunted. "Trying to steal the customer right out my chair, are you?"

Kathy smiled and ignored him.

"I'll let you cut my hair." Charlie stood up. "Don't want to disturb Hal's work."

"I'd love to. Come on over and I'll show you the shop. We're not officially open until ten."

"I think I will." He followed her out the door with Sammy at his heels.

"Hmph. See there. She stole my customer." Hal grumbled under his breath, but apparently his complaints were a ruse. A sly smile betrayed something different.

Unlike most barbers Matt knew, Hal didn't talk while he worked, just alternated between snipping, combing, and appraising. Once the hair cut was done, he prepared to trim Matt's beard.

"Not too short," Matt said. "I've gotten used to it."

Hal nodded once. "I see that. I have an eye for what my customers need. Don't get too many complaints. You be still and don't say a word. Distracts me." With his mouth pinched tight, the cantankerous barber worked with half-shuttered eyes. He surveyed Matt's jaw like an artist might judge his work. Matt couldn't see himself in the mirror with the barber so close to his face as he worked.

When Hal stepped aside to reveal his handiwork, Matt sucked in a breath and stared at himself.

"What? Don't you like it?"

For a moment, Matt was dumbfounded. He recognized the man in the mirror—himself, before Lauren died. "No, it's fine." His voice came out weaker than he'd expected. He observed himself, turning his head from side to side, then looked at Hal. "Thanks. How much do I owe you?"

"I don't take money from dissatisfied customers."

"I am satisfied." Matt pulled out his wallet, then glanced at the sign beside the mirror where the prices were listed. "Here's thirty. Keep the change. I hardly recognized myself, that's all." Matt grinned.

A smile slowly crossed Hal's wrinkled face.

"Have a nice day."

Hal scratched his head. "You too," he called as Matt walked out the door. "Come back again."

Matt walked in next door to find Charlie beaming as Kathy dusted off his neck with a large brush.

She untied the shawl from around his shoulders. "Have a look-see."

"I'll take it," Charlie teased.

Matt chuckled as he looked around. "Hi," he said to the woman he'd seen getting out of Caleb's truck.

"Hi." She approached him. "Can I help you? I'm Kaitlin. Welcome to our shop."

"Matt McLaughlin." He nodded toward Charlie. "I'm with him. Hal has already taken care of me."

"Oh, gosh," Kathy exclaimed when she turned around. "He sure did."

When Charlie paid her, she hugged him and kissed his cheek. "You come back to see us, Mr. Charlie. You know me and my boss next door love it when you come to town."

The door opened, and a well-dressed elderly lady walked in.

"Hey, Miss Margaret." Kathy and the younger woman spoke at once.

"Hi there, girls." She smiled. "Well, my goodness, I see you've been busy this morning. Hey, Charlie."

He grinned. "Good morning, Margaret. Don't you look nice."

"You look good yourself." The two of them hugged in slow motion.

"Are you still trying to single-handedly run the town?" Charlie asked with a chuckle. "I wanna know if you've slowed down yet."

"Charlie, you know I don't want to slow down. If I do, I might rust!" They both laughed.

"Well, you need to take care of yourself."

"You too, Charlie," she said sweetly. "And I don't believe I've met you?" She tilted her head toward Matt.

"I'm Matt McLaughlin. Just visiting here. Charlie's my neighbor."

"Oh, is that right? Well, I know he enjoys having a nice new neighbor." She stuck out her hand and grasped his warmly. "We are mighty glad to have you. Please call me Miss Margaret. Everybody does.

I'm a transplant from Charleston, but this town has been my home for sixty years. Hope you enjoy your stay."

"Thank you."

"I didn't mean to hold y'all up. I'm here for my weekly beauty appointment. It's good seeing you, Charlie."

"You too, Margaret." He turned to the other ladies in the shop. "Girls, you take real good care of this beautiful lady."

"Oh, we will, Mr. Charlie," Kathy said.

When Matt and Charlie walked down the street, Charlie kept smiling to himself. "Well, what do you think of our town?"

"Friendly place. Nice hometown feel about it." They chuckled.

A large vacant lot between buildings at the end of the street served as the permanent location for the farmer's market, which was made up of dozens of stalls along a large center aisle of goods. Charlie spent more time chatting with the locals than he did buying, but he came away with a bag of fresh produce. They stopped at the IGA grocery store and bought a couple more bags of groceries.

As they approached the outskirts of town, Charlie slowed his pickup. "Now I'm gonna buy you the best hamburger you'll ever eat."

"You don't need to buy my lunch."

"I want to. I always get a hamburger for myself anyway on my shopping trip. This place has the best fresh-made hamburgers. Thick and juicy. You won't want to eat another thing for the rest of the day."

Matt didn't argue, and soon they were sitting across from each other at a booth in a little diner, both with a platter in front of them.

"Hal didn't fool you, did he?" Charlie said. "He's really a nice man."

"I caught on to that pretty fast."

He glanced around the diner. "Kathy has worked with him for years. She's more like his daughter. He has children, but they grew up in another state with their mama and a stepdad. And in spite of all the fuss about her shop, he gave her the money for it."

"Wow."

"Yeah, he plays it off. Kathy wanted a shop so she could give her niece, Kaitlin, a livelihood."

"The young woman in the shop?"

"Yes. Kaitlin's daddy is dead and her mother remarried and moved away a few years back. Kaitlin wanted to stay here, and Kathy tries to provide her some stability. She recently opened the shop."

"And Hal financed it." Matt considered the situation. Generosity must be the norm around here. "Your friends are good people, Charlie."

He nodded. "It makes life better to have good people in your life." He wrapped a piece of his hamburger in a napkin and smiled. "And a good dog too." When they returned to the truck, Charlie fed Sammy the piece of burger.

Charlie dropped Matt off at the lake house on his way home, but once he was back in his room, Matt didn't feel like writing after all. He lay on the bed with his hands clasped behind his head, thinking about the morning he'd spent with his neighbor. How he wished he could tell Lauren about it.

His therapist had urged him to imagine conversations with his dead wife. "So you're in the business of promoting insanity?" he'd said. Not the most trusting patient, he'd never wanted to go there. The talking to her wasn't so bad, but waiting for her to reply was a killer.

But today he thought about her and how much she would enjoy the richness of the place and its unpretentious people, and the conversation happened naturally. He told her about his day and the town, about old Charlie and the bass they'd caught, the lake house and the amazing view from his room, and Robin and Callie. If they'd ever had a dog, he would have wanted them to have one like Callie.

When he finished talking, he closed his eyes tight. *Ask her something or wait for a response.* He held his breath.

Her sweet playful voice resonated clearly in his mind. *I'm happy for you, darling. Enjoy yourself … enough for both of us.*

His eyes filled with tears, and he cried. Not gut-wrenching sobs of brokenness, but more like a gentle cleansing rain. At some point, he slept.

When he awoke around three, he wasn't sure if he'd imagined it or if he had actually heard Lauren's voice. It had been so real. Refreshed, his day began anew.

"Thank you, sweetheart," he murmured. "I love you too."

Chapter Seventeen

Jenny had been gone for hours, and Robin continued to scan Caleb's website. Her eyes burned from the strain of speed reading every post and examining the accompanying pictures. Nice pictures too. Kaitlin was a skilled photographer, after all. Caleb looked so handsome and proud, showcased in his ideal environment. The counter on the right of the screen indicated the number of real-time viewers and their location. Obviously, the blog was a valuable component of his current success.

Jealousy pricked her heart. She had been left out, yet another woman was very much a part of it. Surely it meant something that she had been kept entirely in the dark, while Kaitlin had a hand in its creation and maintenance. Robin brooded over it. But she knew she shouldn't.

Picking up her cell phone, she typed a quick message to her sister. *Call me. I have a question for you.*

She sighed. It was time to prepare supper and her goals for the day hadn't been accomplished. She hadn't so much as picked up a pencil or brush, but she had managed to develop knots of tension along her neck and shoulders. Why was she making this such a big deal?

The phone rang once and she answered it. "Emmy!"

"What's up? I got your text."

"I just need to talk. How is everyone?"

"We're fine. I wanted to call you anyway to discuss vacation plans. Was that your question?" But Emily didn't wait for a reply. "Florida. We're going to Florida again like last year. Universal Studios, Discovery Cove. Let me give you the details. I'm assuming you're coming as usual."

"I can't go this year, Emmy."

"What? We have so much fun."

"I know, but I'm making good progress on my illustrations. I want to keep up the momentum."

"But ... Discovery Cove," she whined.

"I know ... swimming with the dolphins. I hate to miss that. And the girls. Darling little angels."

"Aw. Are you sure your decision doesn't have to do with more than the storybook and illustrations? Might a man be a factor?"

"No. A man has nothing to do with my decision." Robin denied it, but she wasn't really sure of her reasons.

"Hmm. Well. What was the question you had for me, then?"

Robin paused, but then rushed ahead in spite of the tinge of embarrassment she felt. "Caleb has had a blog since the fall and he hasn't told me about it."

"Oh." She sounded curious.

"Why didn't he tell me? It's an excellent blog with great appeal."

"He didn't tell you about it." Robin could sense Emmy musing. "How do you know about it now?"

"Jenny, his sister-in-law, told me. She showed it to me today. She's a friend of mine."

"Sure, I met her last summer. And it's a blog he's actively posting content on?"

"Yes." Robin waited.

"Since you're asking for my thoughts on this, I'll tell you." Her sister's tone shifted. "He thinks you wouldn't be interested, so he hasn't bothered mentioning it."

"Emily! Really? You think he thinks I don't care about his passion?"

"I didn't say that exactly."

"Basically, you did. You think he doesn't think I'd have any interest in it, therefore he has never mentioned it."

"Well, yes, that's the gist of it. Maybe he doesn't care about it either. That's just my initial gut response."

Robin considered her sister's remarks. She had learned to trust Emily's judgment. Her know-it-all take was usually spot on. "You might be right."

"Maybe."

"And what if *another woman* helped him develop it and takes the pictures of his adventures and catches."

"Now that could be another situation entirely." Emily's voice sounded quieter and more thoughtful. "Depends on who the woman is, doesn't it? And why she's invested in it?"

The questions hung between them.

"But reason number one could still work," Emily added.

"Okay. As usual, you've been helpful. Your theory hadn't occurred to me. I think the best thing for me to do is ask him about it."

"Absolutely. Open communication is the best practice. You certainly shouldn't be worried about it. In the meantime, no need to speculate. But you might want to show more interest in his work. You know, ask him specific questions about the fish he caught."

"Oh, come on. Do I really need to resort to little ploys?"

"Don't frame it like that. Just show more interest. As a happily married woman, I can tell you, the male ego needs frequent stroking."

"Hah! You are not of this generation, sis." Robin huffed. "Why don't we Facetime so you can see me rolling my eyes right now."

Emily laughed. "I'll spare you my sexist theories."

Thank goodness. "I'll let you know how it goes. Right now, I have to make supper for Professor McLaughlin."

"This is sooo interesting. You're dividing your time between two men and your project. Or is one of them your project? No wonder you're skipping out on our family vacation."

"Never a dull moment," Robin said dryly.

"The girls and I need to come down for a few days to see what's keeping you busy. Meet the *men* in your life and see your work."

"Argh. It's not like that, Emmy, but yes, y'all should come. When?"

"How about the last week of the month? Ryan will be out of town, and the girls and I will be free."

"Yes, please do that. Call or text with the date. In the meantime, I've got to start supper."

"Don't work too much. You know what they say... all work and no play ..."

"Makes Robin tired," she filled in. "I get it." She was ready to end the call, which had failed miserably in allaying her concerns.

"I'll email you the vacation itinerary in case you change your mind."

"Y'all have a good time," Robin said.

"It won't be the same without you. See you soon."

"Thanks, Emmy. Love you."

A talk with her ever-perceptive sister usually made her feel better, but not this time. She actually felt worse about this whole shut-out situation than she had earlier.

What Caleb did every day should be of great interest to her. After all, she hoped to be his wife someday. She admired him for chasing his dream and making it a reality. Wasn't that enough? Or did she have to *like* fishing and hunting? Of course she didn't.

She wanted to dismiss her sister's words, but she couldn't. Emily had touched on a valid point.

As soon as Robin opened the door to go to the house, Callie scampered out and toward the lake. Robin let her play while she went inside and got a box of matches. Grilled chicken breasts on a salad would make a great light supper on this hot night.

After lighting the grill, she stood at the railing and watched Callie chase a squirrel. It was another beautiful summer afternoon, and the scent of mint drew her attention to the herbs in cedar planters along the sides of the deck. She pinched some mint and held it to her nose. It would make a nice garnish for the fruit compote she was about to make.

"Come on, Callie," she called, and returned to the kitchen. She wrapped seasoned fresh corn in aluminum foil, and Callie was waiting for her when she went back out to put it on the grill. "Good girl." She rubbed the dog's head.

As soon as the grill was hot enough, she added the chicken. All she would need to do was turn it a couple of times. Good thing. Easy preparations were necessary after the day she'd had. While the corn and chicken cooked, she sliced peaches and strawberries for compote.

The fruit cooled in a pot on the back of the stove and she was slicing the grilled chicken when Matt walked into the dining area. She stopped, her knife and fork hovering in the air. Something was different. He looked … handsome. *Very* handsome. It took her a few moments to figure out what had changed.

"You got a haircut and trimmed your beard." As soon as the words came out, Robin felt ridiculous for saying them.

Matt looked at her, then grabbed his chin and rubbed his jaw. "I went into town with Charlie. He insisted I get my hair cut while he got his cut."

Robin smiled. "Mr. Hal?" She could picture the old barber shop where her dad used to go.

"Yes."

Matt walked into the kitchen, opened the cabinet, and took out dinner plates. "Why don't I set the table? Will you be eating?"

"Yes." How Matt made himself at home in her kitchen surprised her a little. "We're having chicken salads, roasted corn, and French bread. Dinner plates are all we'll need. Except for dessert. Get those crystal bowls, please." She pointed to some dishes on a higher shelf.

He set the table and proceeded to put ice in glasses while she stirred the fruit compote.

"I'm off schedule today. Sorry supper is late."

Matt shrugged. "That's not a problem to me."

She opened her mouth to explain, then stopped short. Instead, she asked Matt about his day. "You had mentioned you'd be busy today. Did you sacrifice your plans for Mr. Charlie?"

"No. I still got a lot of writing done."

Robin carried the food to the table. "Writing. That's exciting. Mom said you were an author." For a moment, she thought he might say more, but he didn't. She glanced at him. "So you're a published author?"

"I am."

"I'm impressed. What genre?"

Matt sat down at the table. "Mystery suspense … with a little crime and romance."

"Sounds intriguing. Which of those elements do you like the best?"

He laughed. "I suppose the mystery. That's what makes it all compelling, I think."

Robin picked up the water pitcher. "How many books have you written?"

"Four have been published. I'm working on the fifth."

"That's great. I'd love to hear about it sometime." She poured water into their glasses and set a bottle of wine on the table before sitting down. Since Matt only answered her questions without adding more, she realized he didn't want to discuss his writing.

He glanced at her from beneath heavy eyebrows. "Sometime." Then he reached for the bowl of salad and served himself.

She hoped so. It took everything in her not to stare at his face.

"By the way, I have a box of clothing I need to donate. Is there a Goodwill in town?"

"No, those are in the city. But my church has a clothes closet. I can take it next time I go if you like."

"Thanks."

He was quiet as they ate. Robin determined to fill the silence. "I love writing my children's stories. They're simple to create since they were more or less events from my own childhood. There's not much to them, I know, but they delight children. I read them to my kindergarteners. The imagination and creativity that goes into writing a mystery novel amazes me. I'd like to read one of yours."

Matt looked at her and raised his head slightly like he might nod, but he didn't say anything.

For the second time that evening, she felt embarrassed, though she wasn't sure why. Maybe that's why she was talking too much. It covered the awkwardness she was feeling.

"If the stories you create are as beautiful and vivid as your art, you're a talented writer," he said. "Don't belittle the work because you write for children. You create happiness. That's worth something. It's vital."

She put her closed fist to her mouth and looked at him intently, as if reading his face. His eyes shone with sincerity. "You really mean it," she whispered. "I didn't expect that. Thank you for saying that."

"You're welcome." His face relaxed into a smile. "I don't have any of my novels with me, but I could have my publisher send a set."

"I'd like that."

When dinner was over, he thanked her for the delicious meal and excused himself to go back to writing. She washed the dishes and turned out the kitchen lights, all the while basking in the memory of his words. Her mood had lifted considerably. In her life, she'd never lacked love. She'd gotten that in abundance from her family. But as an adult, especially since her dad's death, she'd lacked encouragement as a writer and artist. No one seemed to take her art seriously.

Then when she least expected it, Matt's gift of affirmation touched her heart.

Chapter Eighteen

Robin's usual joyful anticipation of dates with Caleb had dissolved into dread by Saturday afternoon. She was being completely childish and she knew it. What exactly was she afraid of? And why was it that so many real feelings were vague as far as expression went?

She took extra care with her hair and makeup and changed her dress half a dozen times before choosing a short blue striped off-the-shoulder shift. High-heeled espadrille sandals showed off her legs. The least she could do was present a confident façade.

At four thirty, Caleb rapped on the apartment door, and as soon as he stepped inside, his smile vanquished all her fears. He had that easy grace that came from being an athlete, and a glow from good health and lots of sunshine. His eyes twinkled as he held a bouquet of pink Gerber daisies tied with a wide gingham ribbon.

"Oh, Caleb, they're beautiful!" Robin reached for the flowers and he reached for her. "How did I get so lucky?" she murmured as he covered her mouth with his.

"That's my line," he whispered against her cheek.

"You're sweet." She sighed. His kisses made her warm and relaxed all over.

"You're using all my lines." He smiled and drew a deep, dramatic breath. "Let's get them in water before we go." He followed her to the kitchenette and turned to look around the open room while she put the flowers in a vase. "This is a nice apartment. You haven't shown it to me." His eyes followed the spiral staircase and he nodded in the direction of the loft. "What's up there? Your bedroom? Tell me no."

She rolled her eyes and smiled. "Mostly an art studio. And yes, a daybed." She set the flowers on the counter. "Would you like to see my art?"

He reached for her again. "I wish we had time. But our reservations are at seven." His arm hooked around her waist. "We have to stop by and say hi to Rachel on the way." He breathed the words into her hair.

"I'll show you some other time then." She turned and lifted her lips to his for a quick kiss. Instead, he pulled her against his body and encircled her in his arms. His mouth found hers and he kissed her deeply.

"Caleb." She hardly had the will, much less the strength to pull back.

"I'm sorry." He took a step back. "I know. Parameters. We'd better get out of here before I make a fool of myself. You look amazing, you know."

She didn't know what to say. In a flash, she remembered last summer. As soon as their attraction started getting out of hand, she'd pulled back and set parameters. Ultimately, he distanced himself. That wasn't her goal. Yet she knew what she wanted. A beautiful life like her parents had together. Commitment. Marriage. Not a passionate affair. But now she wasn't so sure how to go about attaining her dream without pushing Caleb away again.

She gave him a kiss on the cheek before they walked out her door.

A separate wing of the hospital housed the transitional rehab unit where Rachel had spent the last week. They entered the pristine, quiet facility and walked directly to her room.

"Hey!" Claire and Rachel greeted them.

Caleb smiled from ear to ear. He crossed the room to where Rachel sat on her bed and gave her a kiss on her cheek.

She put her arm around him. "Ah, you're such a prince," she cooed, taking the bouquet he held out. "You're the best." She glanced at Robin. "Isn't he the sweetest?"

"He is." Robin smiled.

"Don't y'all look great!" Claire said. "Caleb has finally found a woman who's as beautiful as he is."

He narrowed his eyes. "These two always make a fuss over me," he said to Robin, jerking his thumb toward his sisters.

"Are y'all going somewhere special?" Claire asked.

He made himself comfortable on the edge of the bed. "We came to see Rachel. And, if you must know, we're having a romantic dinner this evening." He winked playfully at Robin.

Standing beside him, she rubbed his shoulder. "How are you feeling?" she asked Rachel.

"My leg doesn't hurt too much now. Everyone has been great."

"She's having physical therapy daily," Claire added. "Then she'll progress to aquatic therapy. We're pleased with the quality of the care."

"The good news is I'll be here only another week. Then I'll be home."

Claire stood. "Here, let me take your flowers. I'll go find a vase for them and you can have your brother to yourself for a few minutes. Do you want anything from the snack bar?"

Rachel looked thoughtful. "As a matter of fact, could you bring me one of those fruit smoothies? They're addictive."

"Will do." Claire sent her an air kiss, then looked to Robin. "Come with me?"

"Sure." Claire's confident and caring attitude impressed her.

The two of them walked down the hall to the nurses' station and requested a vase for the flowers. The snack bar was at the end of the hall. They chatted amicably while waiting for their order. When they started back to the room, Kaitlin was entering Rachel's room.

Claire grumbled under her breath. "Now there's an accident waiting to happen." She then seemed to remember Robin was beside her. "Sorry."

Her thoughts exactly.

When they walked into the room, Kaitlin had her arms laced around Caleb's bicep and she smiled up into his face. Looking none too pleased, Caleb tried to untangle himself and stepped away.

Claire wasted no time closing the space between the two of them. "Kaitlin, look at the pretty bouquet Caleb brought for Rachel."

Kaitlin's smile vanished. "Oh. Hi, Claire. Robin." She moved around to the other side of the bed.

Caleb squeezed Rachel's shoulder. "We have reservations, so we can't stay, but we wanted to stop by."

"I'm leaving shortly too," Claire added.

Kaitlin looked back and forth between them. "I hope I'm not running y'all off."

"Not at all." Robin smiled. "Enjoy your visit." After witnessing the grimace on Caleb's face in what was clearly a brush-off, she could afford to be gracious. Actually, she felt a little embarrassed for Kaitlin.

Caleb draped his arm around Robin's shoulders and they said their goodbyes.

Robin and Caleb made their way to historic downtown to explore brick-and-stucco row houses. The sultry air forced them to cut their stroll short and duck inside The Tea Olive restaurant, where they sipped tipsy peach tea while waiting for their table. Then a hostess seated them in a cozy dining room permeated with the tantalizing smells of grilling steaks and seafood. Hors d'oeuvres primed them for their delicious meal. While Robin hadn't expected to be seduced by Caleb, the evening, however, worked its magic.

"I've read several rave reviews about this place." She looked around the historic antebellum house that had been transformed into a restaurant several decades before. Each of the lovely rooms was named for a Southern flower. They were seated in the Magnolia Room.

"I thought you'd like it." Caleb smiled at her from across the candle-lit table. "You're such a classy lady yourself."

On the terrace, a guy sat on a high stool strumming a guitar and crooning John Mayer songs. The enchanting fragrance of tea olive wafted across their table from the trees outside. Robin felt pampered in the comfortably elegant surroundings.

"I wanted tonight to be special," Caleb said.

She smiled. "For any particular reason?"

"You." Caleb reached across the table and covered her hand with his, then rubbed his thumb gently over hers as he looked at her adoringly. "I haven't spent as much time with you as I would've liked this summer. I've been working a lot. But if I could put you in my pocket and take you along with me, I would."

"Oh, Caleb," she laughed. "I'm glad we have tonight."

"And finally, it's just the two of us."

The waitress took that moment to bring their orders. Caleb's steak was thick and juicy, and the blackened salmon she ordered was the best she'd ever eaten. She savored every bite. The meal was delicious, but so was the intimate conversation. With the dreamy music playing in the background and the candlelight's soft glow, the evening took on an enchanted feeling. If the table hadn't been between them, she would have melted into his arms. An evening like this was what she'd been waiting for. Rachel had called him a prince, and tonight he was hers.

"The food is exceptional, isn't it?" Caleb asked. "And the atmosphere."

"Yes, I adore the warm atmosphere."

"But this place isn't for those on a tight budget. That's one of the reasons I work like I do. The business is growing, but it hasn't reached the point where I can kick back and enjoy the success. I have to keep up this pace."

"You've done a great job creating your business, Caleb. I'm proud of you."

"I'm making a name for myself in the field. This year has been phenomenal."

How could she possibly bring up the subject of Kaitlin and the blog? Better to leave it alone, she'd thought. And she would have, but Caleb changed the direction of the conversation and she blurted it out without thinking. "Has your blog been a factor in your recent success?"

"It's definitely played a part." Caleb paused and raised his eyes to hers. "Did I tell you about the blog?"

"No, Jenny did. The other day, in fact. I looked at it. It's great."

"Yeah, it pulls in new clients from all over the country. I've even heard from fishermen in Canada."

"Really? And Kaitlin maintains it for you?"

Caleb sobered. "I take care of it myself. I needed Kaitlin's help at first to get it up and going. She wanted to do it. She was going for a degree in web design before she dropped out of college."

"Except she took the pictures of your last clients."

"She shows up all the time with her camera. I think she stalks me by way of the blog, but she does take great pictures." He tilted his head to the side. "That doesn't bother you, does it?"

The dreamy, romantic mood was shifting fast to reality. "No … and yes. Why didn't you tell me about it?"

Caleb twisted his mouth to the side and looked at her intently. He seemed to be thinking through a response. "I'm not going to lie to you, Robin, because you mean too much to me." He paused and inhaled deeply. "If the situation were reversed, I'd be annoyed. Let's face it. I don't like you having a man living in your house. Me letting Kaitlin help seems … hypocritical, and if the truth be known, selfish."

"Mmm." Was he hedging?

"Do you understand what I'm trying to say, honey?" He reached across the table and put his hand over hers again.

Emotions whirled inside her. He'd said a lot, but she hadn't sorted it all out. "Well, I'm not sure. Did you say why you haven't told me about it?"

He shrugged his shoulders. "I didn't want to bring it up. I didn't know how you'd feel about it, and I don't want anything to come between us now that we're back together."

"I don't see how it could,"—Robin scowled as she held his gaze—"unless you have more than a working relationship with her."

"A serious relationship? With Kaitlin?" He stiffened and cleared his throat. "Of course not. You're the woman I want to spend my life with. We're perfect for each other. You're the perfect catch for any man. I wanted to tell you that tonight."

"Really?" She pressed a hand to her chest. When had her heart started racing?

"Perfect, honey. Don't you see that?" His voice had softened, and he stroked her hand.

Robin could feel heat rising in her cheeks.

"Honey?"

"Excuse me a moment, Caleb, please. I'll be right back." Grabbing her purse, she rose as gracefully as possible on wobbly legs and headed to the lady's room.

She rushed through the door, grateful that she hadn't bowled someone over on her way in. One look in the mirror confirmed her flushed face, and she turned on the tap. Leaning over the sink, she patted cold water on her cheeks and dabbed her neck and chest with her handkerchief. All the intense emotions of the evening—desire, joy, anticipation, jealousy—had risen to the surface at once as she forced herself to listen calmly to Caleb. She had listened, finally. She could find no fault with anything he'd said. He had been honest. And she'd been snippy.

What on earth is wrong with you? Get yourself together, girl.

Her recovery took longer than she would've liked, but when she left the restroom ten minutes later, she had regained her composure. By the time she rejoined Caleb at the table, she was practically giddy with excitement. He, on the other hand, appeared apprehensive.

"Sorry for my awkward exit." Robin smiled and sat down. She was ready to hear what he had to say, but one look at him caused more butterflies in her stomach. "Could you repeat the part about us being perfect for each other?"

He laughed and leaned over the table. "Thank God you're okay. I didn't know what had happened."

Robin bit her bottom lip and smiled nervously. "Sorry. Not my most graceful moment. I felt like I might break out in hives."

"Oh, honey. The most important thing is that we are okay. We're perfect for each other."

At that moment, the waitress brought their dessert—over the moon chocolate pie with fluffy marshmallow meringue.

"Are we okay, baby?" Caleb asked. When she nodded, he dipped a spoon into the decadent dessert. "You are perfectly wonderful. I want to spend the rest of my life with you." He lifted the spoon to her lips. "The first bite is yours."

She leaned forward and, without taking her eyes off his, tasted the chocolate and meringue he offered her. "Mmm."

"That's what I'm talking about." He grinned and took a spoonful for himself.

She giggled, he laughed, and they ate the pie slowly as the romance returned.

"Did you just propose to me, Caleb Jackson? It kinda sounded like you did."

"Yes, that's what I did," he said, his voice suddenly unsteady. "But it was a little rough around the edges. Let me try again." He cleared his throat. "Will you marry me?"

"Oh my gosh," Robin whispered. "Yes."

"That's my girl. You've made me a happy man."

"I'm jumping up and down inside, but I'm too weak to move."

"I think that's a good thing." He motioned to the waitress. "Could we get the check, please?" There was a gleam in his emerald green eyes. "Let's get out of here."

She nodded and stood. "I might be a little shaky."

He pressed his hand to her lower back as he guided her to the door. As soon as they walked outside, she turned into him and wrapped her arms around his neck. He slipped his arms around her.

"Hold me tight, Caleb."

"Think you might fall, do you?" He whispered the words into her ear. "You know if you do, I'll catch you."

"Like you did last summer when that shaggy dog knocked me off my feet."

He pulled back and looked into her eyes. "The luckiest catch of my life."

And mine too, she thought, but she couldn't say the words. The only place she wanted to fall right now was into his arms. And she was already there.

Chapter Nineteen

Matt scrubbed his hands over his face, got up, and stretched. The sun had yet to rise, but he wanted to get outside to clear his head. He'd woke several times during the night with too much on his mind.

He pulled back the drapes. The smoky gray water of the lake blended with the dark shadows of the trees and sky. Ready for a run, he dressed quickly and headed out.

The temperature was surprisingly cool, despite the fact that it would be sweltering later. Now, in the early morning, he could breathe. Deeply. And as his feet pounded the path along the lake's edge, he focused on his heartbeat, the sky, and the water. The rhythm of the run brought clarity, and his anxieties subsided. A rush of energy and strength fueled a sense of accomplishment. He could do this. He *was* doing it.

After more than an hour on the trail, he paused beside the lake long enough to snatch off his shirt and shoes and jump in. The jolt of cool water invigorated him. He swam for half an hour before he tired, then lifted himself out and headed up the bank to the house.

This was how he liked to start his day. Three months before he never would have believed he'd become a runner, lose weight, and feel like a man again. Or even more incredulous, that he would stop obsessing about his disappointments and the biggest loss of his life.

The smell of bacon brought a smile to his face as he visualized Robin making breakfast. She had wanted to talk about his work last night. At first, he had been reluctant to share anything about it. His jaw stiffened when she mentioned it, and the wall went up. Lauren had been his writing partner. That had been their private domain. Yet just as quickly as the wall had gone up, it had come down. More evidence of how far he'd come.

Robin had little confidence in her creative endeavors. He'd gathered that from how she spoke about her writing. But he'd seen her art, and it was no less beautiful than that from the most skilled and practiced hands of gifted artists. He recalled those angst-filled days when he'd destroyed his own work almost as fast as he created it, before he believed in his talent, his craft.

He should encourage her. Had it not been for Lauren's encouragement, he wouldn't have accomplished anything in the literary world. Little fish—big pond, he used to think. But so what. An artist had to be true to his or her gift. He'd extrapolated that theory from his grandpa's preaching, his wife's affirmation, and his core belief that people needed to use their God-given talents.

So many of his grandpa's words had come back to him in the last few weeks. So many of his own beliefs, buried under anger, grief, and circumstances, had resurfaced to remind him of who he had been, who he still was. Like a lost penny shining on the street, his faith looked up to him, reminding him, "In God We Trust."

He stepped inside the house and took a deep breath. The breakfast smells made his mouth water. He paused to listen. No little paws scampered toward him. Indeed, he was alone. Robin had already been there and left to begin her day. He went upstairs to shower before eating breakfast.

He was starved when he came back down the stairs. He looked over the breakfast spread and piled generous portions of eggs and bacon on his plate, with a toasted English muffin with cream cheese. As he ate and sipped his hot coffee, he decided it was time to reach out to those who would want to hear from him. Phone calls, rather than email, because he wanted to communicate personally. He glanced at his watch. After he cleaned his dishes, he'd make a call. Those in the Pacific time zone would have to wait until later.

First, Matt called Meryl Duncan. A first-rate literary agent, she cared more about the person than their product. But she knew the business, and if she liked something, it sold. Yet he hadn't spoken to her in more than six months.

"Meryl Duncan speaking. Matt? Is that you?"

"Good morning! It is I," he replied. She squealed with delight, and he chuckled. "Do you get this excited over all your calls?"

"Matt McLaughlin, how are you?"

"I'm well."

"I am glad to hear that from you. You've been on my mind, dear man. I heard you took a sabbatical."

"I needed to get away. New vistas. I wanted to let you know that I'm writing again. It's three years overdue, but do you want novel number five?"

"Of course I want it! You're mine. Don't you dare think of going elsewhere."

"I couldn't do that, Meryl."

"Where are you anyway?"

"I'm staying in a house beside a lake in Georgia. It's secluded. Surrounded by nature."

"And you got over that stubborn writers' block."

"Yes. I'm grateful. Do you want what I have now, or would you rather wait until I finish?"

"Send me as much or as little as you like. I'll get right to it and let you know what I think."

"Thank you, Meryl ... for sticking with me."

"And thank you for trusting me. Most of all, I'm happy you're doing well. It's great hearing from you."

He hung up the phone and ordered books from his publisher for Robin, then returned to his work in progress. After all, people were counting on him to see this project through.

Every day since their romantic evening, Robin day-dreamed about marriage to Caleb. He'd said he wanted to spend the rest of his life with her. Exhilarated at first, her roller-coaster emotions now drifted on the downhill slope after she'd had some time to entertain exactly what he'd said.

He didn't want her to tell anybody. The announcement should wait, he'd said. In the first place, until he was "financially set," he couldn't in good conscience take on a wife. Second, because he didn't need the distraction. After all, they wouldn't get married "for some years down the road."

Down the road! That's where she was living right now, literally and mentally.

He'd said, "Let's keep our happy secret to ourselves." She hadn't voiced any objections. He'd acted like it was a foregone conclusion. So she would keep the secret. Although that might be difficult with Emmy and the girls coming for a visit.

Emily had called first thing that morning. All Robin needed to do was round up the air mattress and clear the visit, more or less, with Matt. Her sister and nieces would keep her delightfully engaged for a few days. But would the little giggly girls disturb her tenant?

As she headed into the house, she racked her brain about the whereabouts of the mattress. If she remembered correctly, it had last been used years ago during a house party celebrating Emily's engagement. Her mom would have stored it in the guest room closet, but her dad would have stored it in the garage. She smiled as she thought of her parents' personalities. Such different styles, yet they'd always made decisions together.

"My bet is on the guest room," she said to the dog at her feet. She glanced up the stairs noting the closed door at the top. Silently she crept up, turned on the landing, and walked down the hallway to the guest room. In addition to the queen-size bed, a set of bunk beds stood along one wall. She'd always liked the room.

A wide mirror-front reach-in closet lined the wall a few feet from the bed. She opened it and looked inside. Stacked neatly on one side were sheet sets, blankets, towels, and extra pillows. Out of reach on the top-most shelf was a bundle that looked like the air mattress. She brought the vanity chair from the adjoining bath to use as a step stool.

Callie jumped up on the bed and pranced like she wanted to climb the closet shelves herself.

"Calm down, Callie."

Standing on the stool, she reached for the bundle. She could only reach it with her finger tips, and as she strained to coax it forward, it rolled off the shelf onto her head. Callie yapped and jumped off the bed, causing her to turn quickly. She lost her balance, and the next thing she knew the stool shot out in one direction and she toppled in the other. Squealing, she reached for the bed, which only served to break her fall. She moaned, clutching the spread with one hand and squeezing her eyes closed, as she slid to the floor.

"Oww!" She rubbed her side along her ribs to her hip. When she opened her eyes, Matt knelt beside her on the floor.

"Don't try to move. Where do you hurt?" He placed one hand on her back and simultaneously stiff-armed Callie with the other. "Move, Callie!"

She inhaled through her teeth, still rubbing her hip with one hand while bracing herself with the other. "The stool flipped over."

"You did too. What hurts?"

"My side. Here." She pressed lightly on the spot. "Oww."

"Can you move?" A frown knitted his brows. "Do you need the EMTs?"

Robin shook her head. "I'm okay … I think. Could you help me get up?"

He held her firmly, one hand across her back and the other on her upper arm. "I'll move you slowly. Let me know if it hurts."

She watched his concerned face as he eased her into a sitting position. "I'm fine." She took a deep breath and let herself feel her body. "Really. That was stupid of me."

They looked into each other's eyes.

She was sorry to cause him such concern. "Are *you* okay?"

He ignored her question. "If you think you're able, let's see if you can stand."

She nodded. The initial stab of pain had subsided to a burning ache.

Matt continued to frown as he lifted her to her feet. "How does that feel?"

"Not nearly as bad as I must look. You look like you've seen a ghost."

"How should I look?" he snapped. "You screamed."

"That's what I always do when I fall from high places and hurt myself," she snapped in response. After a moment, she twisted her mouth into a shy smile. "Thanks for coming to the rescue." She had an overwhelming urge to hug him. They'd both feel better.

She quickly put her arms around him, pinning his arms to his sides and practically snatching him to her. He felt like a mountain of strength, and she smelled his warm woodsy scent. As suddenly as she embraced him, she let him go, embarrassed, and dropped onto the edge of the bed. "I'm sorry I disturbed you."

Matt set the stool upright, picked up the mattress bundle, and started to put it back into the closet.

"I was trying to take that down. My sister is coming for a visit with her two little girls. They'll need the mattress."

"Oh." Matt lifted his head in a nod and handed her the mattress.

"Do you mind?"

"Your sister visiting? Of course not."

"Her two daughters are five and six. I wouldn't want us to disturb you."

"You won't. Are you sure you're not hurt? Stand up and see how it feels. Walk around the bed."

She stood and walked around it, gliding a hand along the bed's surface. When she came to a stop in front of him, she wrinkled her nose and rubbed her hip again. "I might be a little sore." Her embarrassment only worsened.

"You can't move around too much until you're sure you haven't broken anything. I'll get you a glass of water and some Tylenol."

"Oh, please don't bother."

But he'd already left the room.

"It's not a bother," he huffed from in the hallway.

She fell back on the bed with a sigh. *You missed your calling, Nurse McLaughlin.*

When he returned, she took the two tablets and drank the water, promising to lie down for a few minutes before resuming her activities.

His face relaxed and his smoky eyes smiled even though his lips stayed a tight line. "Good idea," he said. "And next time, before you go hurting yourself, please ask for my assistance." He turned and walked out.

She lay there looking up at the light blue ceiling, slightly dazed and amused at how she had gotten there. Her conscience soon got the better of her.

Forgive me, Lord, for misjudging Matthew McLaughlin. He really is a nice person. A much better tenant than I deserve. And most of all, forgive me for misleading him. I have to find a way to tell him the truth and apologize for letting him believe a lie. Thank you, Lord, for protecting me from my misjudgments and silly falls.

Matt sat in front of his computer staring at the screen. He couldn't remember what he had written fifteen minutes before. Robin's scream blew him away. The sight of her lying on the floor tied his stomach in knots. He might have handled it better ... on the inside, since she obviously had been alive and communicating. Especially communicating. Fortunately, she hadn't been seriously injured.

He picked up his cell phone and walked over to the windows. It was another gorgeous summer day. Taking a deep breath, he made the call. "Good morning, Dr. Hess. It's Matt McLaughlin. How are you?"

"Quite well, thank you, Matt. How are you? It's been three months."

"Yes. Three months. I'm doing well. Haven't needed any prescription refills, no nightmares. I'm running, breathing. I've lost weight."

"You're running, practicing the relaxation techniques. Great. And you've lost weight. The unyielding one has become the model patient." He could hear the smile in her voice. "The anxiety has improved. And the anger?"

"Flares up from time to time, but no longer a persistent burn."

"No longer a persistent burn. Very good." She paused and waited in the reflective manner Matt had grown accustomed to in the months of counseling.

"I spoke to my wife the other day, Dr. Hess. Talked to her out loud." Unexpectedly tears pricked his eyes, and he choked up.

"You had a conversation with Lauren?"

He swallowed, trying to regain his composure. "Yes, we talked. Her happy voice came to me like she was there. Thank you for that."

"You are the one doing all the work, Matt. The conversation is a breakthrough. Thanks for sharing that with me."

"I wanted to let you know I'm doing all right. I know you recommended bimonthly therapy sessions by phone or Skype, which I still don't want. Even so, I wanted to call."

"You sound good, Matt. Call anytime, when you want to chat or if you need to share anything. I'm here for you."

"I know. Thank you."

Matt ended the call with a feeling of satisfaction. He appreciated Dr. Hess even though theirs had been a love-hate relationship. The therapist had challenged him to deal with his feelings rather than stagnate in unhealthy ways. Now that the worst was behind him, he saw the wisdom in her counsel.

He had one last call to make.

Tom picked up on the second ring. "Hello."

"Hi, Tom. It's Matt. How's your summer going?"

"Great. It's good to hear from you. The girls and Lydia stay busy at the pool. My department duties are light this summer. How about yourself? How's the weather?"

"Hot. But it hasn't bothered me. I run early in the morning and swim after the run."

"That's great. You're putting me to shame. I haven't been to the gym in weeks. The girls keep us busy."

"That's nice. I like it here, Tom. It's quiet and secluded. I'm writing every day. This has been an ideal place for a sabbatical."

Tom chuckled. "You might not want to leave when the time comes. And what was it about the proprietor? Is she still making your meals?"

"She is. Robin's also an artist. She writes and illustrates children's books. And she's a dream to be around."

"Whoa! How old is Robin?"

"I don't know. Somewhere between twenty-five and thirty. She's fair, a redhead, and probably looks younger than she is."

"And is she easy on the eyes?"

"She's beautiful." The word didn't do her justice.

"You lucky dog. I can't wait to tell Lydia."

"You did well arranging that."

"I don't know what you mean. I didn't arrange that. Give yourself the credit."

"I didn't set this up. You arranged her services as part of the rental deal, didn't you?"

"Nooo. There was no option for a woman." Tom belted out a laugh. "If there had been, I'd have gotten you a masseuse as well."

Matt chuckled uneasily, then held the phone away from his ear. He caught a glimpse of Callie running across the lawn. "How did *this* come about? I can't even recall that first meeting when I got here."

"Well, maybe you don't need to. God is in the circumstances." Tom had stopped laughing.

"Uh ... I thought ..." Matt was stumped. But no need to say any more. "I'm glad I called you today. This conversation has been quite enlightening." He chuckled again nervously. "I also called Dr. Hess and my literary agent."

"How about that. When you left California, you didn't want to talk to a soul."

"I know. Right now, I'm looking forward to the rest of my time here. I'm not going to keep you. Just wanted to touch base."

"Great to hear from you, Matt. I dare say, you sound like your old self."

"Give Lydia and the girls my love."

"Will do. Next time I want to hear more about this beautiful red-haired woman."

As Matt ended the call, he was already clicking through his memories of that first night and the following morning. Robin had showed up and left the dog. He'd frightened her in the kitchen and barely missed getting hit by a spatula. They ate brownies. That was it. He had nothing else.

Robin came into view, walking down to the dock. She wasn't limping. Apparently she'd recovered from the fall. He smiled and shook his head. Today she'd screamed like the first time she'd laid eyes on him. It made no sense that she fascinated him. One thing was for sure, he'd find out how he'd gotten so lucky to have her in his life.

Chapter Twenty

Robin sat in her studio drawing cattails in a pond when Callie started barking excitedly. Her subsequent dance by the door let Robin know they had company. Emmy had arrived. She glanced at the time. Just after noon. She began tidying the drafting table, gathering her pencils and returning them to the proper glass canisters, and putting her drawings out of the reach of inquisitive little fingers. After brushing her hands on her apron, she pulled it off, hung it on a hook, and headed downstairs.

The characteristic glee of children playing brought a smile to her face.

"Help Mommy out, girls!" Emily called. "And I asked that you not be loud." She stood by the van, watching the girls run away from her.

"Whee ... Whee!" Lilly and Bella ran with their arms outstretched like wings.

"I'm a duck," Lilly said. "Quack, quack."

"Quack, quack ... Quack, quack," Bella repeated.

"Girls! Come back here." Emily put her hands on her hips.

When Robin opened the door, Callie darted out and ran down the hill after them.

Robin crouched down as she crept unnoticed toward the girls. "Grr! Grr! I'm a wolf. You'd better fly home, little duckies!"

It was a mystery how two little girls could make such high-pitched squeals. Upon reaching their mom, they flung their bodies at her hips and clung tight.

That's where Robin caught up with them and pulled them into a group hug. "I'm going to eat you up," she said, holding them tightly. "Chomp. Chomp. Give me a hug." The girls dissolved into giggles. "Are you ready to spend a few days with Auntie Robin?"

"Yeah!" They pulled away to turn their attention to Callie. Lilly knelt on the ground with her arms around Callie's neck, and Bella stood over them rubbing the dog's fur.

"So much for the element of surprise," Emily said, taking bags out of the van. "We just shattered the peace."

"Oh, it's all right. Matt knows you're coming. He's rather laidback anyway."

"We're early."

"It's good to see you." Robin hugged her sister. "You're ready for a visit too?"

Emily rolled her eyes. "I'll say. I was ready to get out of the house. I declare, they are getting more and more rambunctious. My hat's off to their teachers—and to you, sis. I've had my hands full this summer with the two of them. How can you manage a roomful of five-year-olds?" She handed a tote bag to Robin. "Come here, girls. You need to get your suitcases." She and Robin gazed adoringly at the girls. "Aren't they precious?"

Robin grinned. "They're adorable."

Bella grabbed the handle of her flowered pink case on wheels, and Lilly grabbed her pink polka-dotted one.

Emily carried the other bags. "Lead the way. Let's go, girls. Follow the leader."

Glancing back again and again at the rolling cases behind them, the girls wove along the path to the studio apartment.

"I think I have our sleeping arrangements figured out," Robin said as she held open the door. "You and the girls can have the air mattress downstairs close to the bathroom. I brought the pink floral bedding the girls like so much down from your room."

"That'll be nice." Emily smiled. "We can set up the room divider to shut out some of the moonlight shining through the patio doors. We'll make it a cozy corner. It'll be fun."

"I thought so. What do you want to do now?"

"They ate peanut butter and jelly sandwiches in the car, but they need a snack. I need to relax a bit. Maybe you could read them some of your stories. We want to swim and take walks and grill s'mores and all the fun stuff. But it's too hot to be outside right now."

"I can think of lots of fun inside activities." Robin led the girls to the bookshelf.

The girls chose books and they read all snuggled together on the sofa. Afterward, they ate goldfish crackers with lemonade before Robin brought out the tiny china tea set she'd used as a child. They had a tea party sitting cross-legged on the floor, serving each other carrot sticks and raisins, while she and Emily chatted.

Emily turned on the iPad when the tea party ended. "Time for our animated kids' shows. That should give us more time. I don't even feel guilty when I let them watch these programs." She handed them the tablet. "Look at their little faces. They're totally engaged."

"Like magic." Robin laughed. "They're really sweet together."

"I allow only one hour in the mornings and one in the afternoons for the educational programs. That makes it special and keeps their attention." Emily grinned. "I have to carve out time to get chores done."

"You're so resourceful." They laughed.

Smart, thoughtful, and self-confident, Emily made others feel comfortable and valued. She loved her husband and children, and life in general, and it showed. They talked about Ryan and his work as a dermatologist, her volunteerism at their church and the girls' school, and the girls' swimming lessons.

"While the girls are entertained, why don't you show me the illustrations you're working on for your story."

Robin and Emily went upstairs and looked at her art for about twenty minutes before the girls ran up looking for them. They decided to put on their sun hats and take a stroll to the manmade beach.

As soon as they stepped outside, the girls ran and played and explored. Bella offered her sister a hand as they walked on the rocks along the shore, then they splashed along the water's edge.

"Isn't that the most delightful sound?" Emily said. "Children's laughter. The girls love playing together. They're best friends."

Robin watched her sister's face as she watched the children. A swell of joy filled her chest. "You're such a beautiful mommy. You're amazing."

"You might be biased. And we did have good examples."

"Do you think Dad can see them? The girls, I mean. I sense his presence sometimes." She drew close to her sister as they watched Lilly and Bella playing in the water.

"Oh, I don't know. I like to think he can. Somehow I feel like he knows what's happening with us." She put her arm around Robin's shoulders. "We're not to worry about things like that though."

The sudden memory of her dad pricked Robin's heart, but the love she shared with Emmy soothed the sadness. "I'm glad I have you," she said, and leaned her head on her sister's shoulder.

"Me too."

Robin inhaled and shimmy-shook her shoulders. "Okay. Time for me to get back to make supper. Hot dogs and hamburgers on the grill."

"My favorite."

"Really?" Robin made a funny face. How did she not know that?

"Yeah." Emily flung out her hand. "Anything I don't have to cook myself."

They laughed.

"Okay, girls! Let's follow Auntie Robin back to the house."

The children stopped what they were doing but only stared at her.

"Who wants to help me cook hot dogs?" Robin yelled.

"Me!" they yelled and ran giggling ahead of Robin on the path to the lake house.

Matt had been forewarned. The sister and nieces were due for a visit. He had even given his consent. What he hadn't taken into account was the exuberance of pint-sized humans. Such squealing and giggling like he hadn't heard in some time spilled out of the van parked under his windows. Writing came to a halt. The mom joined in the racket as did the dog. From where he stood at the window, he counted the number of critters running wild in the yard. The nieces had indeed arrived. Thank goodness there were only two of them.

After the initial shockwave, the noise level decreased to tolerable Saturday-at-the-lake levels, although it was midweek. He could deal with that. Children should have fun. Supper was going to be interesting. He'd heard little voices downstairs for the last hour.

He smiled to himself when he caught sight of the girls in the kitchen. They were whispering and standing close to Robin. *The only thing cuter than a puppy.*

"Hi there." He stopped at the edge of the dining area.

The girls turned to face him, wide-eyed.

The older one raised her finger to her lips. "Shhh. If you want to help Auntie Robin in the kitchen, you have to use your inside voice."

The younger one smiled like a cherub and clasped her hand over her sister's mouth.

Matt paused and nodded, making an "O" with his lips. "How can I help, Auntie Robin?" he whispered.

Robin smiled and leaned down to eye level with the kids. "Girls, this is Mr. Matt. He's the special guest I told you about who writes important books. He's why you need to be very good while you're here." She glanced up at Matt.

"I like that. Your special guest who writes important books." He smiled.

A slender, attractive woman came into the kitchen from the garage just in time to hear his last words. She slowed her pace and sidled up to the girls, an amused expression on her face. "Hi. I'm Emily, the older sister. Not a fellow author. I only write checks and grocery lists."

He stuck out his hand. "It's nice to meet you, Emily. I'm Matt. Forget what you just heard me say when you walked in."

Emily shook his hand and raised an eyebrow. "And these are my daughters. Bella, she's six years old, and Lilly, five going on fifteen."

Lilly held up her tiny hand with her fingers splayed out.

Matt grinned. "Five. Very good. It's nice to meet you, girls. Your Aunt Robin has been head-over-heels planning for your visit." He glanced at Robin.

She cut her eyes at him and frowned.

Emily chuckled. "She told me about toppling off that stool. Glad she didn't break her neck."

Robin turned around and looked from one to the other. She opened her mouth but nothing came out. Finally, she said, "I've made hot dogs and hamburgers on the grill, and there are several sides. I thought we could serve ourselves from the bar and eat cafeteria style—if that's okay with you?" She directed her question to Matt.

"Sounds great."

"This is wonderful, Robin," Emily said. "Let's use paper plates."

Robin opened the cabinet and retrieved a stack of plates and plastic cups.

Emily seated the girls at the table and starting putting catsup and mustard on their hot dogs. After setting their plates before them, she served herself.

Matt picked up one of the china plates Robin had set out and served himself while Robin looked on. She took the pitcher of lemonade to the table, then fixed herself a burger. He wasn't sure why he felt so pleased, but he enjoyed supper with Robin's family. Emily made conversation with him about the contrasts between California and the South, and asked his opinion on several hot political topics, sanctuary cities and wind farms in particular. She asked perceptive questions about the publishing industry and was a good listener. Although he could guess how she stood on issues, she appeared to be open to hearing his point of view. Robin stayed out of the discussions and focused on the little ones.

"You girls ate all your hot dogs. No coaxing required," Emily said and looked at her sister. "This lemonade is wonderful."

"I made it myself. Fresh-squeezed."

As they finished up, Lilly looked around the table. "Is it time now to make them? Can we make them now?"

"The girls and I are making s'mores for dessert," Robin said. "Who wants one?"

"Count me in. I'll take two." Matt held up two fingers for Lilly.

Emily pushed back from the table.

"Emmy, sit back down. Bella, Lilly, and I want to make dessert. Come on, girls." Robin handed them each a plastic bag containing graham crackers, chocolate bars, and marshmallows, then grabbed the tongs and a plate. Together they went outside to use the hot grill.

Matt and Emily watched them leave. He chuckled and poured himself some more lemonade. Then he poured some into Emily's glass. "They are really cute kids."

"I think so. They like being here. Robin is their favorite person in the world."

"I can see that."

"She has that effect on people."

That was for sure. "She does, doesn't she."

Emily turned to gaze at him but didn't say anything.

"Robin said this is a magical place." Makes more sense every day, he thought.

"Yes." Emily smiled and continued to look at him thoughtfully.

He was glad when the girls burst into the room. Robin followed carrying a plate of gooey cookie sandwiches, which were roundly admired. While they ate them, they chatted.

"I feel like we're on a vacation." Emily glanced at Matt. "I'm glad you didn't mind us coming. I hope we won't disturb you while you work."

"I'm sure I'll manage," he said.

Lilly got up from the table and walked over to Matt's chair. She quietly motioned for him to lean down to her level, then cupped her hand beside her mouth and whispered in his ear "You wanna use my napkin? There's something here." She leaned slightly back and tickled her chin, still looking at him with wide innocent eyes.

His brows went up and he smiled. "Thanks." He took the napkin Lilly offered and firmly wiped his chin, which felt surprisingly sticky.

Emily and Robin seemed to be taking Lilly's kind gesture very seriously, and they might have gotten through it without a chuckle had it not been for Bella. She looked at her mother's face and giggled, and then everyone laughed except for him and Lilly, who remained by his side.

"That was a nice thing to do, Lilly, to offer me your napkin," he said, looking into her eyes. "Thank you and Bella for making s'mores. They're yummy. Thank you, Robin, for supper. Now, if you all will excuse me, I'll retire for the evening. I have some important writing to do."

As soon as he got upstairs, he went into the bathroom and looked at himself in the mirror. Tiny scraps of white paper napkin clung to his chin where bits of melted marshmallows had dripped. He splashed off his beard, then roared with laughter. When he paused to catch his breath, he heard laughter resound from downstairs. He laughed even more then, and it felt absolutely wonderful.

"It feels like a vacation to me too," he said to his reflection in the mirror.

Chapter Twenty-One

The next morning, Robin, Emily, and the girls slathered on sunscreen, donned their swimsuits, and pulled summer shifts over them. The necessary hats and towels and equally important swim toys were stuffed into two tote bags, all in preparation for a day out on the boat with Caleb.

"Who's more excited?" Emily smiled at Robin. "Auntie Robin, or Bella and Lilly?" She sat on the sofa in the studio's den.

"I'm pretty excited. I'll admit it. I haven't seen him in five days." Robin wondered how excited Emily would be if she knew they had talked about getting married.

"Not since the dinner last weekend? You've yet to tell me what Caleb said about the blog. I was trying to wait for you to bring it up."

"Oh, don't give me that. Last night you fell asleep when you were supposed to get back up so we could talk until midnight."

"Yeah, sorry about that. Don't take it personally. Ryan complains about the same thing." She chuckled. "The girls wear me out some days, I'm telling you. Just you wait and see."

"Well, there's no time to talk about it now. Caleb will be here any minute."

"But as soon as we get back …"

The steady hum of a powerboat motor grew louder in the cove.

"He's here. Let's go down to the dock." Robin slipped on her sunglasses and grabbed the tote bags. "Just wait until you see him. He's even more handsome than last summer." The last sentence she tossed over her shoulder to her sister, who held each of the girls by the hand. Callie skipped along as they headed down the hill.

"That's not possible," Emily muttered just loud enough for Robin to hear.

Caleb stood up in the boat and stepped onto the dock. He looked like he could've been posing for the cover of *GQ* magazine. "Hey, hey! Good morning to you, pretty girls!"

"Hi, Caleb," Emily said. "It's nice of you to take us for a boat ride."

"I wouldn't miss it. Good morning, honey." He kissed Robin's cheek, took the bags and set them inside the boat, then helped them aboard.

"Now, girls, we need to put our life jackets on before we get started." Robin handed a vest to Emily. "Who wants to go first?"

Lilly stuck her arms forward, and Robin slipped the straps over her shoulders. Bella did the same for Emily, then Robin and Emily put on vests as well.

They sat on either side of the girls on the back row of the boat. After the initial squeals, they enjoyed a tranquil cruise, and the girls especially liked bouncing along the wakes, going under the bridges, passing other boats, and waving at folks. The wind in their hair made them smile. Before the ride was over, Bella stood on one side of the boat in the circle of her mother's arms, and Lilly stood encircled by Robin's on the other.

After the fun ride, Caleb pulled alongside the dock at the beach. They all got out and set up a place in the sand with their towels. Emily swam and played with the girls in the shallow water. When Robin headed to the water, Caleb grabbed her by the hand and pulled her playfully back to the towels. She fell over him, giggling, and it was all she could do not to wrap her arms around his neck and roll into his arms.

"Swim to me, Lilly," Emily called. "Robin, watch how well she swims!"

Robin made a face at Caleb and whispered, "I have to play with my nieces." Then she called, "Super! You can swim like a fish! I'm proud of you!"

Caleb chimed in with words of praise, moving closer to Robin as she tried to observe the kids. "Let me rub some lotion on you, honey. Your shoulders are already pink."

"Really? I put on sunblock earlier. I don't need any more." She frowned at him.

He reached over and plucked the bottle of suntan lotion off the top of the tote bag. "Yes, you need some of this, sweetheart. You're beginning to turn red." He pulled her closer to him on the towel. His chest was directly behind her and she could feel the tickle of his hairy chest against her back. He slowly rubbed the lotion across the top of her shoulders, and then stroked up and down her back.

Her skin tingled. It was impossible to focus on anything but the sensation of his hands over her body. Breathing became difficult. Then he stopped and rested his hands on her shoulders. Robin turned her head slightly to look at him, and at the same moment, he leaned close and kissed her neck.

"Caleb." His name came out as a shaky breath.

"Emily hasn't given us a thought," he whispered, kissing her neck again. "She's looking out across the lake. You're driving me crazy, honey."

Robin turned around and kissed him full on the lips. As he pulled her closer, an orange flying thing whacked him on the shoulder. "Ouch!" He sat up and Robin scrambled to her feet.

"Uhh ... sorry, man. I didn't mean to do that." A skinny boy of about thirteen grabbed the Frisbee from where it lay on the beach and ran to join another boy along the edge of the woods. They kept moving down the stretch of sand.

Robin giggled. "You know, I think I'll just slip my dress back on to prevent over exposure." Certainly, had they been alone, they could have rolled right into each other's arms. In fact, had it not been for that misguided toy, they might have.

A lopsided smile brightened his face as he rubbed his shoulder. "Where would you like for me to take you on Friday night?"

"I'll be happy to go anywhere you like. Maybe dinner and a movie." She shrugged.

"Dinner and a movie at my place?" He raised his brows up and down.

"You! Let's decide another time. We're totally ignoring my little nieces."

"I'll call tomorrow, then." He stood and brushed himself off. Then he ran down to the water. "Who wants to stand on my shoulders and jump into the water?"

"I do!" Bella shouted.

Lilly watched with rapt attention while Caleb lifted her sister up and planted her tiny feet on his shoulders. He strode out into the water up to his chest and turned back to face the beach. Emily walked out and stood several feet between Caleb and the shore.

"Okay, are you ready? One. Two. Three. Jump!"

Bella squealed and leapt from his shoulders toward her mother.

"You did it," he cried.

"Great job, Bella," Emily said. "You swam so well."

"That was fun! I wanna do it again," she said as she swam back to his outstretched arms.

Robin smiled. He brought so much energy to their play.

He flashed her a broad smile, and she blew him a kiss. After Bella's second turn on his shoulders, he grasped Lilly around her waist and hoisted her up. Although not quite as fearless as her sister, she was willing to try.

"One. Two. Three. Jump!" Reluctant to let go, her leap might have turned into a belly flop, but Caleb caught her. She wasn't hurt, but she'd lost her confidence.

Caleb made a frowny face. "Ahh … that's all right. Why don't you show us how you can swim to your mommy?" He supported her body and she moved her arms and kicked.

"Good job, Lilly!"

Everyone cheered, and Lilly felt the triumph.

When they returned to the dock at the lake house, the girls had had enough of swimming for a while. Bella and Lilly hugged Caleb as they said goodbye.

Robin stayed beside the boat while the others walked up to the studio. Seeing him laughing and playing with the girls touched her heart. That was how he'd play with their kids one day.

He took her hand.

"Thanks for playing with the girls. They loved it."

"They're cute." In the next instance, he pulled her into his arms. "You were the one I really wanted to play with."

She willingly leaned into his kiss, and they clung to each other for one unabashed moment before reluctantly parting.

"I'll call you tomorrow," he said. "I can't wait until the weekend when I get you all to myself."

"Me too." She allowed her eyes to linger on him as he drove away from the dock, then gave herself time to regain her composure. She loved watching him. Smiling, she turned and lifted her face toward the house, surrounded by lush green trees and sweet-smelling flowering vines. Taking in the scene, she admired the beauty of nature all around her, plus the architectural beauty of her home with its tall windows and wide glass doors. The gracious porch and decks all facing the lake brought the living space right outdoors.

"Robin, we're going to the shower," Emily called.

"I'm right behind you."

Life was good. Robin had everything she'd ever need right here.

Giggles as bubbly as baby shampoo led Robin to the outdoor cedar shower. Emily had stripped off the girl's clothes, and they were running in place on tippy toes under the cold spray.

"Make room for mommy! I'm coming in," Emily said before slipping into the shower.

"I'll get some clean towels." Robin went inside the house, stopping in the kitchen to listen for sounds of movement upstairs. Matt would have returned from his run by now. In the suite behind the kitchen, she grabbed a bundle of towels, then she scooted back outside in time to wrap Bella in a large fluffy towel. The others she hung on hooks for Emily and Lilly.

"Now let's go inside and get clothes on," Emily said.

Callie barked an excited welcome.

"Whew! That sure was fun," Robin said.

Emily pulled on a shift and then helped the girls into their little outfits. Robin ran upstairs to change. When she came back down, Lilly was begging to watch a movie. "Mommy, can we watch *Moana*? Auntie Robin, will you watch *Moana* with us?"

"It's their favorite Disney movie of the moment," Emily said. "They insisted I bring it so you could watch it with us."

"Sure. But the DVD player is in the lake house. It was awfully quiet over there just now. Maybe I should ask Matt …"

"Why that look?" Emily directed a curious look at her. "He was totally agreeable last night. In fact, he wasn't at all the stuffy stoic I imagined."

"He's changed." Robin remembered how hard and miserable he seemed when he first arrived.

"I like him. And the girls do too."

Robin was busy taking a yellow plastic tablecloth from a drawer, then she smoothed it into place over the kitchen table. After tearing two large sheets of paper out of a tablet, she set them and the water-colors, brushes, and little jars of water on the table. "Girls, would you paint a picture about what we did this morning?"

The girls ran over, climbed up on the chairs, and immediately picked up brushes. Robin stood with her arms crossed in front of her chest and watched them make their first tentative strokes. She glanced at Emily. "It's washable."

"Nice. When they finish painting, the girls and I will go over, since he makes you nervous, and ask Matt if he wants to watch the movie with us."

"He doesn't make me nervous." Robin plopped down on the sofa next to her sister. "It's just that I've been feeling guilty about my selfish plan to stay here. I more or less lied to him by letting him assume that his friend had arranged it."

"Yes, you did. You need to tell him the truth. But it does look like your being here has had a positive effect on the professor you first described as withdrawn and ornery." Emily smiled smugly and wiggled on the sofa like a mama duck settling in her nest.

Robin squinted her eyes. "My presence has had a positive effect on him?"

"That's what I think."

Robin pursed her lips.

Emily sighed. "Now tell me about Caleb."

"Uhh …" Robin shook her head to clear her thoughts and reminded herself not to let anything slip about the proposal. "Well … I don't know what to do with him. He's so … passionate. His kisses blind me."

Emily sputtered out a laugh. "What man between sixteen and sixty isn't passionate. Caleb is gorgeous, and he knows it. He's used to having that effect on women, I'd say."

"You think?"

"Of course. Don't be naive. Don't *you* think he's used to having his way with women?"

"Well, I hadn't thought about that."

"Ha! Okay. What did he say about the blog and the woman who takes the pictures?"

Robin sighed. "He said he didn't tell me because he didn't want to have to explain. Since he doesn't like the fact that a man is staying here, he thinks it's hypocritical of him to let Kaitlin help him and, on top of that, expect me to be okay with it. She does what she does now of her own initiative." Robin shrugged a shoulder. "I believe him."

"He seems like a good guy. You should trust him if you care about him."

"I do. Trust him. Care for him."

"Do you love him? Do you still think he's the man you want to spend your life with?" Emily's voice had dropped a notch.

Robin hesitated. "Sure. We'd have beautiful children. And you saw how good he is with kids."

"So is Matt, for that matter," Emily stated.

"Matt's irrelevant. Caleb loves the lake. His business is taking off, but he's not going anywhere. We could live right here in my favorite place in the world."

"Mmm." Emily nodded a few times. "Sounds more like you're saying you love this place."

"Well, of course I love this place." Robin stood and walked into the kitchen, where she took two glasses out of the cabinet. "How about a glass of iced tea?"

"Sure. That would be nice."

Robin poured the tea and took Emily a glass. Then she stood beside the table and watched the girls paint. A smile spread across her face, and she motioned to Emily to come have a look.

"Oh my. Your pictures are fascinating, girls," Emily said.

She and Robin looked at each other and smiled while suppressing giggles. The boats dominated the pages, and unidentifiable smiley-faced stick figures stood out amid swirls of blue, red, and green. Bella proudly looked up at her mother and aunt.

Robin's phone pinged. She grabbed it off the counter. "Oh, it's Mom." She nodded to Emmy and smiled. "Hi, Mom."

"Hi, my Little Robin. I heard you have some company."

She walked toward the kitchen. "We're having so much fun. Right now, we're watching the girls paint. You should see them. They're amazing."

"I know y'all are busy and I'm not going to keep you. Just wanted to say I love you. I can't wait to see all my girls. I miss you. Talk to Emily about Christmas. I want everyone to come and stay as long as possible."

"Of course. We have to be together at Christmas. How's Grandmother?"

"Very well. She and Aunt Catherine send their love, and they can't wait to see you."

"Thanks for calling, Mom. I love you too." Robin laid the phone on the counter and looked at her sister. "She's surprised me. I thought she would cling, but she's really given me space."

Emily grinned. "I asked her to do that."

"You *did*?"

"I certainly did. She wanted me to come here your first weekend here, Memorial Day, and I told her no. I asked her to let you make your own way, live your own life. You'd been under her for twenty-six years. It was time."

"Oh, Emmy. Thanks."

"Think nothing of it."

They turned their attention back to the girls.

"Will you put our pictures on the fridge, Auntie Robin?" Bella asked.

"Can I show mine to Mr. Matt?" Lilly added.

"Sure, you can, Lilly. We can show him your drawings and put them on the refrigerator in the house where I'll see them every day."

Lilly dropped the brush she was holding, and Bella added one more dash of color before dropping hers too. "Can we go now?" Lilly asked.

Callie barked in excitement.

Emily looked at Robin with lifted brows. "Why not?" She picked up the artwork by the corners and held it out from her body.

"Sure, but let's walk on our tippy toes and use our quiet voices."

As silly as it seemed to her, Robin felt a burst of anticipation. Secretly, she thought it would be fun if the man upstairs joined them for a movie.

Chapter Twenty-Two

Matt had run and swam and had been writing for a couple of hours when he heard the cheerful party at the boat dock. Those little girls giggled non-stop. He stood and stretched before walking over to look out the window. Having dressed only in boxers after his shower, he carefully pulled back the curtain for a glance. Then he froze. Caleb and Robin stood on the dock locked in a steamy kiss. It hit him like a gut punch.

He turned away, grimacing. Anger fueled by jealousy burned within him, bringing out sweat beads on his brow. The sight of her in another man's arms sickened him.

At that moment, his feelings for her could no longer be denied. He was crazy about her. The truth was, he could hardly keep his eyes off her. She was young and beautiful and full of life and hope. Unlike himself. And she had a right to be.

Matt closed his eyes and took a deep breath. The shock brought a wave of sadness.

But if her relationship with Caleb was that serious, why had Caleb been with Kaitlin? He'd seen the girl get out of his truck and stride over to the beauty shop. Was the man the playboy type like he'd suspected all along? While it hurt him to see Robin with him, the thought of the man hurting Robin was even worse. A powerful urge rose within him. He wanted to go to her, to hold her sweet face in his hands, and look into her clear blue eyes.

Robin, he's not the man for you.

Attempting to relieve his distress, he showered again. He got dressed and plopped into the armchair and stared at the wall, but sounds of little girls approaching disturbed his brooding. Were they coming upstairs?

Sure enough, tiny tap-taps, one right after another, sounded at his door. Callie barked excitedly.

Taking a deep breath, he braced himself before opening the door. Emily stood facing him with her arms draped over her two girls shoulders. Callie darted into the room.

"We wanted to invite you to watch a movie with us downstairs," Emily said. "Not just any movie. Our favorite."

"It's *Moana*!" Lilly threw open her arms and joyfully belted out an enchanting line about the sky and sea calling to her.

He watched transfixed as she sang.

Emily burst out laughing. "I'm sorry. She's so spontaneous. Just like Robin."

Matt was totally charmed. "That was beautiful, Lilly."

"I can sing for you too," Bella said.

"You both want to sing for me? In that case, why don't I come down and watch the movie with you."

"That would be great. Robin is going to make grilled cheese sandwiches and popcorn." Emily backed away, taking the girls with her. "Come down whenever you like. We'll wait for you."

"I will. Just give me a minute." Matt closed the door behind them and put his hands over his face. *Breathe ... Breathe ...*

I want to be strong, Lord. Help me rely on you. And Robin, please protect her heart. I'm thankful just to be near her.

Maybe that's why he was here. To keep her from making a mistake.

Matt went downstairs, determined to be good company. Robin was grilling sandwiches and Emily was putting paper plates on the table where the girls were already seated. "Do you girls like grilled cheese sandwiches?"

"Yes, sir," Bella said. "And peanut butter and jelly too."

"Me too," Lilly added.

Robin brought the food to the table and sat down. "Not exactly part of the heart-healthy, low-carb diet I promised you," she said to him with a little smile.

Freckles had popped out on her nose, and he resisted the urge to stare at them. "Cook whatever you want. I've never eaten better." There was a softness in his voice that he hadn't intended.

The girls, eager to start the movie, wasted no time finishing their sandwiches. They hopped down from the table and ran to the sofa to await the movie.

Emily joined them. "I hope I can remember how to use this thing."

"I can help." Matt got up and crossed the room to the couch. After fiddling with the remote, the movie started. He sat down in a rocker recliner and Callie jumped up in his lap. Robin sat on the end of the sofa.

As the movie got underway, Lilly took it upon herself to rearrange their seating. Robin had to sit in the middle of the sofa so the girls could share her. Matt was relegated to the corner of the sofa beside Lilly, while Emily took the rocker recliner where she curled her legs beneath herself.

Matt glanced at Emily, who had watched the maneuvers curiously. She met his gaze and lifted a brow, then smiled. "You're a good sport."

Matt enjoyed watching the girls during the movie. This was a new experience for him. When had he ever watched an entire animated movie, full of singing and fun? Emily made popcorn and brought it to them in large plastic bowls because Robin wasn't allowed to get up. Lilly and Bella sang, and the women did also, loudly and unrestrained. At that point, had he known the words, he might have sung too. He laughed until his belly hurt. More than once, he and Robin's arms brushed against each other. She didn't seem to notice, but he was keenly aware of every touch.

When the movie ended, Lilly had fallen asleep with her head against Robin's lap. The others stirred and stood slowly. Robin gently gathered Lilly into her arms. The brief enchantment had ended, but the contentment stayed with Matt for a few sweet moments after the girls went back to the studio and he returned to the room upstairs in the quiet, empty house.

Not so long ago, solitude was all he wanted. Now, he realized, life held so much more.

Lilly and Bella played on the lake shore with mock fishing poles while Callie took an impromptu swim. Robin and Emily were putting suitcases in the van when the delivery truck came barreling down the drive.

"I'm not expecting a package." Robin shrugged to Emily, then went to meet the driver.

The driver got out with a large box. "Matthew McLaughlin?"

"Oh, sure. You can put it at the front door and ring the bell. Thank you." She went back to helping Emily pack the vehicle.

Soon the front door opened.

"Good morning," Emily called.

"Good morning," came Matt's response.

Robin turned to look at him. "Good morning. There's a package for you." She pointed to the box.

"That must be the books." He glanced up shyly at Robin. "I ordered some for you."

"You did? That's so sweet." She joined him on the porch. "The box is awfully big."

He studied the package. "I'll be right back." Moments later, he returned with a paring knife. "Let's see what we have here." He opened the box and removed the packing paper, uncovering tight stacks of books. "I asked my publisher to send a *set* of my novels for you. I think he misunderstood and sent enough for a signing."

Robin leaned over the box.

"Let me take a look." Emily joined them.

"Take whatever you like, Robin." Matt stepped aside to pet the wet dog that had joined them, leaving her reading the book covers. The girls came to join Matt petting Callie.

"Ooh, they all look fascinating. Listen to this review, Emmy. 'Hypnotic prose, well-drawn characters … keeps the reader turning pages in breathless expectation.' Breathless expectation. Oh my goodness." She leafed through the thick novel. "They're so well done."

Matt took one of the books and handed it to Emily. "Would you like to have one? There's enough to fuel the house this winter." He gave a wry smile.

"Thank you." She hurried to the van and returned with a pen. "Please sign it for me. It will be even more special."

Bracing the book on the hood of the van, he signed his name. Emily held out her arms to him for a hug, and the girls latched onto him as well.

"My," he said. "You girls are so sweet."

Robin smiled. He'd sure won them over.

He picked up the box and turned to go into the house.

"Matt, we're about to go home," Emily called to him. "We enjoyed spending time with you. Thanks for helping entertain the girls."

"It was nice meeting you, Emily. And Bella and Lilly too."

Robin watched him go inside. Then she caught a glimpse of Emily smiling at her. Having caught her eye, Emily propped her hand on her hip and raised a brow cannily. Robin made a face at her before swooping Lilly up into a hug and carrying her to the van. Bella was already climbing into her seat when Robin caught her for a kiss. Robin waited by the door for her sister to get in.

"Thanks, sis. This was fun." Emily held up the book Matt had signed for her. "*The Stranger Between Us.* Read this one first and we'll talk about it. I'll call you when I get home."

"I love you girls," Robin called through Emmy's open window.

Concern furrowed Emily's forehead. "I don't know whether to envy you or pity you."

"What are you talking about?" Robin asked.

Emily held out her hands, palms up, alternately lifting one and then the other. "Caleb. Matt. Caleb. Matt." She giggled.

"I definitely should stop looking to you for advice." Robin stepped back from the van, shaking her head. "Come here, Callie. Out of the way."

Emily slowed down as she drove away and stuck her head out the van. "I really like your professor," she called.

Though dumbstruck, Robin waved wildly and blew kisses to the girls. As she sighed, Callie's wet coat brushed against her leg. She looked down. "Just look at you. You've gotten all dirty. I think the two of us need a shower." Leaving Callie whining at the door, she went inside to get towels.

The box of books sat beside the foyer table. Robin picked up several volumes and examined the covers. *The Unlikely Lover. Dead Lovers Don't Lie.* Interesting. She took one of each title and went to get the towels.

On her way to the studio, an idea popped into her mind. A book signing. She could ask Matt to sign his books at the festival.

She hurried to gather the things she needed for Callie's bath in the outdoor shower. She could hardly wait to start reading the novels.

"The Stranger Between Us," she said out loud. How intriguing was that.

Chapter Twenty-Three

Robin laid aside the novel, reluctant to put it down. She'd read the first one in two days and was well into a second. Emily hadn't even called to discuss the first one yet. Boy, was she in for a surprise. The characters were so real, Robin found herself reading between the lines, imagining their thoughts and motives. Not only was she intrigued by the engaging plots and characters, but the author intrigued her too. From inside the back cover she learned a surprising piece of personal information: *The author is married to Lauren McLaughlin*.

Funny how she had dismissed the idea of a wife right from the start. Not that he couldn't have been married. He'd make a sweet husband. It was just that he seemed … like a man unto himself. Alone in the world.

Catching herself daydreaming, Robin grabbed her purse and headed out to pick up Jenny for the committee meeting. Today they were planning the festival venues and entertainment. After a couple of brainstorming sessions, she and Jenny had great ideas for the projects they wanted to create and oversee.

Jenny hurried out her front door and down the drive to Robin's car. "I was just about to call you."

"Sorry. I lost track of time."

Jenny slid into the passenger seat. "Working on the illustrations?"

"No. Reading a novel, actually." Robin raised her eye brows. "Written by my tenant." She made her voice sound mysterious.

"Really?" Jenny responded in like manner.

"I'm going to pass them along to you. I can about guarantee your eyes will be glued to the pages."

"That good, huh?"

"I had no idea that someone as mild-mannered and introspective as Matt could write such provocative stories. They're old-fashioned whodunits, but he gets the reader right into the hearts and minds of fascinating characters."

Jenny's expression became serious. "Oh my. Caleb doesn't stand a chance."

Robin's smile vanished. "I'm telling you about the novels, Jenny. Not the man. Good grief."

Jenny chuckled. "I'm teasing. It's just I haven't seen you this excited in a while."

Robin sighed. "I need to get excited about this festival. Miss Margaret said the committee has dwindled. They're counting on us."

Jenny grinned. "Girl, we've got this. We're used to managing rooms full of energetic kids.

"Ringmasters! We accomplish great feats." They both laughed.

Absolutely. They could do this singlehandedly.

Their fresh ideas won out. Besides the usual face painting, they would do caricature drawings and have easels set up for finger painting. Anyone so inclined could help create a colossal mural with paint-filled water guns. Robin and Jenny took on much of the hands-on entertainment and the silent auction, while vendors for handcrafted goods and homemade confections fell under the management of Miss Margaret and the faithful few. Mr. Hal was in charge of the live animal and farm events. Miss Susie, the owner of Sweet Confections, was in charge of food vendors. The live music and fireworks show would be arranged by City Hall.

When Miss Margaret heard about Matt's books, she insisted that Robin do whatever it took to get him to participate. "I'm counting on you to get that lovely man to be a part of our festivities," she'd said. "If it's called for, bake him a cake."

On the drive home, Robin and Jenny planned how to get materials and recruit volunteers. Each had a call list and a timeline of what to do in the next two months leading up to the event. Local merchants and civic-minded citizens would contribute materials, cash, or helping hands. "Caleb's top on my list," Robin said. "What could he contribute to the silent auction?"

"Why not a morning on the lake? He can instruct eager novices on how to catch a largemouth." Jenny giggled. "Don't be surprised if lots of women bid on that."

Robin ignored her, instead picturing him reaching for her hand while standing in his boat. In the next second, she saw his handsome face across the candlelit table at The Tea Olive restaurant. His green eyes softened whenever he drew near for a kiss, and especially that night when he'd said they were perfect for each other. She smiled. "I'm not worried about other women, Jenny. We're perfect for each other."

"Things must be going well." Jenny eyed her thoughtfully. "Y'all make a really great couple. You asked him about Kaitlin and the blog?"

"Of course, and everything's fine. He's as serious about our relationship as I am."

"Wonderful." Jenny grinned. "We'll be sisters-in-law one day."

Robin took a deep breath. She was so tempted to divulge their secret, but she bit her tongue.

"What does Caleb think about your desire to be a writer and illustrator?"

Robin twisted her mouth to the side. "Gosh, he still hasn't seen any of my artwork." She couldn't help frowning. "I don't know how I've let that happen."

"Invite him up to the studio. No reason for him not to come over just because there's a renter in the house. If he's anything like Zach though, he'll have zero real interest in the art. He'll think it's cool and be proud of you, but it's doubtful he'll take it too seriously." Jenny gave Robin a sympathetic look. "Nothing against you. It's just their personality. Zach is a numbers guy, and so is Caleb. If your passion doesn't generate income, it's just a hobby."

"He made his hobby into a career. That's exactly what I hope to do."

"I understand perfectly. And I'm probably talking out of turn again. Caleb might think differently on the subject than Zach." Although she didn't sound like she believed he would.

Robin sighed and turned into the drive at Jenny's house.

"Thanks for picking me up. I have to start supper, but you can come in if you'd like."

"No, I need to get back too. I couldn't do this festival without you, Jen. Thanks."

Jenny got out and stood by the SUV. "It's fun. I'll call you. School starts back next week, you know."

"Ugh. Where has the summer gone?" Robin groaned.

"I know. You're so lucky. You get to focus on your passion and your dreamy man."

On the drive to the lake, Robin thought of all Jenny had said. She was a lucky girl. She spent her days doing exactly what she enjoyed, exactly where she wanted to be. She was engaged, albeit secretly, to the perfect man. Matt was a great tenant who had even become a friend. The summer *had* slipped by too quickly.

Why had Caleb not come to see her work? That question bothered her. Grabbing her phone, she called him. He didn't pick up, so she left a voice message. "Would you like to come to my house for supper? We'll grill steaks on the studio patio? You can finally see my artwork. Call me."

She sighed. Why did relationships have to be so complicated? Jenny brought up practical concerns that hadn't once crossed her mind. Opposites did attract, obviously. She just had to look at Jenny and Zach to see that.

When she came to the road to Caleb's place, she found herself turning down it. He probably wouldn't be there, but she couldn't get him and the things Jenny had said out of her mind. Maybe she would catch him at home and invite him over in person.

A dusty black Mustang sat next to his shiny blue pickup when she pulled into his drive. She'd seen that car at the Fourth of July picnic. Maybe Claire was visiting? She should stop in and ask about Rachel.

Just as she was about to knock, the door opened. Caleb stood there smiling at her. "Hi, honey. I saw you pull in." He leaned down and kissed her cheek.

"Hey, sweetheart. I hope I'm not intruding." She leaned around Caleb as he hugged her, peeking into the den. "Is Claire here?"

"No. Come on in." Taking her hand, he led her to his small office. "Kaitlin and I are working on this blasted website."

Kaitlin?

"I'm the one working." Kaitlin sat at his desk, never taking her eyes away from the computer.

"I got way over my head with some of the new regulations."

"Hi, Robin," she said almost as an afterthought.

"Hi."

Caleb shook his head. "I had other things to do today, but I got sucked into this problem. Lucky for me, Kaitlin dropped what she was doing and came over."

"I've figured it out. I'll be done in a little while." She gave a reassuring nod.

"Well, I don't want to interrupt you." Robin looked up at Caleb.

He took her arm and walked her back into the den, where he kissed her again. "Can you stay?"

"I came by because you were on my mind. I'd called and left a voice message."

"I missed your call. Sorry. You know what? I think I must have left the dang phone in the truck. No telling what other calls I missed." He scowled as he moved toward the door.

"I wanted to ask you over for supper. Steaks on the grill."

"I've got to get that phone, honey. Walk out with me." He held the door for her to pass through ahead of him. "We've got a time crunch. Kaitlin has a hair appointment at six. I need her to get the website fixed before she leaves."

"I hope she does." Robin stopped by his truck. "Can you come?"

"No, honey. Not tonight. This website situation hijacked my day."

"I might be jealous of all the time Kaitlin spends with you." She dropped her eyes and pursed her lips, having needed to acknowledge that.

He reached for her and pulled her into his arms. "How are your web design skills, honey?" he asked in a husky voice.

"I don't even do Facebook, Caleb."

He covered her mouth with his. "Well ... you just stick to doing what you do best. Looking beautiful and kissing me like that."

His phone rang from inside the truck. He snatched open the door, grabbed it, and looked at the screen. "Who is this calling me? Oh, I recognize the number. I have to take this." He glanced at her and answered. "Harold!" They launched into a lively exchange about taking Harold out fishing. After a few moments, Caleb glanced up, nodded at her, and continued the loud conversation.

She eased over to her car. No way was she going to hang around and watch Caleb look over Kaitlin's shoulder.

He asked Harold to hold on a second, then turned to her and mouthed, "I'll call you."

She smiled to hide her disappointment.

One thing was apparent. Caleb and Kaitlin were comfortable with each other. Kaitlin's hair was pulled back in a ponytail, and she wore cut off terry-cloth sweatpants and a T-shirt, for Pete's sake. He relied on her for her expertise on web design, just like he'd said. She filled a particular need, and he might even take her help for granted.

But what about her? What had he told her to do? Stick to looking beautiful and kissing him? What kind of thing was that to say? She chewed on her bottom lip. She didn't know whether to be insulted or flattered.

As she pulled onto the road, she saw him take the phone away from his ear and tuck it into his pocket. He swung around to look after her and waved. She smiled and waved back, then pressed the accelerator.

Remembering Jenny's words, she decided to be neither insulted nor flattered. *Nothing against me personally. It's just how he is. Just a regular, gorgeous, outdoorsy kind of guy.*

"Rats," she grumbled. "I forgot to ask him about donating to the silent auction."

She'd do better when she got home. At supper, she'd ask Matt about signing his books.

Chapter Twenty-Four

Matt pressed the heel of his hand to his forehead as he searched for the right word. Any word. Nothing came to him. In fact, nothing had come to him all morning. Writing was at a standstill. For days, he'd struggled to get into the flow. In spite of the fact that ideas virtually flew onto the page all summer, now he grappled with every word. Unable to focus, he found himself alternating between anger and frustration.

That kiss is problematic.

He walked over and stared out the window with his hands clenched at his sides. Nothing came to him but the memory of Robin kissing Caleb. This was a waste of time.

He should go down to Charlie's. He hadn't seen him in more than a week.

Even though it was the hottest part of the day, Matt headed out. Sweat ran down his back as he walked down the dusty dirt road. Not a breath of air stirred to cool his brow. The heat weighed on his shoulders like a fifty-pound sack of field corn.

He shook his head at the memory. He had loaded those sacks into pickup trucks when he worked at the feed and seed store. He was barely thirteen years old, and he wanted that summer job. Boy, he had sweated.

Typically, Charlie sat on the porch. But not today. The weather must have kept him indoors.

Matt knocked and soon heard Sammy waiting on the other side. It took Charlie a long time to answer the door. When he opened it, there wasn't much of a smile on his face.

"Charlie, are you all right?" His old friend didn't look like himself.

"Come on in, Matt. I'm glad to see you, boy."

Matt stepped inside, which put him right in the middle of the dining room and den. He watched Charlie hobble to the recliner. He seemed so much older than usual today. "You look like you don't feel well, Charlie."

"It's my tooth. It hurts like the dickens." He pressed his hand to his jaw on the left and raised his shoulder to meet it. "I've been in this chair for two days trying to get over it."

"Two days?"

"It's hurt me for three. I don't appreciate my tooth letting me down. I ain't had any problems with them in all my seventy-nine years."

"That's amazingly good teeth, Charlie, but you need to go have that one looked at."

"I've a good mind to pull it myself," he grumbled.

"Oh no. That's not a good idea at all." Matt frowned as he watched Charlie stroke Sammy's head. "Let's go into town and visit the dentist."

Charlie grumbled again, and Matt waited.

"You'll ride along with me?"

"Sure, I will. Why don't we go now?"

"Dang it. I reckon I got to." Charlie got up and started walking to the back of the house. "Give me a minute to wash up."

Matt stood in the center of the den and let his eyes wander over the pictures on the wall. A thin brass frame held an Olan Mills portrait of a youthful Charlie and a dark-haired wife posed with a handsome young boy. A large faded picture of an angel shepherding two children across a bridge above turbulent water hung next to it. Matt was inspecting the scene when Charlie came back into the room.

"That's my family." He pointed to the portrait, then to the picture beside it. "And the guardian angel … it's a nice reminder that we're being looked after."

"It is." Matt walked outside with Charlie and headed for the truck. He went to the passenger side and got in.

Charlie stopped beside the driver's-side door. "I don't much feel like driving, son. You think you could drive us?"

Matt's jaw clinched. For a long moment, he sat dead still remembering the last time he had driven. He'd crashed the car into a tree and his wife died. He breathed a ragged breath. "I can." But could he?

He got out and went around to help Charlie, whose strength seemed to have waned. He held the old man's elbow and walked with him to the passenger side, then went back around and got behind the wheel. Time passed. In his mind's eye, he saw the snow drifts and the coyote that sprang into the road. He stomped on the break, slamming his foot hard again the floor.

Charlie was staring at him now. "It's an automatic, son. Don't you know how to drive?"

Matt exhaled the breath he'd been holding, cleared his throat, and lifted his foot. "It's been a long time. I'd feel better if you put on your seat belt." And then he started the truck.

When they pulled into the parking space on Main Street, his hands ached from gripping the wheel. "We made it." *Thank God.*

Charlie nodded. "I had no doubt we would."

Matt hadn't been so sure. "Wait there while I come around and help you."

On the drive back to the cabin, Charlie slept. The molar was abscessed. The dentist sent him home with antibiotics and orders to return at eight o'clock the next morning to have it extracted. "He'll need someone to drive him home after the procedure," the dentist advised.

Matt decided to spend the night at Charlie's and go with him. After getting Charlie settled, Matt went into the kitchen to find something to make for supper. "Charlie, you need to eat something. How about a piece of toast? You've got a loaf of white bread and a lot of canned soup. I'll heat up this chicken noodle."

"That'll be fine. Thank you."

As soon as he'd eaten the toast and a little soup, Charlie went to bed. He was still feeling poorly.

Matt walked out onto the porch with the intention of sitting in a rocker, but the heat was suffocating. He stripped off his shirt and hung it on the arm of the chair. Moments later, he went back inside, picked up Charlie's old black Bible, and began to read where it fell open.

The earth is the LORD's, and the fulness thereof; the world, and they that dwell therein.

Oblivious to the world outside, he read until a persistent bumping demanded attention. He opened the front door to a blast of hot air. The wind had picked up, twisting the tops of the tall pines. Dark clouds were rolling in. The boat knocked into the dock as the water lapped the shore. It needed to be hauled out of the water, covered, and tied before the storm hit. He ran to the water and waded in.

His muscles strained against the weight of the boat multiplied by the force of the wind. He pulled with all his strength. After he secured the boat, the rain started falling. Huge drops pummeled his bare skin. He ran back onto the porch and took a seat in a rocker to watch the storm.

A refreshing breeze blew in as he took his wet shoes and socks off. Rain and wind blew through the thick trees surrounding him. He marveled at how he'd wrangled the boat out of the water. He certainly couldn't have done that a few months ago.

Disrupting his pensive state of mind, a red SUV with its headlights glaring drove up to the cabin in the downpour. Immediately after it jerked to a stop, the driver jumped out, dashed around the vehicle, and up the porch steps. Robin stood there staring wide-eyed at him.

Stunned, Matt said the first thing that popped into his head. "What are you doing here?"

"I came to find you," she said, shivering. Her gaze shifted from his bare chest to his feet.

Adding to the absurdity of the moment, he looked her over from head to toe. Her hair hung in long burgundy ropes, strands plastered to her cheeks and neck, and her legs were splattered with mud. He chuckled nervously.

"What's so funny? I was worried about you. You never came down for supper, and I went looking for you."

Matt couldn't take his eyes off hers. Her sweetness was irresistible. "I'm fine," he said gently. "I came to see Charlie. He's not doing well. I need to take him to get a tooth pulled in the morning."

Robin hugged herself, shivering hard, and Matt couldn't tell if she was cold or if she might cry. But whatever her state of mind, he didn't know how he'd get through the next minute. Her wet clothes clung to her every curve, revealing more to the naked eye than any man had a right to see. With her standing there, water streaming down her body, his natural urge was to wrap his arms around her.

Abruptly, he grabbed his shirt from the arm of the chair and stood. "I don't know if this will help or not." In one fluid motion, he slipped the shirt over her head and shoulders, encircling her with his arms. She tipped her face up to look into his, her trembling body pressed against his warm chest, and she melted against him. For a moment, he forgot how to breathe. Then he closed his eyes and let her go.

When he dropped into the chair, he was shaking. "Sit down, will you. Please sit down." He flung his arm out toward the other rocker.

Robin practically lunged toward the rocker, grabbing its arm for support before plopping into it. They watched the rain without talking for a long time, and rocked while lightning flashed over the lake and the sky rumbled. Eventually the downpour slowed to a gentle shower, and his heart rate returned to normal. The scent of pine filled the air as a misty evening settled in.

"Do you want me to bring you some dry clothes or something to eat from the house?" she asked.

Matt studied her face. She still hadn't smiled at him, but her big eyes were sincere as they searched his. Finally, he said, "I'll be all right until tomorrow."

"All right, then." She stood up, slipped off the shirt and held it out to him.

Without taking his eyes away from hers, he took the shirt. She turned to go. "Robin?"

She turned back, a strange look in her eyes.

"Thanks for coming out to search for me."

She looked away. "You're welcome. I'll see you tomorrow."

Five minutes later, she was gone, like she had never been there. But she left a lonely place in his heart.

Chapter Twenty-Five

Robin made phone calls all morning, and all the while Miss Margaret grew in statute in her mind. How had that lady done all this for fifty years? She'd never realized how many hours went into pulling off a large community event.

But Robin had more than risen to the challenge. She had used all her God-given talents and Southern social graces to get everything she needed. Local businesses and multiple organizations contributed, and volunteers agreed to put in the necessary efforts to set up tents and exhibits, cook the food and sell it, load the hay wagons and haul the kids, and dozens of other essential tasks.

Caleb contributed a day of fishing for the silent auction, as Jenny predicted, and Matt agreed to sign his books. Eventually she'd had the opportunity to talk to him about it. He'd stayed at Charlie's for several days helping him recover from the dental surgery. His attentiveness to their elderly neighbor was endearing. She would've liked to have helped out as

255

well, but Matt turned down her offers for assistance. And she hadn't seen much of him over the last few weeks. Just when she thought she had gotten to know him …

The man had the ability to befuddle her.

As she knew she should, Robin focused on Caleb and the festival. She intended to make sure the festival was a success. Her illustrations had moved to the bottom of her priority list since she started work on the community project. She itched to pick up her pencils again.

For the first time that day, she'd sat down at the drafting table. Within seconds, her phone rang. She reached for it with a sigh. Jenny. "Hey."

"Hi. How's it going?"

"Fine. I marked off the last item on the call list."

"My goodness, girl, you're good. I wish you were on my team here at school."

"That's right, you're at school. Where are your students?"

"I'm on break. It's my miniscule planning period. I just wanted to put a bug in your ear."

"Hah. Go right ahead."

"I overheard Zach and Caleb talking about the festival." Jenny chuckled. "They're concerned we've bitten off more than we can chew. Thus, their gallant promises to spend that entire day with us."

"Are you kidding? They don't think we can manage without them?" Robin clicked her tongue.

"I reckon that's it. I think it's funny. They couldn't do what we do every day with these children."

Robin grinned. "Well, bless their hearts."

"And hunky ones at that." Jenny giggled. "I gotta go."

"Bye." Robin was amused, but not as much as Jenny was. Every little thing about Zach delighted his wife.

Huh. That must be love.

On the day of the festival, Caleb tapped on Robin's door at four a.m., a magical hour when the night chorus blanketed the earth as thick as the misty fog.

"You're sweet to get up so early for me," she said when she opened the door.

"You're totally worth it." He leaned down and lightly touched his lips to hers. "Are you ready to go?"

"Sure am." She smiled and handed him a tall to-go cup of coffee. Listening to the early morning news on the radio, they talked very little on the way to town. Jenny had already texted that she and Zach were on the way.

Caleb parked the truck in the church lot, one of the designated parking areas. They'd already hauled over stacks of folding chairs and a dozen long tables from the Rotary Club for the street café. A section of Main Street had been blocked off, and the owner of the hardware store and his team of volunteers were putting up tables and setting the poles for the tents to cover them all.

Miss Susie had opened her bakery for those setting up. She and four other ladies, all with nets over their fluffy white hair, bustled in and out of the kitchen filling the glass display cases with cookies, cupcakes, and pies. The aroma of hot coffee and fresh baked goods filled the air.

"Hot donuts await," Zach said as he and Caleb headed straight for the counter.

"Would you like some coffee, boys?" Miss Susie asked.

"Yes, ma'am." Caleb took the cup she'd just poured. "Thank you."

Minutes later, the four of them sat outside at a small square table drinking coffee and eating warm pastries.

The October day dawned with baby blue skies and a crispness in the air. The sounds and smells and budding excitement lifted Robin's spirits. All the frustrations and endless details she'd managed over the last several weeks were forgotten. By the time nine o'clock rolled around, the streets had filled with people.

"I'm going to help Mr. Hal with the petting zoo. Some of the animals aren't cooperating. An ornery goat in particular." Caleb leaned down to give Robin a quick kiss on her cheek.

"Ooh, we can't have that. Thanks for being here."

A couple called to Zach to come lend a hand carrying boxes of crafts. Jenny's eyes followed him as he turned to go.

"We've got y'all all set up, babe," Zach said. "I'll be there in a little while."

Jenny smiled. "See you later."

Charlie and Matt were in front of The Bookworm, where Matt was setting up a card table and talking with Miss Elizabeth, the bookstore owner. She'd made a glossy banner introducing the visiting author.

"Hey." Robin waved. "Good morning, Mr. Charlie. Matt. Miss Elizabeth."

"Hi there," Miss Elizabeth said.

Matt smiled.

"Miss Susie has coffee and donuts if you'd like some, Matt." Robin stood with her hand resting on the stack of *Dead Lovers Don't Lie.* Noticing the title, she pulled her hand away quickly and made a silly face.

Matt rolled his eyes. "No, thanks. Charlie, you'd enjoy the company of all those ladies. Go down there and take a seat in the café." The festival atmosphere might have been fostering a happy-go-lucky spirit in Robin, but it didn't seem to be working for him.

"I hope you're going to enjoy your day too," Robin said.

Matt mumbled something as he stacked books on the table. Then he glanced up good-humoredly. "What you wanna bet all these books are sitting here at noon?"

"After I've spread the word? Not a chance. It's more likely you'll be mobbed by women readers and have to take special orders." Looking handsome and sophisticated in his black polo and jeans, he'd certainly attract attention.

Matt wobbled his head. "Right."

"Oh, ye of little faith." She smiled and waved as she joined Jenny.

The two headed to their art stations in the open block usually reserved for the farmer's market. Rows of tents decorated with high-flying balloons, bales of hay, and pumpkins covered the space. She caught a glimpse of Caleb's sister Mary Beth and her kids across the way and raised a hand in greeting.

She was ready for the fun to begin in their creative, free-flowing day.

"Where did all these kids come from?" Caleb asked. "Did you have them bussed in?"

"I know. It's crazy." Robin put the last face-paint touches on a seven-year-old's black kitty nose. A little crowd had gathered in front of one of the tents where they had their supplies.

"Looks like the entire student body of the elementary school turned out," Jenny said.

Robin giggled. "Just think. We've probably inspired some young artists today."

"My dreams tonight will be inspired by tiny super heroes. I'll be painting Spider-Man in my dreams."

"Normally your dreams are all about your Super Man." Zach chuckled. The man laughed at all his own jokes.

"For me, butterflies," Robin said. "And cat whiskers."

"I'm going to find us something for lunch," Zach said. "When are y'all going to take a break?"

"The face-painting supplies are about to run out," Jenny said. "As soon as they do, we're going to walk down to the café. In the meantime, could you get me a corn dog and some fries."

"Sure. How about you, Robin?"

She looked at Caleb. "What are you going to have?"

"They're grilling some mean burgers right next to the hot dogs," Caleb said. "I think I'll have one of those. Can I order one for you, honey? I know how you like 'em."

"Sounds good. I'll meet you at the picnic area."

Ten minutes later, Robin exhausted all the face paint while drawing the last of the butterflies and flowers. Jenny hung a cardboard clock on the tent indicating their return in thirty minutes, and after checking on the volunteers for the other art venues, they hurried to meet the guys.

Miss Margaret waved to them from across the street, where she was displaying handmade quilts. Robin went over to speak to her.

"Oh sugar, isn't this just wonderful? What a turn-out!"

Robin glanced around. "I know. And it looks like everything is running smoothly."

"It is. Thanks to you and Jenny and all the hard-working volunteers."

Robin beamed. The festival had turned out so much better than she imagined it. "See you later. I'll be back down here when the bands start."

A teenaged girl with her head held high posed while Robin drew her profile. She sketched the portrait with quick skillful strokes in five minutes flat, delighting the crowd that had formed around them. When she tore off the sheet of paper and handed it to the girl, her boyfriend handed over ten dollars for the two of them and took his place on the stool.

Robin picked up her charcoal, taking a moment to study her subject.

Jenny sidled up to her. "How many does that make?"

"Too many to count." Robin didn't take her eyes away from her work. "Isn't this fun?"

"Just wait until you see how the mural shaped up. Zach even left his mark."

Robin chuckled and continued sketching the young man.

"You're good," Caleb said from over her other shoulder. "Can I have a turn?"

"Of course. It's on the house if I get to keep the sketch." She smiled up at him. They chatted as she finished the portrait of the boy, and she tore off the sheet and handed it to him.

Caleb walked around and sat down on the stool.

"Mr. Jackson, you *sure* are handsome," Robin drawled.

Caleb gave her a wink.

"Has anyone ever told you to look like Captain America?"

The girls in the group giggled. Some nodded in agreement.

"Captain America?" Caleb laughed.

"I'm going to take my time with this one, folks," Robin said.

About that time, lively instrumental sounds came from the direction of the courthouse, where a stage had been erected for the announcements and live performances. Back-to-back musical groups were scheduled to perform from four to eight.

"Wow. Listen to them," Jenny said. "It's the blue grass band." Someone was fast picking on a banjo, accompanied by acoustic guitars, fiddles, a harmonica, and drums. "They're kicking off the live entertainment."

"I never doubted you girls," Zach said. "But ... will there be groups that don't sound like Earl Scruggs?"

Jenny nudged him with her elbow. "Hush! What's wrong with Earl Scruggs? We had to start with blue grass."

"Yeah. They're good," Robin added. "We worked hard getting this line up."

"Nothing wrong with that kind of music. I'd hoped for a chance to dance with my baby, that's all." Zach shimmied his hips. "And blue grass is a tad too lively, don't you think?"

Jenny shook her head. "See what I deal with every day, Robin. This man!" She giggled before throwing her arms around him.

"I see."

Caleb shook his head. "Y'all are crazy."

"We have country music bands, plus an old-time gospel group, an Elvis impersonator, and the high school chorus." Jenny gave Zach a high five, and they all roared with laughter.

Caleb's portrait complete, he looked it over for a long moment. "Honey, I had no idea you could draw like this. You're really talented."

"You need to go see her work in the studio," Jenny said.

Robin closed the sketch pad and put the easel toward the back of the booth. "Let me finish up here and we'll go listen to the band."

Caleb set the stool alongside it.

"Yeah, I want to get down there by the time the boot-scooting music starts," Zach said.

All four of them packed up the remaining art supplies in a couple of large plastic trunks and closed the booths. The feel-good music beckoned them to the big block party forming on the town square.

As Caleb held her in his arms, dancing around the square, Robin called to Miss Margaret from over her shoulder. "Next year's will be even better! Just you wait and see. I have new ideas."

"That's just what I hoped you'd say, sugar." Miss Margaret smiled brightly.

Fireworks heralded the grand finale. And, as folks have always said in the South, a good time was had by all.

Chapter Twenty-Six

Talk about stupid. Matt had made a fool of himself, and on top of that, he'd come as close as he ever had to picking a senseless fight. If the truth be known, he was still unsettled. Shoving his hands into his jeans pockets, he stood at his bedroom window gazing at the lake and the sky as he thought about the day.

Robin's festival had been a success. Hundreds of people turned out. Children ruled the place. Every copy of his book sold, and the bookstore owner took orders for more. He'd spent the morning immersed in the sounds of gaiety and laughter, and in spite of the magic it worked on his state of mind, his run-in with Caleb wiped that all out. He played it over in his mind.

At lunchtime, Robin came to the bookstore. Smudges of paint on her face only enhanced the glow in her pretty eyes. "Hi, Matt. How's it going? I haven't forgotten I got you into this."

"Well, see for yourself. There're only two copies left." He waved his hand over the table and smiled at her delight.

"My goodness, that's wonderful."

"Yeah, I should hire you as my publicist." He laughed.

"I definitely gave you good reviews." She glanced at the picnic area on the square. "I'm meeting Caleb for lunch. Would you like to join us?"

He jerked up his chin in acknowledgement. "No, but it smells good, whatever they're cooking."

"Bands are going to be starting up soon. You might like that." She smiled. "I'll see you later."

Robin and Jenny joined Caleb and Zach under the tents. Matt's position in front of the bookstore allowed him a clear view of everyone coming and going in the picnic area. He tried to look anywhere besides at Robin and Caleb chatting away. When Caleb started dabbing Robin's face with his napkin apparently to wipe away paint smudges, Matt got a sinking feeling. He breathed a sigh of relief when they got up and walked down the street.

Not long after lunch, Caleb was again over by the picnic tables, this time talking to the girl with pink streaks in her hair. She kept shaking her head and it looked like the two might be arguing. Caleb took her upper arm and they walked away, disappearing from view.

Fifteen minutes later, Caleb sauntered past the bookstore alone.

"Excuse me. It's Caleb, isn't it?" Matt said.

He stopped and turned to Matt.

"I don't usually stick my nose in other people's business ... but I just noticed you with that girl."

Caleb frowned. "Yeah?"

"You and Robin are dating, but I've seen you with the blond girl a couple of times."

"Is *that* right?" His voice sounded strained.

"I wouldn't want Robin to get hurt ... but I suppose she knows about the other woman."

Caleb took a step forward and leaned down slowly, placing the palms of his hands on the table in front of Matt. As they faced off in a stare, heat rose to Matt's face.

Caleb's eyes flashed. "You're messing with the wrong person," he said in a hard, low voice. "It's none of your business *who* I talk to. I'm here today to support Robin—"

"How about that. So am I."

"Hah." Caleb looked skyward a minute, appearing to gather his restraint. "Like I said, I'm here for Robin, or else I'd probably have to get physical—if you know what I mean. Instead, I'll ease your mind. Robin and I plan to get married. I asked her. She said yes." He paused. "You and Kaitlin are the first to know since you both seem to have a problem with that."

Matt swallowed the lump in his throat. "I see."

"And don't think I don't see. You might not like it, but she's going to be my wife."

Matt's head snapped back as the news slammed him.

Caleb laughed derisively. "Stay out of my business," he said before walking off. "Next time I won't be polite."

Matt clenched his teeth and squared his jaw. He hadn't expected that. The anger, yes. The message, no. He had misjudged the situation.

A few minutes after that, the last of his books sold. After a quick farewell to the bookstore owner, he searched for Charlie. He couldn't get away from there fast enough.

And now he stood in his room at the lake house, wondering at the absurd turn of events. Five months ago, nothing mattered. He'd felt dead inside. For all intents and purposes, his career and personal life were shot. The tragedies of his life drove him here. But by some miracle, he'd begun to live again. He looked forward to getting up each day. How had such a transformation taken place? Was it this place? The atmosphere? His writing again? None of that mattered. He'd reconnected to himself ... and God ... and people. The people he'd come to know ... and care about ... and love. Those were the things that mattered.

He shook his head, stripped off his jeans and shirt, and put on his running clothes. He'd go in search of that eagle he sometimes saw and think of his grandpa and pray. Definitely pray. Maybe that would ease his mind and help him come to terms with Robin's plans.

Following the festival, Robin experienced a burst of exuberance and well-being. In all of her twenty-six years, she'd never worked on a project that impact-ed the lives of an entire community. A big moneymaker, the festival had been good for the town, and especially for the individuals who showcased their wares. Miss Margaret had set her heart on bringing Pine Haven together in a big way, and Robin played a role in making that happen.

There had been only one disappointment for her—Matt wasn't there to join in the party on the square. She'd looked for him, but he'd already put away the book-signing table. Mr. Charlie was nowhere to be found either, and Miss Susie informed her he'd left with Matt. She hadn't seen hide nor hair of him since.

As she prepared supper a few days later, Robin determined that she'd eat with Matt and engage him in conversation. What did he think of the festival, and how had his day gone? She'd been painting like a master for two days. The days were cool and clear with sunny afternoons. Life was good.

As soon as Matt's door upstairs opened, Callie ran to meet him and pranced along beside him as he walked into the kitchen. Wearing jeans and a pale blue polo shirt, he looked handsome and fit. How had she ever thought of him as middle-aged?

He turned a lingering gaze on Robin before proceeding over to the sofa. As soon as he sat, Callie rolled over at his feet for her tummy rub.

A surge of satisfaction rose in Robin's chest. "Hi!" Enjoying watching the camaraderie between man and animal, she resisted the urge to chat and put the last touches on the salad she'd been making. The scent of fresh bread wafted from the oven when she opened it. She let it rest a minute while she ladled stew into the tureen and then carried it to the table.

"What would you like to drink? I have a nice rosé chilled and a red wine, if you'd like some." She paused beside the table.

"No, thanks," he said. "Iced tea will be fine."

"Have we made a Southerner out of you, Professor McLaughlin?" Robin propped her hand at her waist and tilted her head to the side.

Matt swiped his hand across his chin and chuckled a little.

"When you first arrived, you drank only water and wine with dinner."

"I hadn't noticed."

"Supper is ready if you'd like to come to the table." Robin returned to the kitchen to fix the glasses of tea.

When she sat down, Matt was ladling steaming stew into his bowl. "My mouth is already watering. I don't know the last time I had beef stew."

"When I have the urge to make recipes like this, autumn leaves are falling." She filled her bowl. "I love this time of year. It's like … pumpkin pie spice is in the air." She glanced up at him. "On Saturday, you left early. I was sorry you missed the music and dancing."

"All the books sold and Charlie needed to get home. He gets tired easily since the incident with his tooth." He didn't make eye contact as he spoke.

"Well … what did you think of the festival?"

"It reminded me of those I used to go to as a kid." He nodded. "You owned it, Robin."

"You really think so? I had so much fun. Did you enjoy talking to people about your books?"

He shrugged. "Sure. At least you didn't have to burn them in the fireplace."

"They're wonderful. I've read them all except *Dead Lovers Don't Lie*. I saved it for last since I have a feeling it's going to be creepy. And I don't sleep well with the lights on." She pursed her lips.

"It's suspenseful." After a few moments, he looked up at her. "How are your illustrations coming?"

"Funny you should ask. Amazingly this week. They're reflecting exactly what I want them to show."

"That's good. You should keep it up. Enjoy your gift. I have an idea about something that might help."

"Oh yeah? Please. Share." She eagerly awaited what he'd say.

"I think you should stop cooking dinner for me."

That wasn't at all what she'd expected him to say. He must have seen the surprise on her face, because he paused, but only for a second.

"Continue making breakfast, but make dinner ... a couple times a week. I can manage fine on my own." A defensive tone had crept into his voice although she hadn't spoken. "How hard is it to make a sandwich? Besides, I won't be here forever. You're spoiling me."

"But ... I'd hardly be earning my keep."

"Don't be silly. You'll have more time for your art and your personal life." A crease formed between his brows, and he turned away to look down at Callie.

Now was the time to tell him the truth, but she was speechless. A lump formed in her throat.

Matt helped himself to a second serving of stew, but she still couldn't make herself open up. How exactly should she say it? She wanted to be near Caleb, so she let him believe a lie? Since that *was* the truth, it was her only option. "There's something I've been meaning to talk to you—"

"You know, Robin, I really need to get back to my writing."

He *interrupted* her. Her jaw dropped slightly before she could think. He'd never done anything like that before. In the next second, he dropped his napkin on his bowl, pushed back from the table, and stood. "If you'll please excuse me." He smiled a quick joyless smile. "Dinner was excellent. I'll get back to my work now."

She stared after him, more than a little confused. And aggravated. She felt like calling his name. He'd cut her off on purpose and behaved much like he'd acted at the beginning of the summer. She would've told him the truth then.

After that evening, she didn't see much of him, and when she did, he acted almost shy. She wanted to ask him what had happened to cause the rift between them, but that didn't make sense. What did she even mean by *between* them? She felt guiltier than ever about being an interloper, less like she had a right to be there.

She went about her days as usual, but like a bruised little toe that kept getting bumped, guilt taunted her.

Chapter Twenty-Seven

Thanksgiving had always been special at Robin's house. Besides the family, there'd be friends from her mom or dad's work and social circle and sometimes she or Emmy would have friends over. Besides the turkey and ham, synonymous with the annual celebration were side dishes such as corn bread dressing, corn soufflé, macaroni and cheese, collard greens with ham hock, pecan pie, and pound cake. Her fingers itched to prepare the meal.

Yet Matt didn't want her cooking for him. Apparently, she wouldn't be making anything for the Jacksons either. At least she'd be helping in the church's soup kitchen after Thanksgiving.

Caleb said she wasn't to bring anything to Thanksgiving dinner at his house. Didn't he know that she couldn't go empty-handed? She called Jenny for her suggestions. "Hi, Jenny," Robin said. "How are you?"

"I have the entire week off. So, I'm great."

"That's nice. I know you're enjoying it. I'll be seeing you on Thursday at Mr. and Mrs. Jacksons'."

"Ah...the family Thanksgiving."

"What dish will you be making to take?"

"What am I *making*? Absolutely nothing. Nada. Zilch."

"I was taught you don't go to a dinner without some little something to contribute to the meal and a gift for the hostess," she explained, "but Caleb said not to bring anything. I don't think I can *not* bring something."

Jenny laughed. "In this case, Robin, take some tea towels and a jar of jelly for Mrs. Jackson. *Don't* make a side. There'll be so much food they won't have a place to set it down."

"But everybody has too much food at Thanksgiving."

"Trust me on this. At the Jacksons', it's over the top. It's like they think it's going to be their last supper." She giggled again as she relayed the information about her in-laws. "They'll eat all their favorites made in overabundance by their mother, sisters, and aunts. Nobody will touch yours, but Mrs. Jackson might take a small portion to be polite. You'll end up having to carry it back home. Who needs a nine-by-eleven dish of sweet potato soufflé after Thanksgiving?"

"Oh, good grief. Okay. If you're sure."

"You'll thank me for this. Really." By her tone, Jenny couldn't have been surer of herself.

"I'll see you Thursday, Jen."

"I'm glad you'll be there. Hugs," Jenny said, and they ended the call.

And since Jenny was already married to a Jackson man, Robin decided to take her advice.

When Robin and Caleb drove up to the Jackson's home on Thanksgiving, lots of folks were raking the front yard of the old four-square mansion. The crowd included Jenny and Zach, Mary Beth's husband, and some others Robin didn't know. Three little kids chased each other around. The weather was perfect for playing in the fall leaves, and the scene brought a smile to her face.

Caleb slid out of the driver's seat and came around to help her down from the truck. She grabbed the gift for Caleb's mother.

"Let's go meet all the family." He gave her hand a squeeze and waved to the relatives outside. "Hey, y'all."

"There's another rake or two if either of you want to join us." Zach stopped and pointed to some garden tools leaning against the trunk of a big oak tree.

"We're going in first. I need to introduce Robin to a few folks."

When Jenny waved, Robin held up the brown paper gift bag holding a bouquet of fresh cut flowers tucked in a Mason jar along with some cute little jars of her homemade apple and pumpkin butter. She wanted to show Jenny she hadn't in a moment of weakness made a casserole.

Jenny gave her a thumbs-up.

As the door opened, warmth and good cheer greeted them. A crowd of mostly men had gathered in the spacious den in front of a wide-screen TV to watch the pregame show. Women young and old filled the kitchen, sitting around the kitchen table, standing at the sink and stove. The French doors leading to the back porch were open, and kids were climbing on a giant jungle gym in the backyard.

Robin smiled at Caleb. "I didn't know your family was this big."

"And it gets bigger every year." He winked at her. "Hi, everyone."

All the women looked when Caleb spoke, their faces immediately wreathed in smiles. Several of them jumped up with happy squeals and rushed to him. He managed to hug them all. Obviously he was a favorite, or they hadn't seen him since *last* Thanksgiving.

"I have someone I want y'all to meet." He reached an arm behind Robin's back and pulled her to his side. Smiling, he introduced her to the roomful of ladies. "Some of you know her already. Some of you don't know she's my sweetheart."

Robin laughed. "Hey, Mrs. Jackson, Mary Beth, Claire, Rachel. Thanks for having me."

"It's about time he brought you back over," Mrs. Jackson scolded, drying her hands on her apron. "It's so nice to see you." She stepped over to Robin and gave her a hug.

"This is for you." Robin handed her the gift bag.

"Thank you, sweetie. How thoughtful of you." She lifted out the jar of daisy mums and held it out for everyone to see. "Oh, how pretty! I'll put some water in the jar and set them right over here." She filled the jar at the sink and put them on the middle of the kitchen table in front of Rachel. "And what is this?" She lifted out the jar tied with an orange gingham ribbon.

"Homemade apple and pumpkin butter. I made it myself."

Mrs. Jackson clicked her tongue and looked at Caleb knowingly. "Really? You made it. That's wonderful. Thank you." She beamed. "She made it, everybody. Didn't I tell you she was talented?"

The other ladies fussed over Robin and her gifts, as well as introduced themselves and explained the family connections. Caleb pointed in the direction of the den and slipped out the room to join the men, leaving her to get to know the women on her own. Unable to extricate herself, that's where she stayed until all two dozen of them, young and old, gathered around the table for the holiday feast.

Jenny was right. On two counts. There was enough food for a church homecoming, and Caleb's family liked the two of them being together. Everyone was enjoying the meal when his mother came right out and said, "So happy our Caleb has found the right girl."

Caleb's granny patted Robin's hand, and he smiled a proud satisfied look. If she hadn't known better, Robin would have thought that somehow everyone had figured out their secret.

Robin laid down her pencil, flexed her fingers, raised her arms over her head, and stretched. For several precious hours, she'd ignored her body's need for fresh air, exercise, and food. She'd been in the zone where originality flowed freely. The illustration before her perfectly reflected the mood and subject. The hues, tints, and light and heavy strokes all combined to beautifully render the scene she visualized in her mind.

Reluctantly, she decided to take a quick walk, shower, and get right back to her drawing. "It's a wonderful day!" she announced to Callie. "Let's go for a walk."

After brushing her hair and pulling it into a ponytail, she changed into walking clothes. Callie barked and planted herself at the top of the stairs.

A firm knock sounded on the door. Robin skipped down the stairs and opened it. Then her cheery mood ended. "Kaitlin. Hi."

Kaitlin pulled her hand away from her chest and let it fall to her side. She looked away like she would have preferred not to look at Robin at all, but only for a moment. "Hi. Can I come in?"

Robin hesitated unintentionally, and then gave a tight-lipped smile. "Of course. Come in. I was just about to take a walk."

Kaitlin stepped inside and turned to her. They looked at each other for an awkward moment. "This won't take long."

"No, no, it's all right. Have a seat. Would you like some tea or water? I can make coffee. I have decaf."

Kaitlin shook her head. "I don't need anything. Except … to talk to you. I've been debating for days about whether or not to come."

"The family missed you at Thanksgiving. Everyone wondered why you weren't there."

"Hmph. They should have asked Caleb. He knew." She kneaded her hands.

Robin shifted her weight from one foot to the other while Callie brushed up against her legs. There was something foreboding in Kaitlin's manner. "Would you like to sit down? Let's sit at the table." Feeling nervous all of a sudden, she pulled out a chair, but no one sat.

"Caleb told me he's serious about you … that y'all plan to get married."

"Oh. Yes. I'm surprised he mentioned it."

"Just let me say what I need to say." The color in Kaitlin's cheeks was rapidly changing to that of the streaks in her hair. "Caleb doesn't know what he wants as far as a marriage. He's too caught up with his business. You're not the right person for him."

Robin felt the sting but didn't want to show it. "That's very presumptuous of you, Kaitlin. Especially since you don't even know me." If looks could kill, Kaitlin would have drawn her last breath.

"But I *do* know Caleb," she said, not taking her eyes away from Robin's. "I've known him all my life."

"If this is what you came to say, you shouldn't have come." Robin started toward the door. "I hate to be rude, but—"

"He's too concerned about his brand. His grandiose plans for his business. He thinks he might eventually be televised. Did you know that? And you make him look good. Better than he already does."

"Oh, Kaitlin." Robin slowly shook her head. "That's just mean. To Caleb and me."

"Look at you!" Kaitlin held out both her arms. "Look at this place. You fit his image of himself. He's hot for you, but you and I both know, that's meaningless. You won't make him happy."

Robin's gasped and her mouth fell open as her stomach tanked. For a second, she couldn't speak. Then, in the most condescending voice she could muster, she delivered a barb. "Oh, so now, among your many skills, you've added fortune telling. You might want to hang a flashy sign at the beauty shop." She glared at the woman in front of her.

"I knew you wouldn't understand. But I'm right about this." Kaitlin's face had turned red, and tears pooled in her eyes. "And if he decides to give up on this venture—because Caleb will only accept the best from himself, will you follow him wherever he has to go to find a job as an engineer?"

"Yes!" Robin said sharply.

"You would not! But I would. Because I love him. I love him so much." Kaitlin gasped, and tears spilled down her cheeks. "You don't. He's just part of your fantasy world." She sounded devastated, but that only angered Robin more.

She stormed over to the door and opened it. "You need to leave. I can't believe you're saying these things to me."

Kaitlin moved to the door, but paused in front of Robin. "I'm going," she said, straightening her shoulders. "But I'm warning you. If you break his heart, I'll pull every single hair out of your hoity-toity head with my own two hands."

A strangled noise in her throat was the only sound that Robin made. If she'd had the wherewithal, she might have slammed the door behind Kaitlin with all the hellacious fury she felt. Instead, she just stood there, shaking from head to toe like an electric charge surged through her. Never in her life had anyone talked to her like that.

Kaitlin had gotten in her car and driven away before Robin could turn loose the door. When she did, she walked over to the table, sat down, and tried to think. Her thoughts were spinning. For a long time, she sat, staring at nothing, searching for calm.

Callie's imploring eyes begged her to get with the plan. Finally, they took a walk as she'd promised. Robin hoped it might pull her out of the confusion Kaitlin dumped on her, but try as she might, she couldn't forget the things Kaitlin had said—or her tearful profession of love for Caleb.

Suddenly, a disconcerting flash of intuition came to her. No amount of her soul searching revealed that kind of passion for the man she intended to marry—the kind that could bring forth such heartfelt tears for the love of him. The thought left her apprehensive and embarrassed, but she didn't know what if anything she could do about it. In the meantime, she wouldn't say anything about the encounter to Caleb. It was her problem, after all.

When she got back to the studio, she brewed herself a cup of green tea and carried it onto the patio, where she sat watching the clouds. There was no need to waste her time going up to the studio. No way was she getting back into the amazing flow she'd been in before today's seriously unpleasant episode.

Chapter Twenty-Eight

In the morning, the sky was dusty gray. Robin didn't mind the much cooler temperature, snuggled in bed in her soft flannel pajamas. She was tempted to roll over, close her eyes, and pretend she didn't have a care in the world—that her mother would make breakfast and together they'd sit in front of a fire sipping hot coffee.

Maybe she was missing her mother for the first time in a long time. She needed a little reassurance. Kaitlin's visit had thrown her out of kilter. Still, she couldn't let it spoil another day. Mustering her resolve, she rose, reminding herself how much she enjoyed making breakfast and having the morning cup of joe that awaited her in the kitchen.

Robin expected to be busy all afternoon at church, and she and Caleb were taking in a late movie. It was the fourth Saturday of the month, and like every fourth Saturday, Robin would be preparing and serving food at the monthly soup kitchen. These meals usually consisted of homemade soups, salads, breads, and desserts, but today's menu would include traditional Thanksgiving favorites. She looked forward to helping and especially since she hadn't had a chance yet to make any holiday dishes.

When she arrived just after noon, the hall already perked like a smooth-running cafeteria. Turkeys and pies were in the ovens. Bundling her hair into a large clip, she set to work making several pans of macaroni and cheese. Green beans and collard greens simmered on the stove. Ladies were making pear salad, broccoli salad, cranberry relish, and ambrosia.

The hours passed quickly until serving started at four. She was dishing up the guests' food choices behind the hot serving line when Mr. Charlie came into the hall. He was a soup kitchen regular. Matt followed him through the door, and Robin couldn't help the swell of happiness in her chest when she saw him. Mr. Charlie would miss him when the sabbatical ended.

Robin continued to serve guests with hardly a pause, pleased to see familiar faces, many of whom she only saw at these meals.

"Hey, Birdie," Mr. Charlie said. "It's nice to see you here today."

"You too, Mr. Charlie. I'm glad you came. What can I get for you?"

"Give me a little of everything and gravy on the cornbread dressing. I sure didn't want to miss this. Matt kindly got me here."

"That was good of him." She glanced up to see Matt thoughtfully observing her. She smiled, feeling a flush in her cheeks.

"I hope you're going to sit down and enjoy a plate yourself, little lady," Mr. Charlie said. "Thank you for doing all this." He walked away to one of the round white tables.

"You know it's my pleasure," she said, pointedly glancing at Matt. "I like to cook for people."

Matt nodded, then looked away, and followed Mr. Charlie across the room.

As much as she enjoyed serving the guests, Robin was glad when the line closed at six thirty. Her back and feet ached like she'd run a half marathon. She plopped into a chair in the kitchen, taking a break before she started washing the dishes. Some of the volunteers were having their dinner and chatting with the guests who lingered in the social hall.

"Coming through," Matt said as he walked into the kitchen carrying a large stainless-steel pan. "Where do you want me to set this?"

"Oh." Robin hurried to clear a spot on the counter by the sink. "Put it here if you don't mind. After I dish out what's left, I'll slide it into the sink."

"Well, there's not much left. Everything was delicious." He stood beside her while she dished the food into an aluminum-foil pan and covered it with a paper lid. When she started to lift the large pan into the sink, he did it for her and watched while she washed it. "I have a couple more to bring." He turned and went back out, returning with another. "You have to wash all these pots and pans?" His eyes scanned the counter.

"I volunteered." She smiled, lifting her eyebrows. "Didn't seem like a big deal in June when I signed up."

"I can help. At least until Charlie is ready to leave. I'll be right back." Matt returned with the last pan. After gathering dirty pots and spoons, he set them on the counter beside the sink.

"The dishwashers are already full. I have to wash the big stuff."

She washed and rinsed, and Matt dried. When she walked away to bring other items to the sink, Matt slid over and took her place washing. They'd worked through that rotation a couple of times when Mr. Charlie peeked his head in the kitchen.

"Hey there, Matt. What you think about us going on home?"

"I'll be right out, Charlie." Matt dried his hands on a dishtowel.

Robin nodded at him with a smile. "You go ahead. Thanks for helping. And take one of the pans of leftovers for Mr. Charlie."

Matt returned the smile. "You're a special person, you know that?"

"Well, gee. Thank you." She looked at him thoughtfully.

"I'm glad I brought Charlie," he said before walking out of the kitchen.

Not long after he went out, the other volunteers came in. "Robin, what are you doing in here?" one asked. "You should have eaten supper with us." The kitchen supervisor pulled on rubber gloves and came to her side. "Move over, sugar. Let someone else have a turn."

Robin chuckled, happy enough to relinquish her station. It was time to go home and get ready for her date with Caleb.

Since Caleb and Robin were both Marvel Comic fans who looked forward to each new release, they'd been looking forward to the latest film. As soon as it was released, Caleb purchased tickets for the late movie.

Robin had just enough time to shower and change before he knocked on her door. Dressed in slim jeans with lace-up suede boots and a navy sweater with green and pink stripes, she opened the door.

"All ready to go? You look good, honey."

"Thanks, Caleb." She placed her hands on his cheeks, and they stared into each other's eyes and kissed. She liked his kisses, but it seemed he couldn't get enough of hers. "Hey," she murmured, easing back. "We're gonna be late."

"Okay. Let's go, but sit close to me in the truck."

Robin laughed. "Will do."

As they walked out the door, Caleb let his eyes trail down her body. "I like those jeans."

After the two-hour adrenalin rush from the movie, they walked out hand in hand into the cold night air. He draped his arm across her shoulders as they chatted about their favorite scenes and compared characters and films.

"Let's go to my place," Caleb said when they reached his truck. "I'll build a fire."

"That sounds nice, but I'm so tired." She yawned. "And we have church tomorrow."

"I'll rub your footsies," he teased.

"Ahhh … they're aching too. You're sweet. But I need to get home."

He sighed. "I'll be glad when that tenant of yours in gone. I can take you home and we can cozy up like normal couples."

"He leaves the first week in January. It won't be long."

"I can't wait." He opened the door for her and then closed it behind her.

She waited until he got in to say more. "He was at the soup kitchen today."

Caleb abruptly turned to her. "Why would he be at the soup kitchen? I wouldn't think he'd be down on his luck."

Robin sighed feeling sleepier by the minute. "You know the meals are a service to our community. They're for anybody who'd like to come, not just for those down on their luck. Actually, he brought Mr. Charlie. They've become close friends."

"Is that right."

Silence settled around them. As they left the parking lot, Robin snuggled against him in the dimly lit truck, listening to the soft rock playing on the radio.

"I googled him."

She glanced at Caleb, unsure of what he had said, and observed his face in the glow of the dash lights. "Huh?"

"I googled your tenant."

This time she understood and sat up straighter. "Why? I thought you'd gotten over your mistrust of him."

"How can I forget a man who's staying in your house? Don't you want to know what I found out?"

"No, I don't think I do. He's a private person. I think he'd consider our snooping into his background terribly intrusive."

"Come on. You're kidding me. You're protecting his feelings about something he won't even know about?"

"I guess I am."

"Well, he's rather generic after all. He's a professor."

"Of course he is." Robin's back stiffened and she shifted toward the passenger-side door. "Are you really so mistrusting?" She pursed her lips and looked out the window.

"Apparently, those novels of his do well. The last one was a *New York Times* bestseller. Interested now, would-be author?"

Robin didn't respond. Her chest tightened. She found Caleb's stubborn disregard of her feelings distasteful. And that last remark sounded like he was mocking her. She didn't like his angry tone.

"Oh, come on." He reached for her. "Stop pouting."

She couldn't hide her annoyance. "I'm not pouting. I told you his novels were good. He signed copies of them at the festival, remember?"

"His wife was killed four years ago in a car accident. *He* was the one driving."

Robin gasped as her hand flew to her face. She squeezed her eyes shut and her head dropped forward. "His wife was killed. How awful. How truly awful." She shook her head as grief closed in on her.

Caleb hushed immediately. After a miserable silence, he patted her arm and rubbed it gently. "I'm sorry, Robin. Really, I am," he said in a quiet, repentant voice. "I'm so dense sometimes. Please forgive me. I won't bring up anything about it again."

Robin forced herself to lift her head and look at him. "You felt badly about the boating accident. Can you imagine how Matt must feel? His wife *died*." Tears pooled in her eyes and spilled down her cheeks.

He grimaced. "Oh, honey. I am sorry."

Just the same, she couldn't help herself. She wasn't being reasonable and her feelings now were tangled up with her own loss, but still. What did reason have to do with it anyway? What Matt must have suffered saddened her. He'd more than likely come here to heal. And the fact that Caleb acted so glib about the whole thing was terribly hurtful. The urge to protect Matt rose within her.

"I'm sorry, honey," Caleb murmured. "I shouldn't have blurted it out like that."

Robin swiped her fingertips across her cheeks and eyes. She shook her head to discourage the apologies. She didn't want to talk.

"Look, I know this is about more than the tenant. I'm sorry you lost your dad. I don't know if I've ever said that. But I mean it, sincerely. I'm not sure why I came across with so little sympathy for the man's loss. I guess I'm intimidated by his being there close to you every day."

Robin looked into his eyes. "Thank you for saying that about Dad. I know you mean it. But ... I'm shocked by what you just told me. You don't know him like I do. How Matt's wife died must have crushed him. Apparently he's here attempting to get over his loss."

"So it's Matt, huh? You've become close friends too?"

Robin searched his dark green eyes. It hurt to see his disapproval and lack of empathy. "Don't you dare be mean to me. It's bad enough you drop this horrible news on me. And Kaitlin came to me yesterday to tell me how shallow I am, how wrong we are for each other."

"She did *what*?" Caleb twisted to look straight at her.

"Please, look at the road." Immediately she regretted snapping at Caleb, her misguided reflex in response to her own personal pain. "I'm sorry I mentioned it. I didn't intend to bother you with it. But ..." Robin sniffled. "She said some insulting things about the two of us."

Caleb stiffened. "Robin. What did she say to you?"

"Uh ..." Robin couldn't think with both of them so upset. "It was nothing. You'll have to ask her."

"You can bet I will!" Robin had never seen him so furious, and never had his anger been pointed at her. "I'll tell you what I said to *her.* I told her to stop coming on to me."

Robin stared at him. "Oh. I'm sorry that was necessary. But I trust you, Caleb." She moaned. "I shouldn't have mentioned it. Now we're both upset."

Neither said much on the way back to her house. Caleb turned down the drive, and as soon as the truck came to a stop in the driveway, he pulled her to him and held her without saying anything.

She could feel tension in his arms and chest. She didn't pull away, and eventually she relaxed a bit in his arms, but little comfort came. She wasn't thinking of him. She was thinking about Matt.

His lips brushed hers softly, and she kissed him back, but she didn't press closer. Caleb leaned in to give her another kiss and met with the same apathy. He frowned. "I'll call you tomorrow. We'll make plans for the week."

Robin nodded. She leaned in and kissed him quickly before rummaging through her purse for her keys.

He reached for his door handle.

"No. Don't get out," she said. "I'll walk myself to the door."

Caleb hesitated. "Robin," he implored, and then he sounded frustrated. "Okay, if that's how you feel."

"We'll talk soon." She attempted to smile, but couldn't. Before she was inside, he sped out of the driveway, leaving a cloud of dust and rocks in his wake.

She stood in the darkened foyer with her back pressed against the door and her chest heaved as she fought to push down a torrent of emotions. She struggled to breathe. All the while, Matt filled her heart and mind. The poor sweet man. All this time grieving for his wife. He had come here to be alone. She realized that even more clearly now. And to this day she hadn't had the nerve to tell him the truth about how she had deceived him. She'd thought only of herself, only about what she wanted. His intentions never crossed her mind.

She dropped her face into her hands and wept.

Chapter Twenty-Nine

Having given up on writing early in the evening, Matt had finally fallen asleep only to be awaked by something. Obscure sounds had come to him through the veil of sleep. Then he heard Callie bark and recognized her lively steps in the foyer. Robin had come home. He listened but heard no sounds from her. Callie whined. Then gasping sounds followed making his chest tightened.

He sat up, threw back the sheets, and swung his legs off the mattress. He hurried downstairs to find Robin leaning against the door, shaking, with her face in her hands.

"Robin," he whispered. "What's wrong?"

She looked up. "I'm … so … sorry," she said through her tears. "I'm sorry your wife died."

Her words jolted him. He grasped her shoulders to steady the both of them. "Robin, it's okay. Don't cry. Look at me."

She lifted her eyes to his. "You came here to grieve for your wife," she whimpered, her face collapsing again.

"I came here to decide whether to live or die. I hated myself for living when she had died."

"Oh, Matt." She sniffed. "I'm sorry."

He raised his hand to her cheek and gently stroked her hair away from her face. "It's all right. I'm better now." His throat tightened as tears pooled in her eyes. "Please stop crying, Robin. You're killing me," he whispered, his face close to hers.

She sucked in a shaky breath. "But I lied to you. I wanted to be near Caleb. I let you think it had all been arranged for me to stay here. That wasn't true. I shouldn't have stayed at all."

"I've known for some time that you duped me, Birdie. Good thing you did. I needed someone to throw me a line. You were the only one who could." His voice was low and gentle.

"Oh, Matt." He felt her breath on his lips. "Can you forgive ..."

It was impossible to say who moved first. He leaned closer and she rose up and slid her arms around his neck and his lips touched hers. Not letting him move away, she pressed her lips to his with urgency. Before he could think, his arms slipped around her slender body and they clung to one another. Soft, eager kisses became longer, deeper as his desire met hers. Lost in passion, she trembled in his arms.

Callie barked and skittled at their feet.

With a tender cry, she touched his cheek, curling her fingertips into his beard. They searched each other's eyes. "I've messed things up so badly," she said, closing her eyes tightly. Then she pulled away from him and hurried through the kitchen.

"Robin, wait," he called. "Don't go."

But she had gone. Leaving him trembling from a flood of emotions both pure and passionate coursing through his veins. He could feel his heart breaking. With an anguished sound, he clenched his jaw and sank down onto the bottom stair, burying his face in his hands.

Robin tossed in bed and fussed with the blankets for what seemed like hours before sleep came. Morning found her more exhausted than she'd been the night before. She struggled to sit up. The memory of Matt's arms around her warmed her. The memory of his kisses made her tremble, wanting to relive every detail. But the realization of the mess she'd caused stabbed her conscience.

How had she been so selfish and shallow? She should have told Matt the truth from the start. And she had ignored all the signs that something was happening between them. All the stolen glances, the tender moments. The way she looked for him to come into a room. The way he made her heart quicken whenever she saw him. Her sins bore down on her like a stone.

"I have to fix this," she muttered.

Lord, forgive me. I failed. I lied to Matt, and, in a way, I lied to myself and Caleb as well. Now this is all my fault.

She jumped when her cell phone rang, but ignored it anyway, reluctant to turn her attention anywhere but to her mistakes. She would take steps to sort through this confusion. She would talk to Matt. She had no idea what she would say, but she'd have the humility to ask the Lord to direct her steps.

And she would talk to Caleb. She hadn't been fair to him either. Her plan had worked. She'd gotten exactly what she'd wanted. Caleb wanted to marry her. And now she realized her feelings for him had changed. She shouldn't have lashed out at him. She'd overreacted. She was the one who'd been awful. And to top it off, she dumped the can of worms about Kaitlin onto him, making matters worse.

In spite of a headache and fatigue, she dressed and headed over to the kitchen to make breakfast. She put the breakfast quiche she'd made earlier in the week into the oven and took special care even when making the coffee. When it was ready, she sat at the table and sipped her coffee, hoping Matt would come down. But now that the weather was cooler, she didn't walk so early and he left later in the morning for his run.

When the timer sounded and he still hadn't come downstairs, she decided to take her walk.

The air was brisk and fresh, giving her a bit of a boost. Georgia's fall chill meant perfect temperatures for hiking, watching football games, making hearty soups, and snuggling by a fire. She enjoyed the seasons, and she was glad Matt could experience fall after the long, hot summer.

The words he had spoken last night were unforgettable. He'd come to the lake house to decide whether to live or die. How sad he must have been when he first arrived. She'd seen pain in his eyes. Had she truly rescued him from despondency? If she'd been honest from the start, maybe she wouldn't have stayed at the lake. Maybe she would have realized months ago that a relationship with Caleb was just an immature fantasy she'd clung to. But she had stayed, and Matt said that had been a good thing.

Could she really blame herself for going for Caleb? He fit her ideal of the perfect mate. He was living his dream, something she aspired to do. She admired him for that. He was devoted to his large family, exactly what she wanted one day. And the physical attraction between them was palpable. They were so perfect for one another, except in one crucial detail. He wasn't that one person in the world she couldn't live without. He wasn't her heart's desire. Last night, when Matt held her in his arms, she understood the meaning of heart's desire.

She race-walked back to the house, hoping to find Matt still eating breakfast. The empty coffee pot indicated he'd already been down and headed out. She would lie down until he returned from his run.

She went back to the studio, sat down on the side of the bed, and petted Callie. Then she noticed the forgotten cell phone. Picking it up, she remembered the early morning call.

Emily had left a voice message. "Robin, Mom called. She's fine, but Grandmother has had a stroke. Mom needs us to come. Can you get to the airport in two hours? If so, you might be able to take the same flight with us. Oh, I hope you get this message soon. Call me. Love you, sis."

Noting the present time and the time of the call, she groaned, chastising herself for not answering it. The return call to Emily went directly to voicemail. They'd probably be going through security.

So sorry Emmy for missing your call, she texted. *Driving to Virginia with Callie. I'll see you tonight. Will call en route with ETA.*

She stared at the phone, giving her brain a chance to focus, knowing her mom would be stressed to no end. *Lord, please by your grace restore Grandmother's health and give her and Mom a little more time together. Pour your love on all those taking care of her.*

Robin hurried to the house for her suitcases. She packed what she needed from there, then went back to the studio to gather the rest of her things. Matt hadn't returned. There was no way of knowing how long she'd be in Virginia, but under the best of circumstances, it being the first week in December, she'd be there all month.

After gathering her toiletry items, Robin put away all of her art supplies. Matt hadn't returned. Chances were, he wouldn't be back for at least an hour. Maybe … she could wait.

She was packing the car when her mother called.

"Robin, dear. Emily said you'll be driving up."

"Yes, Mom." She closed the tailgate door with one hand while holding the phone in the other.

"Snow is expected. The roads might be bad. Please be careful."

"I will. I'll be on the interstate most of the drive. How's Grandmother?"

"She's sleeping. The doctor said it's precautionary that she's in intensive care. They have an excellent neurology center here." Mom sounded tired. "It's too early to know how she's doing. If she gets worse …" Her voice broke.

"We're praying, Mom."

"I know. Be careful."

"I'm leaving in ten minutes."

"I'll feel better with you here. You stayed with me when Daddy was sick. You gave up so much for me. Have I told you how much I appreciate what you did?"

"Of course. Don't think about that now. Go to the chapel in the hospital. I know they have one."

"I love you, Robin. See you tonight."

"I love you too." She needed to get to her as soon as she could.

Back inside she scribbled a note.

Dear Matt, I need to drive to Virginia for a family emergency. My grandmother is in the hospital. I don't know when I'll be back. Probably not until the end of the month. I'll be in touch. I'm taking Callie with me. Robin

She closed her eyes and pressed between her eyebrows, then put the note on the refrigerator above the picture Lilly had painted. As she hurried to the car, she wanted nothing so much as she wanted to go search for Matt, beg his forgiveness for lying to him, and ask what those kisses meant.

That conversation would have to wait. She had to get on the road.

By the time Robin arrived in Richmond, it was dark and she could barely keep her eyes open. Exhaustion on top of more exhaustion from navigating black ice and snow flurries weighed on her. Callie needed to be dropped off at her grandmother's house before she went to the medical center downtown.

Driving down the tree-lined streets decorated with evergreen wreaths and twinkly lights, she smiled for the first time all day. Her grandmother's stately brick colonial housed a wealth of warm memories. How she'd loved visiting at Christmas and especially for summer holidays. Growing up, she explored in the huge backyard, running free, safely surrounded by the lime-washed brick fence that encircled the property. She'd sat straddle-legged on branches of the huge cedar trees, flying away to worlds unknown while her parents and Aunt Catherine and Grandmother sat on the veranda whiling away the time. Emmy usually lost herself in some quiet corner with one of the books on her required reading list. And there was always a little spaniel to play with.

Emily opened the door for her and gathered her into a hug. "I'm so glad you're here. I was beginning to worry about you."

"Where are the girls?" She looked around her sister but didn't hear them anywhere.

"Aunt Catherine has them snuggled in bed. She's reading *The House at Pooh Corner* to them."

Robin chuckled. "She loves that book. How many times did she read it to us?"

"At least a dozen. Aunt Catherine came home from the hospital when we did. Mom wanted to stay so she'd be there when Grandmother woke up."

"Bless her heart." Robin rubbed her eyes.

"Come on into the kitchen and sit down. You look pale." Emily laid her hand on her shoulder. "Are you all right?"

"Just tired." She gave her sister a little smile. "Soup kitchen was yesterday. How's Grandmother?"

"She's stable. Hopefully you can rest tonight too. There's homemade vegetable soup. Would you like some? How about a cup of coffee?"

"Sure." Robin went over to the stove and lifted the lid. "Smells good."

Emily ladled soup into a bowl. "The doctor said all of her vital signs are good, and she's sleeping. There's no brain tumor or signs of anything other than a mild stroke. When it happened, she and Mom were sitting in the den talking."

"Poor Mom. She would've been terrified."

Emily brought a coffee to the table and sat down across from her. "Grandmother's speech became slurred. Mom said she looked horribly confused, and then she couldn't speak at all."

"Oh my. That would have been frightening. How's Aunt Catherine?"

"She's fine. She was very attentive to what the doctors had to say. That allayed many of her fears. Mom wasn't listening well. She kept fussing over Grandmother."

"I can imagine." Robin finished the soup, then took a few sips of the coffee. "Watch Callie while I'm gone, please. I'm going to go ahead to the hospital."

"Sure, go on." Emily chatted all the while as Robin got ready to leave. "If I don't see you later tonight, I'll see you in the morning."

Robin put on her coat and they said goodbye. As soon as she got out of the driveway, the phone rang. Caleb's name appeared. She closed her eyes and drew a deep breath. "Hi," she answered sweetly on a sigh.

"Hi, honey. I want to come over and pick you up. We need to talk. I've been thinking about you all day."

"Me too. But I can't. I'm in Virginia."

"Virginia?"

"I just got here. I drove all day. Grandmother had a stroke. She's in intensive care."

"Oh no. Will she be all right?"

"It's too early to know. I didn't have time to call you after I got the news. I was planning to call you tonight."

"I understand." He paused. "Robin, about last night. I'm sorry I upset you. Apparently Kaitlin had upset you already. I've talked to her, and she won't be interfering in our business again."

"I suppose she did what she thought she had to do." Robin's stomach fluttered.

"No, she stuck her nose into our business and said things she had no right to say. Forget it ever happened."

"But, Caleb … maybe some of what she said was worth thinking about." She let the words settle. "Are our feelings for one another deep enough?"

"*Deep enough*? You *have* let her get to you!" He'd raised his voice. "Forget it. Of course they're deep enough. I want to marry you."

"That's what I wanted too, but now … I'm wondering if we want to be together for the wrong reasons."

"Wrong reasons? What *wrong reasons*? You aren't making any sense. Either you love me or you don't."

The words hovered out there. Neither of them spoke. Robin held her breath.

"Well? Do you love me?"

"That's just it … I love you, but I don't know if I love you enough?" A wave of nausea washed over her.

"You don't know if you love me enough?" Hurt and confusion sounded in his voice.

"Do you love me?" she asked weakly.

"Of course I love you. I'm with you, aren't I?"

"But you've never said it, and—"

"I'd like to wring that girl's neck," Caleb snapped, recouping some of his forcefulness. "Everything was fine before she stuck her nose in, and that man in your house hasn't helped either."

"Oh, Caleb. I don't want us to argue. Please. I'm sorry. Let's just take this time while I'm up here to think about our relationship and decide where we need to go with it."

"This is incredible. I can't believe I'm hearing this from you. I don't know what to think."

"Caleb …" Robin regretted starting this painful conversation. "I'm on my way to the hospital."

"Argh. Go on then, and be careful. Call me please, as soon as you can talk."

"I will. I'm sorry. Really sorry. Bad timing for this conversation."

"Robin, I love you. Call me."

"I will," she said, her voice as weak as water.

She couldn't believe she'd said those things to him. Sadness filled her heart. She'd dreamed of the babies they'd have together. What if she lost him now only to realize later that they should be together? But what else could she do? She couldn't lie about her mixed-up feelings. Not anymore.

Not to herself. Not to Caleb. Even when the truth hurt.

Chapter Thirty

Matt slowed to a jog, then stopped with his hands on his hips. In spite of the long run, his mood was no better than when he started out. The memory of Robin kissing him filled his thoughts. She *had* kissed him. A kiss like no other.

He'd tried to change the status quo when he learned she was engaged. Seeing less of her hadn't changed his feelings. But after last night, he was sure she had feelings for him too. She'd responded with such sweet passion. Was she in love with him? Well, he wasn't going to ignore that elephant in the room. He'd give voice to his feelings for her.

He walked inside and glanced toward the kitchen. Without hesitation, he continued out the back door and over to the studio. All was silent. He pressed the doorbell, then rapped on the door. He knocked again. Why wasn't Callie barking and scampering near the door?

Sighing loudly, he turned his face to the sky. Then he walked down to the dock and looked out at the lake. She must be walking and he'd missed her. He resolved to talk to her as soon as she got back.

He returned to the house and went upstairs to shower.

Matt spent the entire morning writing, more productive than he had been in weeks. He kept an ear tuned to the sound of Robin's footsteps, or her voice calling to Callie, or the dog's bark, but he never heard them. After having a sandwich, he lingered in the den, built a fire, and sat enjoying its warmth and thought of her. If she felt for him a fraction of what he felt for her, he'd be a fool not to try to make her his.

Still, she didn't come in. A sinking feeling came over him. He stood and walked slowly to the kitchen and through the back hallway to the garage. He swore when all he saw was an empty place where her car should have been. She must have been gone all day, must have left when he was out for his run.

He returned to the sofa to sit by the fire and watched the flames flicker until they burned low. Why had she left? Because she wasn't earning her keep or some such nonsense? Because she'd *messed things up*?

He feared the truth was apt to be she needed to put distance between them since she was engaged to another man.

After a brutal night, Matt staggered down to the kitchen for coffee, hoping Robin would be there, knowing that she wouldn't be. He stepped on a piece of paper.

Dear Matt …

Gone to Virginia. Be *in touch*.

He swore under his breath. It was going to be a long month.

Something about the smell of the hospital took Robin back to the time her dad was dying. The sober looks on the faces in the silent corridors, the swoosh of the elevator up to the intensive care unit. It might have been yesterday. She needed to find Mom, knowing she too would be experiencing her own déjà vu.

In a small windowless room, her mother sat staring at her hands in her lap. An older man and someone who might have been his daughter sat on a couch, dozing on each other's shoulders.

Mom stood up, stretching out her arms. "I'm glad you're here. You look tired, dear." She wrapped her arms around Robin, and they stood there for a long moment.

"How are you? You look tired too." They sat down, thighs touching, holding hands.

She gave Robin a wan smile. "I'm fine. I was waiting for you. The doctor came by already. He said to come back in the morning. If she does well during the night, she might be in a regular room."

"That's encouraging."

Mom nodded. "Let's go home."

Robin stepped back and looked into her eyes. "It's good to see you, Mom."

She smiled more genuinely. "I've missed you, sweetheart."

Robin carried boxes filled with all kinds of garlands, wreaths, and ornaments down from the attic. She and Emily were decorating for Christmas before Emily and the girls flew back to Georgia. "Put these in the living room." Robin handed her the cardboard box. "We'll set up the new pre-lit spruce there."

Emily made a face. "I don't see the need for four or five trees this year. Besides, it's too much for Mom and Aunt Catherine to deal with since they'll be taking care of Grandmother."

"I agree. Mom won't complain. But we have to put up these wreaths and garlands." Robin handed her another box.

Having finished their breakfasts, the girls came running into the room. "Ohh, look at the big tree," Lilly said. "It sparkles."

"Can I help?" Bella asked. "*May* I help?"

"Of course you can. Wait for Aunt Robin and me to sort through the ornaments. Sit there on the rug and we'll show them all to you." Emily opened the first box and lifted out garlands of gold leaves and bows. "We can use these." Pushing aside the packing paper, she lifted out a porcelain angel dressed in white satin and tulle, trimmed with pearls and narrow gold ribbon. "Do you remember this, girls?"

"Oh, she's perfectly pretty," Bella said.

"She's the angel for the top of the tree." Emily set it on the coffee table. "You can look at her, but don't pick her up. She's very old."

"Like Grammy?" Lilly asked.

Emily laughed. "Yes, like Grammy."

Robin opened a box filled with strings of lights. Reclosing it, she set it aside. "We won't be using those this year." She opened another and smiled. "Ah, here's the treasure trove. The ornaments."

"I love the ornaments," Emily agreed. "Each one is unique. Girls, I'll set some on the chair for you to hang. But first I need to stand on the stool to decorate the high places. Then you can hang yours. Can you be very patient?"

Smiling, they nodded their heads.

"Okay, my little angels. You'll get your turn in a few minutes."

Emily and Robin hung the heirloom ornaments, delighting in their childhood favorites. In spite of the happy task, Robin couldn't stop thinking about Matt.

After several minutes in which Robin disappeared into her thoughts, Emily caught her eye. "You haven't been yourself since you got here. You seem far away. Is everything alright?"

Robin twisted her mouth to the side and looked down at the ornament in her hand. She should have known Emmy would detect something wasn't right.

"Is it Dad? Are you missing him?"

She shook her head and sighed.

Emily glanced at her but continued hanging ornaments. "If you don't want to talk about it, it's okay."

Robin turned to her. "So much has happened in my life in the past few weeks. I'm afraid I've made a mess of things."

Emily's brows rose and she stepped down off the stool. "You mean in your personal life?"

Even her sister's gentle probing made Robin fear she'd lose the grip she had on her emotions. "It's complicated."

"Life generally is."

"Does love have to be?" She closed her eyes.

Emmy touched her arm.

"It's not only that I've messed things up for myself, I've messed things up for other people."

"I see. Sounds serious." She glanced at her daughters, who still sat on the floor watching them. "Why don't we talk about it when the girls take their naps?"

Robin nodded.

With the upper portion of the tree decorated, the girls started hanging the less fragile ornaments on the lower branches. Robin placed the skirt underneath the tree. Beautifully realistic and festive, they were delighted with the tree.

When Emmy placed the angel on top and lit the tree, they all cheered. But in reality, her cheerful moments were short-lived. Loneliness for the love she'd left in Georgia filled her heart.

Robin sat in her bedroom sipping a cup of hot tea when Emmy rapped quietly and pushed open the door.

"Hey … I'd like a cup of tea too. Do you want to go down to the kitchen?"

"Sure." She got up. "Are the girls asleep now?"

"Shh. Keep your fingers crossed."

In the kitchen, Robin sat at the table while Emily made a cup of raspberry tea. She joined Robin at the table. "The girls might not sleep long. You want to tell me what's going on?"

"Oh, Emmy, I don't know where to start."

She lifted her hands palm up and shrugged. "At the beginning."

Robin pressed her forehead with her fingers and shook her head. "Okay. I think I broke up with Caleb. No, wait. I'll start at the beginning. Kaitlin … she's the woman who helped Caleb create his blog. She came to see me the day after Thanksgiving. She's in love with him."

"Ooh. Naturally." Emily smirked and blinked her eyes.

Robin told her the whole story, down to the last detail, including Kaitlin's threat to tear her hair out if she broke Caleb's heart.

"No way!" Emily clamped her hand over her mouth.

"But she started me thinking. She really believed what she said. Not only that, but I can't find that depth of passion in myself for Caleb. I wanted to. I think he's a wonderful person. He would make an excellent husband, but …"

"You don't love him," she whispered matter-of-factly.

Robin shook her head. "I had a terrible crush on him in my teens. Then last summer when we met again, that spark reignited. I've fantasized about him for years."

"You projected your fantasy onto him," Emily said, her eyes wide.

Yes. Exactly. "I think I have. In August, he told me he wanted to spend the rest of his life with me. Just what I hoped would happen, happened. But something had changed. Instead of moving closer to him, I was pulling away. I care about him. I really do."

They sat silently for a long moment while Emily studied her face.

"Could that something be Matt?" Emily asked. "I saw how the two of you looked at each other."

Robin put her hands over her eyes. "I should have told him the truth from the start, and maybe I could have seen what was happening. Now I can't bear to explain this to Caleb. He'll think there was something more going on between Matt and me than warm fuzzy feelings."

"He might at first maybe. That's understandable. And you never told Matt the truth? I thought you were going to do that weeks ago. Are you saying sorting through all this is the big mess?"

"It's even bigger than that. I'm not sure what this is I feel for Matt or what he feels for me. He kissed me a couple nights ago and I thought I had died and gone to heaven."

"He kissed you?" Emily's mouth fell open and she reached across the table for Robin's hand.

"I told you. It's a long story," she said weakly.

Emily looked up at the ceiling and listened. "The girls are still quiet."

The two of them talked for over an hour. When the girls woke up, Emily and Robin continued the discussion. They prepared the evening meal together, peeling back layers of past encounters and sorting through scenes to figure out what had happened with Robin and the men in her life.

"Well, you have to call Matt," Emily said, pressing her finger tips to her temples. "You can't leave him hanging for weeks."

The front door opened and their mother and aunt walked in.

She and Emily glanced at one another, then went to the doorway into the foyer. "Come on in where it's warm," Emily said. "Dinner is almost ready."

"How's Grandmother?" Robin asked.

"She's doing better than we could have hoped," Mom said once they were all in the kitchen. "We can bring her home tomorrow. Next week we'll start taking her to rehab, specifically speech. The Lord willing, she'll be much better in a couple of months."

Thank God.

"She can come home. Isn't that the best news?" Aunt Catherine said.

Lilly and Bella grabbed Aunt Catherine and Mom by the hand and pulled them into the living room. "Look at the tree," Lilly squealed.

"We made it all beautiful," Bella added. "The angel's on top. Grammy will like it."

Everyone laughed.

"She will, Bella," Mom said. "I'm sure she will. Just look at it. It's beautiful. Thank you for decorating our tree."

"Mommy said we have to go home tomorrow, but we'll come back for Christmas. Daddy can see the tree then too."

"Yes." Mom smiled as she hugged her grand-daughters. "You'll come back. We'll all be together to celebrate Christmas."

For the first time in days, Mom looked happy.

Chapter Thirty-One

While her grandmother made steady progress, Robin put the last touches on the Christmas decorations and printed address labels for her mom's Christmas cards. She had called the lake house several times, but Matt didn't answer. She didn't know his email address or his cell phone number. At first, she was reluctant to call. Now she felt antsy. What must he be thinking?

Her need to speak to him had grown immeasurably. As much as she wished she could avoid it, she was going to have to ask Mom for his contact information. Since the real feat would be doing so without raising her suspicions, Robin strategically timed the request.

With her purse and keys in hand, she tapped lightly on her Grandmother's door, then stuck her head in. "Is she sleeping?" she whispered.

Her mother sat on a chaise near the bed. "Yes. I'm going to stay here and read."

"I'm on my way to the post office to mail these cards. Is there anything you want me to get for you while I'm out?"

"No, thank you, dear."

"Would you do me a favor, Mom? I need the contact information for our tenant. Can you look up that information the next time you're at your computer and forward it to me in an email. I want to check on things at home."

"Oh. Sure. I'll do that."

"Thanks. I'll be back in a little while." Robin turned and exited the room before her mother had an opportunity to say more.

As she drove to the post office, she thought of her situation. Another phone call from Caleb had left her feeling sad. Naturally, he wanted to talk with her in person and asked to come up for a day or two. With a heavy heart, she'd said no. It wasn't without regrets. She hated upsetting him. Of course she enjoyed spending time with him. But it wouldn't be fair or honest to him. And moreover, there were her feelings for Matt.

She couldn't think of Matt without getting shaky inside. At that moment, she'd like to gaze into his dark eyes and touch his face. That would be enough. Was she in love with him? How could she have fallen in love with him when he was a most unlikely fit for her plans? His kiss had turned her world upside down. They were both trembling when she pulled away from him, he asking her not to go. Over a week had gone by. She had to get his number.

After her errand, she prepared dinner. Her mother and aunt were busy enough taking care of

Grandmother and accompanying her to therapy. They all gathered to share the evening meal, but Mom didn't mention getting the information she'd requested.

Several days passed and still Robin hadn't received his email address. She made another call to the house that went unanswered. She thought of Mr. Charlie and Jenny, but she couldn't bring herself to call them with messages for Matt.

While she stewed about it, her mother came into the den putting on her coat and tying a scarf around her neck. "I'd like to go for a walk. Would you join me?"

Robin looked up. "Sure. A stroll in the neighborhood or a race walk?"

"Just a leisurely stroll. I need some fresh air. Your company would be nice."

"Give me a minute." She retrieved her coat and Callie's leash from the hall closet. "It's a nice day for a walk. The sky is mostly clear. Callie's not used to the cold though. You think she'll be all right?"

While Robin fastened the leash, Mom talked to Callie. "Wanna go for a walk? Wanna go for a walk? We're going to get fat sitting around here."

Robin laughed. "I suppose she'll be all right. We won't be out long."

"It's a little cold, but this will be good for us." They stepped outside, and she smiled, pointing out the lovely decorations on the neighboring homes. "I might be getting into the holiday spirit after all."

"Bella and Lilly will put us all into the Christmas spirit." Robin linked her arm through her mom's.

"You're right about that. They're delightful children. I miss them. Still, I'm glad I came to Virginia. Mom and Catherine and I have reconnected. I've enjoyed it more than I could have imagined."

"I'm so glad."

"It's made me feel more alive to be needed. Not like the nuisance I was becoming treating you like a sixteen-year-old."

"You were never a nuisance." She gave her mom a little smile.

"And how have you been, really?"

"I'm happy at the lake. It's the perfect place for an artist's retreat."

"Your dad thought so. How is your relationship with Caleb?"

"Fine. Interesting. I don't know what to say. It's gone better than I planned on one hand, and on the other it's shown me how complicated relationships can be."

"Well, that's quite an answer. You're right about that." She pressed Robin's arm tighter to her side. "Love relationships are wonderful, complicated creatures. Just mind that heart of yours."

"Will do." Robin gave a playful nod.

"And after Dr. McLaughlin returns to California, if you get bored, just come up and visit me."

"Thanks, Mom. After he leaves, I might forget to eat I'll be working so diligently on my book. It's nearing completion. I want to focus on it."

"I'm proud of you. Dad and I always admired your talent. By the way, I couldn't find the information you wanted regarding the professor. I emailed Marjorie at the realty office. I'll forward it to you as soon as I hear from her."

"Thanks."

Mom picked up the pace and gave Robin's arm a tug. "Let's get back. My feet are getting cold."

"Mine too. Callie's too. Wanna race back?" Not waiting for a reply, she glanced at her mother before sprinting down the sidewalk with Callie in tow. Her mom closed in behind them.

They stopped on the front walk to catch their breath.

"Oh, I have a stitch in my side," Mom said, grimacing and smiling at the same time. "I'd like a hundred dollars for every time your dad sprang that on us."

They both laughed, remembering happy times with Dad. They might just have a merry Christmas after all.

When they were back inside, Robin made a phone call. Miss Margaret needed to know she was in Virginia. She'd see to it that Matt and Mr. Charlie wouldn't spend Christmas alone.

In spite of the stressors that had dominated the weeks prior to Christmas, the actual day was a marvel of good cheer. The girls' excitement delighted the entire family. Robin and Emily spent three days baking cookies and making delicious food for the holiday meal. Grandmother was moving around on her own and making progress with her speech. Signs were promising for a healthy happy new year.

On Christmas evening, after her nieces and grandmother were already in bed, Robin sat chatting in the den with her mom and aunt, her sister and brother-in-law. Peace filled her heart. Amid so many unknowns in life, her family's love and the faith they'd celebrated that day were the bedrock she counted on.

"Robin, I've finally gotten an email from my real-tor friend Marjorie. They're in Hawaii for the holi-days. I forwarded her message to you this morning."

"Great. Thanks, Mom."

Tomorrow she could call Matt. It would be such a gift to hear his voice. Robin excused herself by giving everyone a kiss on the cheek and wishing them all a good-night.

To Robin's dismay, the message from Mom's realtor contained the contact information for Tom Morgan and only a mailing address for Matt. Not his phone number or email address.

Then she'd have to call Matt's colleague—after noon since he was on the West Coast. To pass the morning she took a long walk, enjoying the new-fallen snow and the lovely historic neighborhood. Then she had breakfast with Emily and the girls while Ryan slept late and her mother and aunt spent time with Grandmother. She hadn't watched the clock so closely since the day Emily gave birth to Lilly.

At precisely noon, nine o'clock in California, she went upstairs to her bedroom and closed the door. She hadn't spoken to Matt in three weeks. Three weeks since he'd held her in his arms, melting her heart and dissolving all her plans. An absurd amount of time had lapsed. Well, better late than never. She would explain everything when they finally spoke.

A man answered on the third ring.

"Good morning. Mr. Morgan? This is Robin Lancaster."

"Oh. Good morning, Robin. And merry Christmas."

"Merry Christmas to you too." Robin sat down on the bed. "I've been trying to get in touch with Matt. He hasn't answered the landline when I called the house. I hoped that you might get him a message for me."

"Certainly. I'd be happy to. I'll be seeing him in a few hours, in fact."

What had he said? "In a few hours? You'll be seeing *Matt*?"

"Yes, I'm picking him up at the airport."

Her throat nearly closed. She swallowed hard. "The airport? In San Diego?"

"Yes. He's flying in around three."

No. There had to be some sort of miscommunication. "But … I thought he was staying at the lake until January."

"Uhh … I don't know. What was the message you wanted me to relay?"

Robin struggled to find her voice. Her sunny outlook had turned dark. "I wanted …" *To tell him I'm coming home tomorrow—that I want to see him, to be in his arms again.* She wanted to say all that and more but couldn't.

"You wanted …" Tom repeated. "Are you still there, Miss Lancaster?"

"Yes, I'm here. Sorry." She took a deep breath. "I wanted to tell him merry Christmas. I'm afraid I left suddenly without his contact information."

"I'll let him know. I'm sure he'll appreciate the call. I'll give him your number as well."

"Thank you. And merry Christmas and happy New Year, Mr. Morgan."

"And to you as well. Goodbye now."

Nausea washed over her as she lay down on the bed and curled into a ball. She'd thought there was still time …

At that moment, Matt was in an airplane flying to California. He wasn't at the lake running along the shore or writing his novel. He hadn't waited for her return. The sabbatical was over.

He was gone.

Chapter Thirty-Two

Never again. Going through the Atlanta airport the day after Christmas might become Matt's new worst nightmare. Couples struggled to put on happy faces as they juggled babies and children with all the kid-related minutia. Young professionals dashed to make connections. Lonely looking business men with briefcases and coffees milled through the terminals lacking in good cheer. He could relate, alone in an airport the day after Christmas.

He simply could no longer stand waiting for Robin's return. She'd left, and while that was due to her grandmother's illness, she hadn't even called. Caleb accompanied her, no doubt. Why hang around another week? Without Robin and Callie there, the place had lost its magic.

Charlie wanted to eat Christmas dinner at home, so Miss Margaret had brought over ham and casseroles and a plate of holiday cookies. Earlier, Matt had driven him to Hal's for a traditional slice of Hal's rum-soaked fruitcake and an afternoon chat in keeping with the spirit of the season. He then said his goodbye to Charlie, who invited him to visit in the summer. They'd go fishing again.

Matt watched the baggage claim turnstile crawl by for the umpteenth time. He propped his elbow in one hand while he kneaded his jaw with the other. Some giggly little girls burst by, reminding him of Bella and Lilly. Then he saw their parents. Tom and Lydia stood not thirty feet away from him, holding hands while looking up at a flight monitor. They hadn't noticed him. He waved to grab their attention, but they looked right past him, calling to the girls.

So now I'm the invisible man. He glanced at the turnstile again, then back at them. Finally, his bags came around. He pulled them off and dropped them at his feet. He waved again. "Tom!"

Tom and Lydia turned toward him, then exchanged a confused look. She tugged her husband's hand and pulled him along. "Oh, my goodness. Matt, I didn't recognize you." She placed her hand on his shoulder and they kissed each other's cheeks. Tom just stood there grinning.

"It's nice to see you, Lydia."

"Merry Christmas, old pal." Tom pulled Matt into a hug. "Is there a fountain of youth in Georgia?"

Matt chuckled and shook his head at their unexpected response. He hadn't considered how much his appearance had changed since May. "Thanks for meeting me."

"Absolutely." Tom hugged his daughters, who had latched onto his legs while he talked.

Matt smiled at the little ones. "Hi, girls. Did Santa come to see you?"

"Uh-huh. He did!" They immediately started telling him all about their Christmas.

"Now, girls," Lydia said. "Give Matt a chance to catch his breath. You'll have plenty of time to tell him about your gifts when we get home. He's coming to our house."

Together he and Tom loaded the bags into their van. The kids' constant chatter controlled the conversation and bumped endless thoughts of Robin to some corner of his brain. Their home was so well decorated that it looked like a gingerbread house, which thoroughly made up for the total lack of holiday display at the lake house. While he enjoyed the time with friends, when Tom drove him to his condo several hours later, he was ready to be alone.

"Matt, you look great," Tom said before he got out of the van. "We should all take sabbaticals."

"It was your brilliant idea. Thanks for forcing that bitter pill down my throat. There's a good chance I'm human again because of it."

Tom laughed as Matt unloaded the back seat of the van. "Do you need me for anything else before I go?"

"I'm perfectly fine. Go home to your family." He carried his luggage to the door and waved as his friend drove away.

Once inside the foyer, he looked around. The place looked foreign to him. He left his bags by the door and wandered through the tidy rooms, flipping on lights as he went. In the kitchen, he started a pot of coffee. Not because he particularly wanted a cup.

He wanted to smell the aroma, to assault his senses with something more appealing than the smell of a house that had been closed up for months. Then he sat at the kitchen table drinking cup after cup. He needed to be perfectly alone and still while he re-hashed what Tom had told him about Robin's call.

She called to say merry Christmas. *Merry Christmas?* Well, if that didn't take the cake. If that was all she wanted to say to him, there wasn't much point in pining for her and the new life he had started to believe they could have. Thanks to her, he had come through his valley of the shadow. Thanks to the house beside the lake. Thanks to God. He'd do his best to hang on to what he'd gained and make the best of life as it was now.

He dropped his head back and stared as if he could see through the ceiling to the bedroom above. Sooner or later he'd have to go up there. With a sigh, he pushed back from the table. He grabbed one of the bags in the foyer and went up the steep stairs to the bedroom. Their bedroom.

He flipped on the light and looked around. Famil-iar. It should have been. He'd slept there for ten years. Still, it felt strange. He didn't live here any-more. That was the catch. He didn't *live* here. It was like a tomb. He thought of Lauren's picture in the drawer, but he didn't move toward it. His legs re-fused to take him there.

Drawing a shaky breath, he turned in the door-way, crossed the landing, and went to the guest bed-room, flipping on lights as he went. The queen-size bed would be comfortable and serve his needs. He would sleep there.

With his bag dropped inside the door, he went downstairs for the others. He unpacked enough to retrieve his toiletry items, made a trip to the bathroom, and then crawled into bed.

No matter that every light in the house was still on.

When Callie got excited as they approached the house, Robin almost fussed at her. She felt like crying herself. But she had already cried for half of the drive home. She'd wrung out her emotions by reliving every moment she'd spent with Caleb. What made matters worse, she'd done the same with every moment she'd spent with Matt. The tears came then, at times falling so fast she could hardly see the road. She'd swipe them away, but new ones slid down her cheeks. As they approached the house, her apprehension rose higher.

"Matt's not here, Callie." She stopped the car in front of the porch instead of pulling into the garage. Callie jumped out as soon as the door opened and ran up the steps to the front door. Robin didn't want to go in yet, so she walked down the drive to the mailbox. Callie followed and lingered along the edge of the woods on the way back to the house.

But there was no use avoiding the unavoidable. She turned the key in the door, opened it, and stepped inside. It was silly, but she couldn't help pausing a moment to listen for him.

Maybe he had left a note.

She hurried to the kitchen and scanned the counters and the front of the refrigerator. Nothing. She tossed the mail on the counter and put fresh water in Callie's bowl. The dog had disappeared up the stairs. Robin found her sniffing around Matt's room, which held the lingering scent of him.

She went back downstairs and sat at the table, staring through the windows at the wintry lake. Callie came downstairs looking as dejected as she felt, and Robin laid her head on the table and let the tears come again. She didn't care how pathetic she sounded.

And that's when the front door opened. "Robin, honey?" Caleb. She hadn't heard him drive up.

He stood in the foyer when she looked up. Even through the tears, she saw shock on his face. She swiped her cheeks with both hands and struggled to pull herself together.

"Are you okay?" His voice was full of kindness and concern.

Robin shook her head and sniffed. "What are you doing here?"

"I saw your car. I wanted to see you." He moved toward her but only came halfway.

The pained look in his eyes made her stand. She wanted to comfort him, to allow him to comfort her, but something held her back.

"You're so upset. Tell me what's wrong."

"It's not really a good time." She pushed her hair back from her face and smoothed her sweater.

"Is your grandmother ..."

"She's much better." She stayed where she was and so did he.

"Robin, I really needed to see you."

She couldn't make herself reply.

That's when he began to pace. He looked up and must have noticed the open door at the top of the stairs. "Are we alone? Can we talk privately?"

"Yes. Matt's gone. Back to California." Speaking the words aloud made tears threaten again.

"Great!"

Robin scowled at the satisfied look on his face. "Why is that so great? He's a nice person." She took a deep breath and walked to the bank of windows. The sun sitting low in the sky cast a golden shimmer that ran across the lake straight toward her.

"Uhh ... sure." Caleb stopped beside her. "The lake is beautiful, isn't it? We love this lake." He looked down at her.

"Yeah." Regaining her composure, she gave him a half-hearted smile.

He put his arm around her shoulders then and pulled her gently against him. "I've been lost since you went to Virginia. I don't understand what's happened."

Robin shook her head. "I'm sorry, Caleb. It's all my fault."

He didn't say anything, probably waiting for her to go on.

"After Kaitlin came here, I started thinking about what she'd said. I realized I had built us up into a fairy-tale fantasy and tried to fit us into some pre-conceived mold ..."

"That again." He exhaled. "We care about each other, Robin. We have great chemistry. There has to be more to it than that. I thought we were perfect together."

"I …"

They stared into each other's eyes for a long moment.

Suddenly, a knowing look came into his. "Wait. Does that man have something to do with this?"

Tears sprang to her eyes again and her chin quivered. "I'm sorry. I didn't mean for it to happen. It wasn't something I expected or sought. It just … happened."

Shock and humiliation contorted his face before he dropped his arm and turned away. "I'm not used to being made a fool of."

"Nothing happened between us. It wasn't like that. He doesn't know I have feelings for him. I don't even know what it is I feel."

"I can't believe this. It's a good thing he's back in California." With his back to her, he crossed his arms. A moment later, he headed for the door.

"Wait. It was as much a surprise to me as it is to you. Caleb?"

"I've got nothing to say to you." The door closed behind him.

Guilt and regret swirled inside her along with a multitude of emotions. She wanted Caleb to understand, but that was asking too much. She didn't understand herself. She hadn't meant to hurt him. But somehow her heart was broken too, and it had shattered a little more when he turned his back and walked away.

Yet in reality, she knew. There was nothing else that either of them could do. No apologies would fix what they were going through.

Chapter Thirty-Three

For several days, Robin slogged through her routine. She watched the sun rise. She and Callie walked in the woods by the lake. She drew. She watched the sun set. All the while her thoughts circled around Caleb or Matt, especially Matt, stirring her emotions.

Amid the hours of melancholy, moments of clarity shone forth. Moments of joy. She was beginning to understand. She loved Matt McLaughlin. But just as a life with Caleb wasn't meant to be, neither was a life with Matt.

One afternoon when the sky was clear and the weather was unseasonably mild for Georgia's coldest month, she put on her socks and boots and grabbed a jacket for a walk to Mr. Charlie's. With Matt now gone for weeks, he would be lonesome. Callie ran ahead of her, darted off the dirt road, and scared up a covey of quail. Then she trotted back toward her looking proud as the birds flurried away.

Robin laughed. "Showing off, are you?"

Mr. Charlie was bundled up on the porch, sitting in a rocking chair. Sammy stood and barked as they approached, his tail wagging.

"Hey there, Birdie," Mr. Charlie called. "It's about time you came to see me."

"Sorry I haven't been to visit." She walked up to the porch. "It's a nice day to sit outside."

"Yeah, I was tired of being cooped up in the house. Can you stay a while? Sit down."

Robin climbed the steps and took the chair beside his.

"How's your grandma? Matt told me you had to go to Virginia to see about her."

"She had a stroke, but thank God it was a mild one. Mom and Aunt Catherine are taking her twice a week to outpatient rehab. Her speech was most affected, but she's making progress."

"Good. We missed you at Christmas."

Robin smiled. "I missed y'all too." Before her mind could take her to sad and lonely places, she looked around for something else to think about.

"And now our visitor has gone back to California." He inhaled and let out a sigh. "I'm sure glad he came and stayed a while."

So much for occupying herself with something else. "Me too. I'm glad he was here."

He studied her face. "Y'all missing him too, huh?"

"We are." She swallowed and cleared her throat. "I guess Callie and I will have to come visit you more often."

"I'd like that." He smiled. "Matt made me feel like a grandpa. I asked him to come back in the summer to go fishing with me."

The summer. Her mind started running through the days. "Wouldn't that be nice. What did he say about that?"

"That he'd think about it." He began rocking as he gazed at the lake. "We'd have a fish fry. You'd get an invite."

"I wouldn't want to miss it." A wave of affection touched her heart. She couldn't help smiling, remembering the camaraderie between the two.

Memories of a certain stormy night on the porch stunned her anew, and she rocked in silence as emotions filled her heart.

She stayed for two hours, until Mr. Charlie felt a chill and needed to go inside for his nap.

"You can be my grandpa too," she said, giving him a hug. "Next time I come, I'll bring you some beef stew. It was one of Matt's favorites."

He thanked her as she and Callie started home. She turned and waved to him, but already her thoughts were flying ahead to summer.

Wouldn't it be wonderful if he came again in summer?

One thing she knew. Summer would come again. She wouldn't be grieving over lost love forever. But right now, grieving seemed to be the only thing she could do.

Matt kept telling himself that in a matter of days he'd snap out of it. That he'd get back to the routine that had worked so well for him at the lake house. But it was getting harder to lie to himself. He could no longer deny the regression when he caught himself munching potato chips in the middle of the night.

Brushing the greasy crumbs off his keyboard, he growled in disapproval. But while mindlessly munching on them, he finished the novel soon after returning to California. He'd sent it off to his agent right away, knowing it was the best he'd written.

His agent loved it. "You put a lot of yourself into this one, Matt," Meryl said after a quick read. "I could almost feel your pulse."

"I'm glad you like it."

"I *love* it. And not only me. The publisher loves it. Readers will too."

"How much ... for the advance?"

She chuckled. "Hold onto your hat. The editor's barely had time to read through it. Let's give him a week or two to mull over it. I don't think you'll be disappointed. We certainly weren't."

"A couple of weeks, then." When the call ended, Matt resumed planning lectures. He'd never found his classes to be as boring as they were this semester. Just the same, he counted on them to fill the hours. Coffee with Tom provided a nice diversion on campus. If he didn't stop by Tom's office, he could count on Tom to stop by his.

On his next visit, he dropped a plastic grocery bag onto Tom's desk. "For you."

"What is it?" Tom nodded at the chair in front of his desk. "Make yourself comfortable while I finish replying to this message."

"A bag of snacks." Matt sat down and sipped the coffee he'd picked up at the coffee shop down the hall.

Tom finished typing, glanced up, and raised his brows. "Huh?"

"Snacks. Two packages of Oreos, a box of cheese crackers, a large bag of Cheetos, and a half-eaten giant bag of potato chips." Matt hadn't cracked a smile.

Neither did Tom. "Do I look like I need cookies? Lydia has me on a diet. I think it's one of her new year's resolutions. Shrink the husband to pre-nuptial size." He eyed the offending bag.

"Give it to the kids."

"We aim for nutritious foods for the girls, Matt."

Tom wasn't making this easy for him. "I don't care what you do with it. Help me out here. I'm on a junk-food binge."

Tom enjoyed a hearty laugh at his expense. "Are you still struggling to hang on to those good habits? Life must have been pretty sweet in Georgia." He folded his hands on the desk. "Are you running again like you did there?"

"No." Matt smirked.

"What's up with that? Was it just to impress the girl?"

"Of course not. I plan to get back to it. I've just felt a little sluggish since I got back."

"It's that bad, huh? Matt, you're missing her. You know that, right?"

"I thought you were a sociologist. Take off the psychiatrist hat."

"I've known you for how long? Fifteen years?" Tom held his gaze for several moments. "Which is it? Are you missing the place and Robin, or just Robin?"

"Both. I'm missing all of it."

"That's what I thought. Well? What's wrong with that? Now the question is, what are you going to do about it?"

What could he do? "Nothing. Absolutely nothing." Matt stood up.

"Come on." Tom scowled.

"She's engaged. Now let's drop the subject."

"Uhh, that stinks. I'm sorry."

"It's life. I'll figure it out. I think I'll go buy myself a new pair of running shoes." *And a car.*

"Good. You're taking action."

"Maybe. I'll see you Monday." Coffee still in hand, Matt turned to leave.

"You just got here. Sit."

He shook his head. "I've really got to run. No pun intended." And he left before anything else could be said.

Matt bought the new car, the first he'd owned since the accident, surprising the heck out of himself. He bought the new shoes and ran every day that week, determined not to crawl back into the same dark hole he'd inhabited before he took the sabbatical. He'd even started turning off all the lights before going to bed.

Still, he knew he was only going through the motions of life. The condo no longer felt like home. He longed for something he'd had for a brief time across the country beside a lake. There he'd had a different state of mind. He couldn't accept that this was his new normal.

With these thoughts in mind, Matt entered the hospital complex. He hadn't made an appointment with his therapist, but he knew if he didn't stop by right at that moment, he wouldn't be able to make himself go back. When he and Dr. Hess had last spoken, Matt was confident he no longer needed her counsel. Right now, he could admit he needed something.

He pushed the button and waited for the elevator. The doors opened, and he looked right into Callie's warm chocolate eyes. He inhaled sharply, suddenly disoriented. Then a smile spread across his face. Of course it wasn't Callie, but the Cavalier King Charles puppy pictured on the poster had markings identical to hers. Memories of the sweet-tempered dog and their happy companionship touched his heart.

Do you need some puppy love? the poster asked.

Absolutely. He chuckled. The poster was an advertisement for a farm that specialized in raising the breed for therapy dogs. By the time the elevator came to a stop, the address and phone number were in his phone. Two people got on and pressed the down button, but he held his spot instead of getting off. When the elevator came to a stop, he exited and headed out of the building.

Dr. Hess approached the hospital's automatic doors as Matt walked through them. "Matt!" she called. "Were you looking for me?"

He stopped. "Actually, I stopped by to say hello, but something else has come up. It's good to see you just the same." He shook her hand. "I'm doing well."

"You look well. Sorry I wasn't in. Make an appointment and we'll talk."

"Thanks." Matt waved and headed for the parking lot.

As soon as he got into his car, he put the address in his navigation system and called the number. In forty-five minutes, he should be there.

Let's see where this takes me. He laughed out loud.

The following weekend, Matt got the call he'd been waiting for from his agent.

"Good morning, Meryl." He divided his attention between the phone held to his ear and the puppy who had just bounced out the door of her crate. She wiggled playfully around his feet on the kitchen floor.

"Is this a good time, Matt?"

"Sure." Jumping up and down on his ankles, the puppy alternated adorable whines, barks, and growls.

"I just sent you an email with all the details. Look it over and get back to me as soon as possible. Sounds like you have company."

He laughed. "That's Penny, my new puppy. She's a little tyrant."

"A puppy? Success must have mellowed you."

"Ha! Desperation forced my hand." He chuckled. "We're establishing a routine, but so far so good. We've bonded and I'm smitten."

"Ah, that's sweet. So back to this news you've been waiting for. How does six figures sound for the advance?"

"No kidding? Outstanding. That's better than all the others put together. You're the best, Meryl. Thanks for everything you're doing for me."

"You know I love you," she said. "Now, how about the next one?"

Matt groaned. "Let's not go there yet. In the meantime, I have a favor to ask of you."

"Of course."

"The woman who owns the house in Georgia. Robin Lancaster. She's an exceptional artist and a children's writer. She's illustrating her children's book. Would you consider looking at her work and recommending an agent? She deserves a break. I'd like to help make that possible for her."

"Sure. I can do that for you."

"That means a lot to me. When I reply to your email, I'll send you her contact information. Thanks, Meryl."

As soon as they hung up, Matt picked up Penny and held her to his neck. She nuzzled his beard, licking his face and ears. He closed his eyes and enjoyed the puppy's breath and tickles. He must have chosen the most adorable charmer in the litter.

He and Penny walked around the yard and then sat on the floor and played until the puppy fell asleep. After he opened his computer to read the message from Meryl, he ordered gifts for Robin and wrote an overdue thank-you note. Then he went to his recliner in the living room. Eyes closed and hands clasped behind his head, he leaned back and traveled in his mind to the place he hoped she'd be.

Never would he forget her and their friendship. Her beautiful smile could make his day. He hoped she'd stay just the way she was forever, even when she became Mrs. Caleb Jackson.

Chapter Thirty-Four

While the tea kettle whistled on the stove, Robin blew her nose and shuffled back to the kitchen to make herself a cup of orange spice tea. Her shoulders ached as she poured the hot water into the cup. Rather than drag herself back to the bedroom, she took the nearest seat at the table. A fire would have been soothing, but she didn't have the energy to make one. The house seemed vast and silent since Matt left. Even after a month, she hadn't gotten used to the emptiness.

Her cell phone chirped and she stared at the name on the screen. With a sigh, she picked it up. "Hi, Emmy."

"You're *still* sick?" Her sister's voice was a mixture of surprise and alarm.

"How could you tell?"

"You sound dreadful."

"This cold is hanging on. My whole body aches."

"So it's more than depression now. You've let yourself get sick. That settles it. I'm having Ryan's mother come over here in the morning, and I'm coming down to spend the day with you. I'll stay overnight too."

Robin grimaced when she swallowed. Her throat hurt. "That's not necessary."

"Yes, it is. For my peace of mind, if nothing else. It's crummy to be alone when you're sick. You could get dehydrated."

Robin rubbed her eyes and realized they were teary. "Okay. I'll see you in the morning."

"I'll be there around ten. In the meantime, be sure to drink plenty of water and hot herb tea with lemon."

"Got it."

"Bye. Love you, sis."

"You too." Robin put aside the phone and laid her head on her folded arms. It really *was* crummy to be alone, sick or not.

Callie barked.

"Sorry, girl. No walk today. I guess you would like your supper though." Robin returned to the kitchen, where she filled Callie's bowl with dog food.

Then she eased her way back to bed to bury herself under the warm blankets and wait for her sister to arrive.

When Callie barked and Robin heard the front door open, she breathed a sigh of relief. She'd wanted Emily to come all along.

"Robin? Are you sleeping?" Soon Emily was beside the bed, touching Robin's forehead.

"I'm glad you're here," she said without opening her eyes.

"I think you have a fever. Did you eat anything today?"

Robin shook her head.

"How about anything to drink?"

"I didn't want to get out of bed."

"I'll be right back. I'm going to find the thermometer and get you something to drink."

She heard drawers being opened in the bathroom and the kitchen. Robin opened one eye but closed it immediately.

"You should have told me you were this sick," Emily whispered, beside her again. "I'd have come sooner. You know Ryan's mother loves to babysit and have her son all to herself. I can be here whenever you need me."

She opened her mouth to grasp the thermometer that wavered over her face.

"I'm sorry to be so bossy. But you let yourself get really down in the dumps and you haven't been taking care of yourself."

Beep-beep-beep.

Robin opened her eyes when the thermometer sounded.

Emily pulled it out of her mouth. "One hundred and one. Just as I thought. You probably have the flu."

Emily fussed over Robin, trying to make her as comfortable as possible, and then sat in a chaise with a book for a couple of hours while Robin dozed. Robin woke to the aroma of something cooking, but nothing about it smelled appetizing.

"I've made chicken broth with carrots and on-ions," Emily said. "You need to eat some. I have a clean pair of pajamas here for you. Let's see if you don't feel better after a warm bath and something nourishing in your stomach."

"Gosh, you sound like Mom." She pushed herself into a sitting position and sat there a few minutes. Her head felt woozy.

Emily took her arm and walked with her to the bathroom. Robin refused a bath, but took a warm shower while Emily remade the bed.

"By the way, there was a large box beside the front door when I got here," she said when Robin came out of the bathroom. "I brought it inside."

"Okay. Thanks." Dressed in fresh pajamas, she ate some of Emily's soup. It was tasteless, and being out of bed for so long exhausted her.

She went back to bed and slept.

On the third day of Emily's visit, Robin woke feeling almost normal. She got out of bed without coaxing and sipped a glass of juice while eating applesauce and toast.

"You haven't been sick like this in years, Robin." Emily watched her from across the table. "Your re-sistance was low. It's that mind-body thing, you know."

Robin rolled her eyes and wished she could avoid the inevitable conversation.

Emily leaned slightly toward her. "You haven't talked to him yet, have you?"

Robin pursed her lips and stared into her bowl of applesauce. She didn't have to ask who she meant.

"Oh, Robin. Why not? You're in love with him. And he's probably in love with you."

She shook her head. "He hasn't contacted me, Emmy. Shouldn't he have contacted me? At least to say he enjoyed his stay here."

"Give the guy a break. He probably thinks you're with Caleb." Emily sighed. "Did you send him the painting you made for his Christmas gift?"

Robin shook her head.

"Well, I can see you don't plan to take any initiative. You sure took some when it came to having a shot at Caleb. What's different this time?"

What *was* different this time? She hadn't really considered that. But ... "There's just too much at risk," she whispered.

"Like what? What's holding you back?"

"I'm scared. If this is love, where can it lead? He's in California. This is my home. And if this is love, why is it I can hardly function? What if he doesn't love me back?"

"I told you to trust your heart. Remember?" Emmy's voice had softened. "Does your heart tell you he loves you? You've been physically sick, but right now you're miserable because you're heartsick. What if he is too?"

For once she wasn't so sure her sister understood. "Too many things happened at once. We should talk, I know. I'm still working up my courage."

"Bless your heart. Well, I'm taking Callie for a walk and getting the mail. I need some fresh air. You work on your courage while I'm out."

She had little else to work on. Emily had done the laundry and dishes. In fact, she'd taken care of everything so well that no chores remained for Robin. Her sister had helped her express some of her feelings too, which gave her a little relief. Now she needed a distraction.

Drawing. For the first time in days, she wanted to work on her art. She went over to the studio, and immediately her eyes fell on the picture she had painted for Matt. The scene was perfect. It reminded her so much of him standing down by the lake gazing out over the water. He looked like he belonged there. She smiled but still felt sad.

When Emily came in a while later, she was working on a new illustration. Callie sprinted up the stairs and ran to her, putting her paws up on her knees.

Robin petted the soft head. "You enjoyed that walk, huh, girl?"

"Yes, we did." Emily smiled as she walked toward her. "When was the last time you checked the mailbox?"

Robin shrugged. "A week … at least. Was there a lot? I was sick, remember."

"Yeah. Junk mail, grocery store fliers, a few bills, and *this*." She tossed what appeared to be a greeting card on the drafting table.

Robin glanced at it and back to her work before doing a double take. She looked up at her sister.

"He's written, Robin! Close your mouth that's hanging open, blink your eyes, and open the card. Please."

"Oh my gosh," Robin whispered, pressing the card to her chest.

"I'm outta here. Going back over to my room so you can read it." She pointed at the picture Robin had painted for Matt. "That painting is phenomenal, by the way." Then she disappeared down the stairs.

Robin's heart pounded as she looked at the envelope. *Thank you, Lord. No matter what he's written, I'm happy he wrote.*

She slowly opened the flap to reveal a lovely thinking-of-you card.

Dear Robin,

Thanks for the best retreat of my life. I know. Officially, it was a sabbatical, but it achieved far more than its original intent and proved to be my saving grace. You're a wonderful caretaker and a great cook. Thanks for taking care of me for six months. If the sabbatical had been any better, I couldn't have left. As it is, classes have resumed and I'm lecturing to halls full of eager scholars. Not! You'd think I handed out sleeping pills at the door.

The novel is finished and off to the publisher.

I hope your grandmother is well and this note finds you enjoying life beside the lake.

Could you visit Charlie for me and be sure to give Callie some extra tummy rubs on my behalf?

With fondest memories, Matt

P. S. During the second week of February, expect one or two deliveries as a small token of my thanks.

Robin clasped the card to her chest again and took a deep breath. He'd practically written a letter. A wonderful letter.

She jumped up. "Let's go show this to Emmy," she said to Callie. "She'll be so pleased."

Robin sat beside the fire sipping hot tea and looking out at the clear blue sky over the lake. The lake looked lonely in winter, but today she didn't mind that. She'd recovered from the flu and had been drawing since Emily left two days earlier.

If the sabbatical had been any better, I couldn't have left. She remembered a line from Matt's card, the words of which she knew by heart, and wondered what he had meant by that.

When she heard the delivery truck, she almost squealed. She and Callie met the driver at the door. The name of a local farm and nursery was displayed on the side of the truck.

"We have a delivery for Robin Lancaster," the driver said as he got out.

"I'm Robin."

He walked toward the back of the truck. "Where can we set it up? Where do you want the boxes?"

"Boxes? What needs to be set up? I didn't place the order. It was sent as a gift, so I don't know what you're delivering." She clasped her hands together.

"You want to come take a look? We have a greenhouse. We're supposed to set it up wherever you want it. And the other boxes contain plants."

A greenhouse! "How delightful. I have the perfect place for it." She walked outside and over to the corner of the deck. "Set it up right here. You can put the boxes over there so I can see what's in them."

"It's up to you." Another man got out, and the two started setting up the seven-foot-square transparent greenhouse. Robin snapped a couple of pictures with her phone and sent them to Emily. One box contained an herb garden with individual square cedar planters, while the long box contained a six-foot-tall lemon tree. She went inside to get a box cutter, then opened the smaller box and took out the wooden planters and then the packages of herbs.

As soon as the men left, she called her sister. "My delivery arrived! Did you see the pictures?"

"I did. What exactly is it? A greenhouse?"

"Yes. And there are pots for herbs and a lemon tree. They'll be beautiful after I get them planted and into the greenhouse. And that explains the large planter delivered when I was sick. He must have sent that for the lemon tree."

"Matt knows you well. He chose perfect gifts for you." She sounded almost as excited as Robin felt. "How thoughtful."

He sure was. Robin picked up the package of thyme and smiled. "By summer, the herbs will be awesome. I've already thought of other seeds I want to get started in the greenhouse."

"Yay! That should cheer you up."

"It already has. Now … I'll get busy working on this. And it's easier to get in touch with him now. I'll send him a thank-you card along with the drawing."

"Do it, Robin. The sooner the better. He'll love the picture. He'll want to know everything has arrived in good condition too."

"At least. Thanks for helping me through this, Emmy."

"Of course! What are sisters for?"

Robin spent the afternoon setting up the plants in the greenhouse and thinking of Matt. Just like the roots of the lemon tree, hope was alive. And tomorrow ...

Tomorrow she would write to him.

Mission accomplished. Robin had mailed the picture to Matt along with a card. Leaving the post office feeling positively cheerful, she zipped her jacket against the chill and walked down the street to finish her shopping.

She was just about to get into her car in front of Fred's General Store when Caleb came walking down the other side of the street. He, Kaitlin, and Rachel were about to enter the café. Robin paused and must have smiled. The next thing she knew, he'd stopped, grinned, and started walking toward her. Rachel and Kaitlin waited, but he waved them on into the café. Wearing a long-sleeved plaid shirt and jeans, he looked amazing.

"Don't you think of getting away from me that fast," he said, striding toward her. As they stood face-to-face, he took both her hands. He was obviously glad to see her, and she expected that her expression told him the same.

A lump rose up in her throat. "Oh, Caleb. You are a prince."

"Hey," he said in a low voice, standing close and giving her hands a squeeze. "Your hands are cold. Are you okay?"

Robin nodded. "Uh-huh. Are you?"

"Getting there." He looked into her eyes. "You did the right thing."

"I wasn't fair to you. You deserved better."

"So did you. I never came to look at your drawings. I wanted to. I meant to. I was too caught up in my business. Come here." He pulled her into a warm hug. "I blame myself for that. I didn't give you what you needed."

She drew back to look at him. "I don't know why things happened the way they did. I was caught off guard. Please forgive me."

"Aw … honey." They held each other again. "I've figured out what happened," he whispered into her ear. "I didn't set the hook. I should have run off with you that first summer we met."

"Oh, Caleb, you're going to make me cry." She tilted her face up to look into his. Then she glanced toward the café.

He shrugged. "They can eat without me. I'll text Rachel." He took out his phone, punched in a message, and then tucked it back into his pocket.

"She's walking without a limp now," Robin said, brightening.

"She's a hundred percent, and as soon as I get through kicking my butt for not marrying you when I could, I'll be a hundred percent." He offered a wry smile.

"And I so would have married you." She hugged him again. "You're an amazing man."

"You're an amazing woman." He rubbed her back. "We'll see each other around. Let's go for pizza at Joe's sometimes?"

They laughed at the mention of Joe's.

"I'd like that." Robin breathed deeply and smiled. "I'm glad you stopped me. I've needed to talk to you."

"Me too. I miss you. But the truth is, I wouldn't have been ready for marriage for years. I don't need a wife and kids until I'm satisfied my business is all set."

So he really hadn't changed on that point after all. "I understand."

He hesitated, then leaned down and gave her a tender kiss. A simple lingering one, perfect for one's serious flame after the fire has burned out. He stepped back and started to walk away, then looked back at her.

"Tell Rachel and Kaitlin hello for me," she said.

"You can tell 'em yourself. I'm not gonna let you be a stranger. Call me when you're ready for that pizza."

"I will." She lifted her hand and watched him walk across the street, admiring him as much as ever.

At one point in time, she had wanted to be his wife, and she could have been. But God apparently had other plans.

Chapter Thirty-Five

One of the best things about San Diego was the weather. Under clear skies and with the temperature at a glorious sixty-seven degrees, Matt went for a run. Afterward he lay on the sofa and cuddled Penny, who wiggled and climbed on him, intermittently chewing his shirt and growling.

"Ouch! Careful, Penny!" He rubbed the spot the puppy had nipped through his shirt, then held her to his chest and stood. Together they went upstairs. He needed to shower and change before Tom and the girls arrived on their way to the park. They were eager to meet the new puppy.

Matt pulled on his shirt as the doorbell rang. When he opened the door, the mail carrier was climbing into his truck.

"I left a package beside the door," he called. A square box leaned against the condo's outer wall.

"Have a good day!" Matt picked up the package.

Robin's name and address were in the top left-hand corner. Huh. What had she sent him? *Fragile* was stamped on the box.

By the time he looked up, Penny had meandered halfway down the walk toward the street. "Penny! Stay!" Still holding the box, Matt sprinted to swoop up the puppy.

Tom and his daughters drove up at the same time. Having spied the fuzzy animal, gleeful shrieks and giggles erupted as the girls jumped out of the car. He led them through the house to the back door so they could play with Penny in the yard.

Tom laughed, shaking his head, as Matt closed the screen door behind them. "You know what you've started, don't you? They won't let me rest now until they've convinced me we have to have one of our own."

"I'm defenseless." He laid the package on the kitchen table. While he poured lemonade in plastic cups, Tom eyed the box. "Are you reading my mail?"

"Sorry. I couldn't help myself. The name jumped out at me."

"You and me both."

"Why not open it?"

"Not with you standing over me." He gave Tom a firm tap on the shoulder. "Grab yourself something out of the fridge. The lemonade is for your girls." He went outside to the patio.

The girls had dropped onto the grass, delighting in Penny's licks and clumsy tumbles. Before long, all three of them were lying prone in the grass.

"That's a cute puppy," Tom said as he joined him. "Has she helped? Get your mind off Georgia?"

"She's entertaining, that's for sure." He sat down on a lawn chair. "And place is irrelevant. It's what I left there I can't stop thinking about."

Tom nodded. "People get unengaged, you know. Did you tell her how you feel?"

The two guys looked at each other for a minute.

Aggravation rose in Matt, but he let it go. He needed to talk. "I wanted to, but it didn't work out. She left."

"But she had to leave, right? Her grandmother was ill."

True. But … "If she'd felt what I feel, she wouldn't have run away when we kissed."

Tom tapped his fingers on the arm of the chair and looked unconvinced. "You choked. You're the one who left."

"It wasn't that easy."

"You have her phone number. You could call her before it's too late. Love is always a timely gift."

Matt leaned his head back. "You sound like a Hallmark card." Just the same, he considered his friend's words. True enough maybe, but he couldn't imagine himself calling her. Not now. It was too late.

After a long pause, Tom stood up and walked toward the girls. "The puppy is sleeping now," he whispered. "Let's leave her napping while we say goodbye and go to the park."

Amid gentle protests so as not to wake the puppy, they begged to come again. When Matt agreed, they ran to the patio and sipped their lemonades before saying goodbye.

"You're welcome to come any time. Thanks for coming to meet Penny." He walked them back through the house and out to the driveway.

"Thanks for inviting us. Right, girls?"

"Have fun at the park."

"You'll figure it out," Tom said before getting into the car. "You've come a long way."

Matt nodded and watched them drive away. With his hands stuffed into his shorts pockets, he went back inside. Penny still napped in the grass, so he walked over to the kitchen table.

Maybe I'll have a look right now. He retrieved a paring knife from a kitchen drawer. Slowly drawing it along the edge of the box, he opened the flap and pulled out something hard covered in bubble wrap. As he removed the wrap, a framed picture unleashed a memory.

He wasn't prepared for the jolt to his heart. Like magic, the scene took him there. Robin had drawn the lake with him and Callie standing near the dock from the perspective of the lake house. He closed his eyes. He wanted to hold the image in his mind and breathe the essence of contentment represented by Robin's work. But loneliness quickly replaced the wonderful feeling.

He'd lost something precious and unique in all the world. He'd left a piece of his heart in Georgia.

Robin sat at the drafting table with her hands in her lap as she watched clouds drift across the sky. She didn't know it was possible to miss someone as much as she missed Matt. She marveled at the powerful pull of the heart and how again and again memories of him captured her thoughts. She offered prayers for unknown others separated from their loved ones by life events or death. Her pain seemed to lessen while she prayed for them.

Her phone rang, interrupting her meditative moments. She grabbed it but didn't recognize the number. "Hello?"

"Hello, is this Robin?"

"Yes."

"My name is Meryl Duncan. I'm Matt McLaughlin's literary agent."

"You're his agent?" she said. "Oh. Hello."

"It appears we have a mutual friend. He's asked me to get in touch with you."

"Really? Well, it's nice to speak to you." Robin managed to control the surprise in her voice.

"Matt has told me of your exceptional talent as an artist and children's writer."

"I'm ... flattered."

"He thinks you ought to be published and asked me to help get you in touch with people who can help make that happen. What do you think of that?"

"I'm so surprised, I hardly know what to say. That's awfully kind of both of you."

"If you have a few minutes, we could talk."

A half hour later, the call ended. Robin had never felt so encouraged and validated as a children's book illustrator and writer. Meryl's proposals sounded promising. And if nothing else came of it, she treasured their votes of confidence.

She read over the notes she'd made during the call and created a must-do timeline according to Meryl's requests. Inspiration energized her thoughts and plans. But before she went any further, she had a call to make.

Jenny had left a voice message while she'd been out on her walk that morning. The last time they'd spoken to each other, she and Caleb had just broken up. Now Jenny was ready for a friendly chat.

And Robin was happy to have something exciting to share besides a recount of her mistakes.

Robin admired the bouquet of pink and yellow snapdragons delivered that morning. The colors were so vibrant and fresh, and their subtle fragrance sweetened the room. She looked at them from every angle and reread the note.

Can't thank you enough for the wonderful drawing. I'll treasure it forever as well as my time with you and Callie. Love, Matt

She called Emily.

"Oh my gosh, what's wrong?" her sister asked at hearing her greeting. "Was that a sniffle I heard?"

"No," Robin chided. "Not right now anyway. Nothing's wrong. Matt sent me flowers."

"I thought you'd stopped crying over him in January. According to my calendar, it's almost April."

"I wasn't crying. My nose got a little stuffy. That's all."

"If you say so. Last time we talked, you were so excited about the call from the agent. Be happy!"

Her lecture over, her tone changed. "Why did he send flowers?"

"For the drawing. He wrote that he'd treasure it forever."

"Oh my. The picture was evocative. I'm sure he loves it. But the thing is, I don't understand what's keeping the two of you apart. You're not even talking to one another. Cryptic notes back and forth, for Pete's sake. In my opinion, neither of you has the nerve to reach out, and there's three thousand miles between you."

Robin sighed. "I know … but like this, it's manageable. I was wondering though … about summer vacation. Haven't you always wanted to go to California, visit Napa Valley and San Francisco?"

"Yes. But why are you asking about what I want?"

"What about us planning a trip to California for summer vacation? We can visit all those places you've wanted to see and more."

"Hmm. And we could go to San Diego and visit Matt too." She burst out laughing. "I can't believe you're saying this."

Robin put her face in her hand as she waited for her sister to calm down. "I can't believe you're laughing at me."

"Don't you see what you're doing? You're trying to figure out a way to see him, without letting him know you want to see him, without telling him your feelings."

She blew out her breath. "I just can't stop thinking about him."

"If that's the case, why are you doing nothing about it?"

And *that* was the question. Why was she doing nothing? "If he'd only call and open the door just a teeny bit."

"You know you could fly out there and see him. You don't need me in order to go."

Robin considered that. "I know."

"Well ..."

"I'll think about it. If I still feel this way in June, I might book a flight."

"Whoa! I know I'm suggesting it, but for a girl firmly dug into her place in the world, that would be a bold move."

"If I saw him, I think it would be easier to talk to him and risk telling him how I feel."

"Maybe you're right. In spite of all this noise I'm making, I'm really sorry you're sad. And Mom was so sure that Caleb would be the one to break your heart. Isn't it amazing how life works out sometimes? But you know, Robin, sometimes it works out better than anything we could have planned." Emily's voice had softened. "You're going to be all right. Somehow everything will work out."

"I know. My life is great. I just miss him." Neither of them spoke for a long moment. "It's always good to talk things out with you, Emmy. Thank you."

"You're welcome. Besides, aren't I right 99.9% of the time?"

Robin laughed. "Yes, you are, know-it-all sister."

And she really hoped she was this time.

Matt pulse quickened when he saw the envelope with Robin's sister's name on it. Why would she be writing to him? Was Robin okay? He ripped open the envelope.

Dear Matt,

I hope all is well for you in California. I've been holding on to your address since your note to Robin in February. I thought it might eventually come in handy if it became necessary for me to lend a hand. I'm writing you this note to let you know that you are missed. Robin hasn't been the same since you returned to California. I thought it might interest you to know Robin broke up with Caleb Jackson on December 27th, the day she returned to the lake house from Virginia. She realized what most of us already knew. He wasn't the man for her.

It's a shame to me that you and Robin haven't talked about what was going on between the two of you during your stay at the lake house. Something was going on between you two, wasn't it?

The older sister, Emily.

He dropped the card on the table. With his heart rate ticking up, he paced the kitchen floor. Intermittently he stopped and gazed at the note, only to begin pacing again. Penny bounced and tumbled, endeavoring to follow along. Finally, he began to relax, the pacing stopped, and he exhaled loudly. Penny came to rest at his feet.

"Thank you, Emily," he said aloud. "I knew we understood each other."

Robin wasn't marrying Caleb. Of course she wasn't.

Chapter Thirty-Six

A week later, Matt stood in Tom's office with a coffee in his hand, watching Tom scribble red ink across a student's exam.

"Hey. Sit down. Don't you love red ink pens?" Tom glanced up and chuckled. "My wife gives them to me for Christmas." He dropped the pen on the stack of papers and pushed them aside. "Where have you been? I came by your office yesterday and you'd already left for the day." His brows lifted as he studied Matt's face.

"I've been busy." Matt sat across from him and set his coffee on the desk.

"Another novel in the works?"

"No." He smiled a wry smile. "Something more earthshaking."

Tom held his gaze, his expression blank. "You sure know how to build suspense. What the heck's going on?"

"I've put the condo on the market."

"What? That is major."

"The condo was home to Lauren and me. It's time to start over."

Tom nodded slowly.

"The sabbatical gave me enough space to realize that our life together is in the past. I have a future." They stared at one another, and then Matt smiled. "And that's not all. I resigned my faculty position."

"I think the earth just trembled." Tom gripped the arms of his chair. "What about tenure?"

"Means nothing to me now. California isn't home anymore." Matt picked up the red pen and squiggled on a note pad.

"Effective when?"

"The end of this semester."

"Wow."

"I need to go back to Georgia. A good friend once told me people get unengaged. Last week, her sister confirmed that for me."

"Robin's not engaged anymore?" Tom threaded his hands behind his head and kicked back in his chair.

They both started laughing.

So many doubts and fears had been turned upside down. "I've got to follow my heart. You said so yourself." Matt couldn't stop grinning.

"Absolutely, man. And it's going to take you right back to her. I knew you missed her. We're going to miss *you*. But I have a good feeling about this."

"Yeah, so do I, and basically you engineered the whole thing with the sabbatical."

Tom smiled. "What a life changer. Lydia will be over the moon. Let me know what we can do to help. We'll want you over for dinner before you go.

Bring Penny." Then he stood and came around the desk to shake Matt's hand. They gave each other a slap on the back and a hug.

Joy and a sense of well-being flooded Matt's heart as he walked out of Tom's office. He knew exactly where he was going.

On a balmy May afternoon, Robin sat on the porch making preliminary sketches of her new children's story. She had fulfilled all of Meryl Duncan's requests and awaited news of potential representatives for her work. In the meantime, she'd written a new children's story.

The acrid smell of smoke wafted from across the lake, where the neighbors had a fire pit near the water. As her attention shifted to the spiraling silver plume, it transported her back to the year before when fire had forced her and her mother out of their condo.

What could have been devastating had led to transformative change for both of them. Mom was experiencing renewed *joie de vivre*. Grandmother had recovered. And for her, what an amazing year it had been. In a way, she'd grown up. Thanks to Matt, it was confirmed she was a caretaker at heart. She'd experienced her first true love and the pain of its loss. She'd also proven that she could live happily on her own creating beautiful art and stories.

Callie's barking disrupted her reminiscing, snapping her back to the present. Callie pranced along the edge of the screened porch, then jumped up, pawing the screen.

"No, Callie. Stop that! What's gotten into you?" Robin sprang up and went to her. In the yard below, a frisky puppy ran willy-nilly on the slope to the lake. "Oh! I see why you're so excited. There's a puppy down there. Give me a second and we'll go see."

Callie was howling in delight by the time Robin picked up her tennis shoes. She started toward the chair to put them on, but stopped short as her heart leaped into her throat. The real cause of the dog's hysteria was ... *Matt*. He was following the puppy to the lake shore.

Staring, she dropped the shoes. He was really there. He wasn't a dream. She pressed her hands to her cheeks as her stomach fluttered and her heart began hammering.

He turned, looked toward the house and began walking back to it. Then he lifted his eyes to hers. A smile spread across his handsome face. "Aren't you going to come down?" he called, his deep voice mellow and sweet. "I have someone I want you to meet."

Tears of joy sprang to her eyes and Robin practically raced to the door. Callie darted past and already waited there to spring out as soon as it opened. Yapping with excitement, the ecstatic animal sprinted to Matt. He knelt down as she sprang up to greet him, then laughed as wet kisses covered his face and ears. The puppy playfully pounced into the mix.

Robin stopped eight feet away and watched, adoring every move he made. His beard was neat and his dark hair long enough to curl on his neck. He looked happy.

He stood, never taking his eyes away from hers. "This is Penny. She's five months old." By his wavering voice, he was every bit as shaken as she was. "She was meant to fill a gaping hole in my heart, but it was an impossible task."

Robin shook her head, smiling. "She's the cutest thing."

Matt continued to study her face. "You're beautiful."

"I can't believe you're here." She motioned to the silver SUV with a U-Haul behind it in the drive, but no words formed.

"California didn't feel like home anymore."

"So … you're moving."

Matt nodded, his steel gray eyes soft and smiling.

"But what about your teaching assignment?"

"No longer what I need in my life." He took a step closer. "I'm a full-time writer now. I can work anywhere."

A tear trickled down her cheek, but she didn't bother to wipe it away. "I've missed you. Every day."

"I've missed you night and day. Getting Penny didn't come close to replacing you."

"Oh, Matt," she whispered.

He took another step, closing the gap between them. And then he reached for her, cupping her face in his hands.

She tipped her face up to his and felt her knees go weak as she breathed the words, "I love you."

"I love you too." He brushed his lips against hers.

In the next marvelous moment, sweet kisses covered her face. He held her so close, she felt his heart pounding against hers. She wrapped her arms around his neck and clung to him for joy. This is where she'd yearned to be ... forever.

Callie barked and growled possessively, demanding the place at their feet where Penny had settled. They pulled away from each other to see Penny detangling her own feet before scampering away down the slope to the lake.

Matt laughed and grabbed Robin's hand. Together with Callie, they walked toward the lake to join the exuberant puppy.

"Everything I love is here," he said as the puppy pounced onto Callie's head.

"Me too, Matt. Me too."

Robin leaned her head against his shoulder and for several moments they stood silently in the sunshine gazing at the sky and lake.

"There's something I've been wanting to ask you," he said, leaning down to look into her eyes.

"Anything."

"Might you have a pet-friendly room for rent?"

She watched the smile in his eyes spread over his face. Then she laughed, and so did he.

"I thought you'd never ask." She raised up on tiptoes to murmur against his lips. "For you, I do."

Acknowledgements

I owe my heartfelt thanks to many people who helped in the writing of this novel. I was incredibly blessed to have the talented and generous assistance of so many supportive individuals. To my mother, its first critic and fan, who discussed characters and plot tangles with me over long conversations on the phone and front porch. To Maggie Brendan, Debbi Crowson, Christy Distler, Evelyn Elliott, Susie Joyner, Anne Marie Keith, Liz Talley, and Melanie Viebrock, who read and reread every word and made my writing shine. A very special thank you to my daughter, Melanie, who became my critique partner *exceptionnelle*. Even though four time zones and almost five thousand miles lay between us, she read every chapter as I wrote it and gave me her unbridled, insightful, and all-together delightful feedback. My sincere thanks to my editor, Christy Distler, who critiqued the novel and edited the final work. And finally, to my wonderful readers. Thank you for loving my characters and their stories so much you clamored for more. You inspire me. May your appreciation for my work never wane.

ABOUT THE AUTHOR

Rose Chandler Johnson is known for her heartwarming, inspirational writing. In addition to works of fiction, Rose has written an award-winning devotional: *God, Me, and Sweet Iced Tea.* Connect with her on her blog, www.writemomentswithgod.blogspot.com, Amazon, https://amzn.to/2cEecdo, or Twitter @ rechanjo.

CPSIA information can be obtained
at www.ICGtesting.com
Printed in the USA
FSHW021939060619
58828FS

9 780998 493312